HOW TO KILL YOUR FRIENDS

PHIL KURTHAUSEN

In case, I'm frirst
on the lust :) *[signature]*

BLOODHOUND
— BOOKS —

Print ISBN 978-1-912986-79-8

ALSO BY PHIL KURTHAUSEN

Don't Let Me In

1

Meredith couldn't be sure, but she felt like she was being watched. She smiled hesitantly at the elderly couple who were waiting for her to finish the sentence she had just begun before her senses interrupted with the danger signal.

The man leaned forward a little on his bulbous, white, day-off-the-cruise-ship sneakers, and his wife, Susan, a retired optometrist from Milwaukee, placed a gentle hand on his arm, arresting any chance of a topple. It was August hot, and Meredith had seen more than one of her marks fail to complete because they had passed out or had to return to the ship to rest and rehydrate.

She risked a glance out at the throbbing crowds in Plaça del Pi and didn't spot any obvious watcher, yet still, she could feel something was wrong.

'You were telling us about the Peni– Pene– oh I forget what it was called, that wine, deary?'

Meredith smiled. She knew that this affected people, both men and women, and made them want to please her. Her father, may he burn in hell, had told her once that she looked like the girl from a Pepsi commercial in the eighties. She had been curious enough to check out the ad on YouTube and he had been right, she looked almost identical: Californian sun-kissed blonde locks, freckles, but not too many, on her cheeks, and a wide mouth that together with her shiny white teeth and sparkling green eyes allowed magic to happen. Like now. Tom – that was the man's name she remembered – leaned further forward, pushing against his wife's arm, to get closer to her smile.

'Penedès, and well-remembered, Susan.' She reached out and gently touched Susan's exposed, liver-spot-covered forearm. 'I can tell you've heard all about it already but as you know it is a famous Catalan wine region around an hour from here in Barcelona and this is where you will find the finest whites and reds in the country. Not many people in the States have heard about this wine region so when you take a few cases of this back home folks will be mighty impressed by your taste and knowledge.'

Tom seemed to be in a daze and was just staring at her, but Meredith was used to this and in any event, it was Susan she needed to charm, although she could see from a similar look in her eyes that this was a foregone conclusion.

'But we couldn't possibly bring cases back to the ship! We only have a 'captain's delight' cabin.'

Suddenly, there it was again, the sense of being watched. This time Meredith looked up straight away and across the square and caught the eyes of a young man at a table outside Bar del Pi. He was wearing a blue polo shirt and red trousers that must be killing him in this heat. He quickly looked down at the espresso he was nursing. A flash of recognition hit her. She knew this man but couldn't place him.

Meredith made a quick inventory of who might be watching her. A friend of her father's? Impossible, he had none. At his funeral, the only mourners had been her and his half-sister, who had been there hoping to find out if there was any money in the estate (there wasn't).

The police in Australia might be interested in talking to her about some minor transgressions but surely that couldn't be it. And as for the local police, the *Mossos*, they wouldn't be concerned with a young American woman sending tourists to buy grossly overpriced cooking wine in bottles marked as various 'Gran Reserva' from Alfonso Martinez. In the stupefying heat and the cauldron that was Barcelona in August, it was all they could do to keep the lid on the tensions of hundreds of thousands of tourists packed into the Barri Gòtic and the sharks that fed on them. Cheap wine dressed up as expensive vintages was the least of their concerns.

So, maybe the man watching her was just looking at her in the way that many did during every one of her days. But she didn't think so. There was something else she had seen, not the usual shame at being caught, but the look of dawning recognition on his face. This man knew her, maybe he even knew who she really was.

'Missy, did you hear what I said? Our cabin, it's too small for cases of wine.'

'We got you covered, Susan! We ship it via FedEx, bubble-wrapped but insured 100 per cent in case some careless baggage handler at General Mitchell International drops it. But don't worry: that has never happened to me yet!'

Susan turned to Tom who was still staring at Meredith. 'What do you think darling? Should we get a couple of cases? It might be nice to see the Olufsen's faces when we invite them round for dinner. Do you remember the fuss they made about that Riesling they brought back from their river cruise? Tom?' Susan tugged at the flesh that hung loosely from Tom's elbow.

Tom jerked to life as though he was wakening from some deep faerie spell.

'What, oh yes, absolutely.' He looked back to Meredith, his eyes widening. 'Will you come with us?'

She glanced up again. The man in the blue polo shirt was no longer sitting at the table watching her.

'Well, Tom, lucky for you, I get to pass you into the hands of the real expert. Just follow me. You guys are in for a real treat.' She wanted to get out of the square quickly.

She led them down a narrow alleyway that most tourists ignored due to it being dark, almost hidden and the type of place the guidebooks told you to avoid at night. Here was Alfonso's bodega, as she described it to the tourists who answered positively to her cheery greeting, 'Hey do you guys like wine?' – which was, of course, almost all of them. Who doesn't like wine when asked by a beautiful young woman whose smile is reminiscent of all that is wholesome in the world?

The bodega was a hole in the wall that led down to a cellar that Alfonso rented off the shawarma shop owner whose premises it sat beneath. Alfonso had added a few old wooden barrels and five hundred cases of cheap wine which he would spend the summer selling to the Tom-and-Susans of the world. Normally, Meredith would accompany the marks down into the cellar but the man in the blue polo shirt had worried her and she didn't want to be in a basement with only one way out.

'Alfonso will take care of you. You really are in for a treat. What he doesn't know about Spanish wine isn't worth knowing.'

Alfonso knew next to nothing about wine. He was a car mechanic in Badalona during the off-season. What he did know was how to dial his Spanish-accented English up to ten and play the romantic Spanish wine merchant.

'It's at the bottom of the stairs.'

'Are you not joining us, deary?'

'Yes, you must!' said Tom.

'I'm afraid not. Alfonso has the last of the 2012's I was telling you about so I have to try and source some 2013's quickly from our growers in the south. I have an appointment in half an hour. They are not as good as the 2012's you are about to get, but they will do.'

Tom looked crestfallen.

'Thank you so much, deary. You must come and visit us if you are ever in Cedar Falls.'

Meredith deployed the smile again. 'Sure will! Alfonso will give me your email address and I'll be sure to drop you a line next time I am Stateside. We can enjoy a glass of one of those 2012's together. Alfonso's waiting.'

She looked back towards the square. No one was following her but she wanted to get away from here more than anything in the world.

Tom looked at her and didn't move. She pointed towards the door and the stairs that descended to the basement.

'Oh, okay.' He began to turn around but lost his footing on the cobbles. Meredith dashed forward and caught him in her arms before he fell. He looked up at her like she was a visiting angel and grinned. 'I'm having such a lovely day.'

Susan took his arm. 'I've got him now, deary. Thank you for all your help.' Her tone had turned a little harder, possibly because she had just noticed her husband's infatuation. This happened a lot as well.

Meredith resisted the urge to push them towards the stairs but she kept smiling and nodded towards the entrance to the basement.

They took the hint and as soon as they turned their backs Meredith's smile disappeared. Cause and effect Meredith understood. She wondered if Susan and Tom had seen any change in her face when she first noticed the man watching her. Meredith had tried hard to keep the muscles set. She had practised in front of the mirror for many years, and she hoped her muscle memory was stronger than her fear. She made a mental note to check her smile later that day when she went back to her apartment in El Raval.

She hurried up the alley. It was cooler here than the square, and normally she might have lingered for a while and had a cigarette in the shadows, but not today. When she reached the top of the alleyway, she looked behind her and waited for a second, but the alley remained empty and still. Once she was happy no one was following her, she stepped out into another, slightly wider, alley lined with boutique shops, bars and restaurants. She was immediately enveloped by the hordes of tourists who coursed through the Barri Gòtic's alleyways like fat cells through arteries, giving and killing at the same time.

Meredith didn't hate the tourists, or *guiris*, as most of the Barcelonés called them. She saw them as camouflage or sometimes they reminded her of the herds of wildebeest you saw on a wildlife documentary, meat in ready supply with their stupid herd-like behaviour, following the same migratory path from dock, airport to the Barri Gòtic, La Rambla, and to stand outside the Gaudí buildings looking at everything and seeing nothing. They didn't evoke any positive or negative emotion in her. They were like the weather, just there.

Today, she was grateful for their bovine presence as they allowed her to move and blend with them as they gawped at gaudy fridge magnets or followed their phones to well-reviewed churro houses where they queued, as they queued for everything in this city, waiting for their five star experience.

She glanced back and with a swooping rush of fear recognised the man in the blue polo shirt some fifty yards behind her, struggling through the crowds, trying to reach her.

Meredith felt sick. She liked Barcelona. She didn't want to have to leave another place and begin again.

She ducked into the entrance of a ceramic shop, full of Gaudí-inspired ceramics. Pots, cups, vases, and the ubiquitous Gaudí lizard, all cast with multicoloured mosaic tiles, covered every surface and hung from the roof. Meredith felt like she had stepped into a kaleidoscope. The air conditioning knifed through the summer heat as she crossed the portal into the shop. Like every shop in the Barri Gòtic in August, it was full of sweating red faces and smelled of body odour, aftershave and stale alcohol.

Meredith walked briskly to the stairs that led to the base-ment, not pausing as she grabbed hold of a Gaudí-inspired pencil from a Gaudí-inspired cup. She gripped it like a dagger. If it came to it, she could plunge it somewhere soft and vulnerable.

She pretended to study a row of ceramic fish on one of the racks. They, like the rest of the items, were covered in small glass mosaics. From here she could see the stairs and anyone who came down them. If she was being followed, he would have to come down here.

She felt a tug on her shorts and looked down. A small child, a girl of about four or five, looked up at her. 'Do you know where my mummy is?'

Meredith didn't understand children or people's responses to them. She had never had a decent conversation with a child or seen them contribute something other than stress to people's lives. This child was following the usual pattern. Although Meredith didn't understand people's responses, she did know how to mimic them.

She smiled but the child didn't seem affected in the same way adults were and instead she screwed up her face and began to cry.

'Be quiet kid!'

The child sobbed even louder. Meredith squeezed the pencil tighter in her hand.

'I want my mummy!'

Meredith glanced at the stairs and then looked around the small basement. There was just one other customer, an elderly man doing his best not to knock any pots off the racks, but no one who fulfilled the criteria of a mother. Meredith knelt down until her face was level with that of the child. 'Listen, my beauty, see that man over there?'

The child glanced over at the old man.

'Well, he's put a spell on your mother and captured her in a dark castle in a dark forest.'

The child started to shake and sob even more.

Meredith took hold of her hand. 'But don't worry: you can break the spell. All you have to do is go over there and smash this' – she took down the ceramic fish – 'on the floor next to him. Once you've done that you will have broken the spell and your mother will return just like that!'

'Just like that?'

Meredith didn't bother smiling. 'Sure, just like that.' She placed the fish in the child's hands. 'Now off you go. Go on, go and break the spell.'

The child looked down at the fish, then back at Meredith and finally across to the old man. 'Okay,' she said, although she looked unsure. It didn't matter. Meredith just wanted her gone and she watched the child scamper away towards the unsuspecting old man.

'Nancy, is that you?'

Meredith's fist tightened around the pencil. She stood up and turned round to face the owner of the English accent. It was the man in the blue polo shirt. Late twenties, good-looking, over groomed, but despite this, he was displaying the redness around the gills common to all new Northern European arrivals. She still didn't recognise him, but he recognised 'Nancy' and that placed her at a disadvantage and made her feel vulnerable and sick.

Meredith smiled and put the hand holding the pencil behind her back. 'Oh my God! Is that you?' Meredith said, her brain working furiously to try and place this man who knew her as the long-discarded identity of Nancy.

The man held his arms out. 'Well, duh, yeah! I thought it was you in the square but I wasn't sure. You seemed to be selling something to tourists and I thought, that cannot be our Nancy.'

Meredith did some quick calculations. 'Nancy' had been her chosen name for about two years in her late teens and early twenties. 'How long's it been? It must be what? Ten years?'

The man looked at her quizzically. 'You must have checked your phone today! It's unbelievable, the memories popped up on Facebook, ten years to the day and then boom, I'm having a coffee in the square and I look across and spot you selling stuff to those tourists.'

'Unbelievable. I was just helping them with directions.' *Ten years.* That put her in Thailand. The Nancy years. The handsome face in front of her, cut-glass cheekbones, high forehead. Was it possible that this was the diamond hidden in the long-departed flesh of someone she used to know?

'Tubs?'

The corners of the man's lips dropped a little and his face, although it seemed impossible that it could, went a little redder. 'I prefer Richard these days.'

A rapid stream of memories was accessed. Beach parties on Ko Pha-ngan, lots of bad drugs and talk of Buddhism, and a plump English boy known as 'Tubs' to everyone, sitting on the sidelines, glumly wearing an oversized Hawaiian shirt, watching everyone else cavorting and enjoying each other. 'Of course, that was a special time. And look at you! You are looking really well.'

There was a loud smash from the corner of the room and an old man began to swear loudly in Catalan.

'Gosh, what was that?'

'That adorable child just smashed a vase. Nothing to worry about.'

Meredith could see the old man talking to the child and now a tired, middle-aged woman had turned up and picked the child up. The child pointed at Meredith.

'Listen, you must join me for a drink. I have some amazing news about the gang which I think you will love.'

Meredith couldn't think of anything she wanted to do less than discuss 'old times' with Richard, someone who she had only been dimly aware of even when she 'knew' him.

The woman made her way through the racks of ceramics towards them. She was shouting abuse in Catalan, most of it centred around Meredith being the 'daughter of a whore', something which Meredith had no knowledge of either way to confirm or deny.

'What's that woman saying? She seems angry.'

Meredith put the pencil in her rear shorts pocket and with her other hand grabbed hold of Richard's elbow and propelled him towards the stairs.

'You know what the Spanish are like. It's the heat, it makes them all crazy. Come on, let's get that drink.'

2

Sick with boredom, Meredith compiled lists in her mind of how she could either kill Richard or herself in order to stop the one-sided conversation that she was being forced to endure.

It had seemed to make sense to drink a vermouth and then move to red wine. Meredith believed in Hemingway's view that drinking made other people more interesting but this truism had met its match with Richard.

The more he drank, the fewer insights he made. His previous small talk seemed profound by comparison with his now alcohol-suffused conversation. Even in the late summer afternoon, La Alcoba Azul was cool and dark, lit by candles and it was one of the reasons that Meredith liked it. You could sit at the bar, or at a table in the corner, and the world wouldn't know you existed. The barman, Jordi, was the taciturn type, a man who realised that what his customers most appreciated was the space to breathe away from the craziness of the city. In hindsight, it had been a mistake to bring Richard here as he was the opposite of everything the bar was.

His voice, now lazy due to heat and alcohol, was loud and

booming. Meredith had forgotten how annoying the British public-school accent could be. It seemed alien here where she was used to low, conspiratorial whispers about politics, life and sex.

Richard had been through his repertoire of false memories, one by one, in great detail. The beach parties, which Meredith could barely remember, had in his mind been cleansed somehow of the humiliation he must have felt at being fat and on the outside. The group, who Meredith remembered as being the usual self-obsessed Eurotrash, had assumed life-changing status in Richard's mind.

He had talked long and loudly about drugs, immediately placing him in the category of total bore, compounded by his even louder assertion, and one which made Jordi pause for a second from cleaning a glass and catch Meredith's eye briefly, that he was now a vegan and this explained the change in his appearance. Meredith declined to add that the last time she had seen him he had been vomiting a Full Moon cocktail onto the sand behind a rock whilst simultaneously sobbing loudly about the fact that the boy he had been obsessing about had just made out with one of the girls in the group. What had been her name? A face popped into her mind, tanned, young, entitled. She would need more than that to narrow it down.

Richard was talking about someone called Daniel (she had no memory of a Daniel) who was now a big thing in the city, which was a good thing, but had a huge coke habit, which was a bad thing. Although the way Richard's voice picked up when talking about the coke habit suggested that he was quite happy about this dark cloud attached to Daniel's silver lining.

She let him drone on. There was just a little wine left in his glass and once it was finished, she would pour him into a cab and rejoin her life in the city. Alfonso would no doubt be on the warpath because of her vanishing act. She could rely on Jordi never to mention the fact that Richard had been calling her Nancy since they had walked into the bar.

'You know everyone is coming here. Even Amy will be here. Well, obviously that's the reason everyone will be here.'

Amy, the girl who had got together with Richard's love interest back on Ko Pha-ngan. Meredith remembered her now. She hadn't been the centre of attention back then but she had been best friends with the girl who was: Olivia. Meredith recalled them being joined at the hip.

Meredith's involvement with them had been the usual backpacker relationship borne out of sharing the same hostel, going to the same bars and taking the same drugs. Nothing more and something that Meredith had replicated all over the world – two-week friendships that meant and signified nothing to her. But to Richard it had obviously meant something more.

'Oh my God, they are going to be so stoked to find out you are here. They won't believe it, I can see their faces! Here's Richard with one of his stories again... But then no, you walk in and everyone will freak out! Here's Nancy! You haven't changed a bit. It will be so amazing.'

Meredith felt nauseous. She looked at the bottles of spirits at the back of the bar, rows of enchanting greens, yellows, and reds glistening in crystal brilliance. She could start ordering Orujo and get Richard very drunk. They could walk back to his hotel via Port Vell. Every year drunken *guiris* fell into the dock and drowned. It was an idle thought only and she would get him into a cab instead and promise to keep in touch, knowing full well that she would never speak to him again.

'So, Amy is coming here, and Olivia also?' asked Meredith, more as a verbal placeholder whilst she figured out what to do with this boy.

'Oh yeah, sponsored of course, by her brands. We are all in

Soho House. It's going to be so much fun. I can't wait for you to see them all again. Oh my God, think of the posts!'

This particular group dynamic hasn't changed much in ten years, thought Meredith. Richard, despite the weight loss, was still just a spear carrier for Olivia and Amy.

Meredith wondered about her own life. Had she changed since she knew this group? Ten years had added some physical changes, despite what Richard said, but what about her character? She tried very hard to change, to grow and understand more about herself and the world and she thought she had, but meeting someone like Richard made her question her assumptions. Richard, no doubt, thought he had changed, and physically he had, but Meredith suspected in every other way he was just an amplified version of those character traits he had demonstrated ten years ago.

'Her brands?'

Richard looked up perkily from his drink. His eyes were now as red as his face. 'Oh my God, yeah. You know Amy is massive now?'

Meredith shook her head. She didn't know anything about Amy or the rest of them and had never wanted to know anything. 'For all I know you guys are still on that beach partying hard.'

Richard put his hands to his cheeks. 'Oh my God, you haven't heard, where have you been?'

Richard was clearly the type who liked to be the first to give news. Meredith stored this nugget of information. One way in which she had changed from the girl ten years ago was that she read people better. It helped her understand and improve herself.

Meredith gave Richard half a smile and cocked her head to one side. This made people want to please her and believe that she liked them.

Richard nodded. 'You always were the quiet one.'

She kept the smile in place despite wanting to scream, *You don't know me! You never knew me! You never will know me!*

'Old Nancy, I can't tell if you are teasing me or not but assuming you've not been on social media for the last ten years, which we both know isn't true...'

It sort of was.

'...then you've only missed out on the rise of our Amy as one of Europe's most well-known fashion vloggers and influencers. Amy is everywhere. She's a one-person industry.' Richard slurred the last syllable and Meredith nodded at Jordi, who filled up his glass.

Richard continued, 'She has the magic million on Instagram.'

Meredith could tell that she was supposed to be impressed so she let out a low whistle.

'And this has made her rich? She was doing well enough back in the good old days as I recall.'

Richard nodded and took a large slurp of his red wine. 'This is good stuff.'

It wasn't. On the off-chance she would be stuck with the bill – and given she currently didn't have enough to contribute to the monthly rent she owed on her shared apartment, because even anarchism needs rules to make sure someone bought garbanzos – she had taken the precaution of telling Jordi in Catalan that her friend was already drunk so the 'house' would do. He kept it in a white plastic container in the back and decanted it into a bottle before serving.

'Oh yeah, she is like' – he splayed his hands on the bar – 'huge. Daddy helped, of course, pictures in paradise or with supercars don't come cheap, especially if your "selfies" are taken by a professional photographer! But fair's fair. She is the face of her face and she spreads the love around.' He raised his glass. 'And that's why I'm here and meeting you right now. To Amy!'

Meredith raised her glass. She recalled a drunken, drugged evening on a Ko Pha-ngan beach and Amy making a clumsy attempt to kiss her. Nancy/Meredith had observed almost as though it wasn't her being kissed. She had politely told Amy that she wasn't attracted to women, which wasn't always true, and there hadn't been any awkwardness. But maybe there was something to be said for rejoining the orbit of someone successful and wealthy.

Perhaps she shouldn't pour Richard into a cab. Maybe it was worth drinking some more and talking about the old times until their mythology became the basis for something else entirely. Meredith smiled at Richard and asked him to tell her all about Amy and her business.

3

Meredith flopped down onto the bed and lay there crushed by the heavy heat and still air. Her fan wasn't in her room which meant that one of her flatmates had probably borrowed it to help their stoned afternoon slumbers. She couldn't be bothered going to find it as this might mean having to engage one of them in some sort of mind-numbing small talk.

It didn't make you sweat lying still but she was sure her blood was thickening and slowing, pooling in her muscles and making it impossible to move or to sleep. She dug into her pocket and pulled out her mobile phone. Meredith had always avoided social media. She briefly had a Twitter account in a false name which she used for searching her other name to see if it received any mentions concerning her father's demise, but after a few years of checking in, she had stopped using it.

She quickly downloaded the Instagram app and set up an account using an anonymous email account. She used a free random image from Shutterstock and named the account 'XYZ45X'.

She had no intention of posting anything but she wanted to

use it to lurk and see exactly what Amy had been doing that had made her so successful.

Amy's profile was easy to find and, at first, Meredith couldn't see what was so special about it. Why had it attracted so many followers, 1.3 million at the current count? It seemed indistinguishable from all the other profiles of attractive young women in their twenties posting pictures of themselves posing in front of the pyramids, capturing the setting sun between their forefinger and thumb, looking impossibly glamorous on Mount Kilimanjaro and splayed around various hotel pools. But the more Meredith scrolled through the images the more she began to see a narrative.

There were images of Dylan (Amy's boyfriend, she learned from the posts) and Amy holding hands or having a romantic dinner.

This would be immediately followed by an image of Richard falling into a pool or off a banana boat. He was the fool of the group, the court jester.

Then there was Olivia. The photographs of her were always stagier and more serious. She would be looking out across the bay of Naples for example, wistfully contemplating Vesuvius and, just in case you were in any doubt about this, the caption would tell you 'Olivia wistfully contemplates love and Vesuvius'. Olivia was the elder, wiser stateswoman of the group, its head not its heart, and the message that Meredith took – but she was sure it was not the intended message – was that she was the tragic counterpoint to the joy and success of Amy.

She wondered what this supporting role had done to Olivia. She had always been the leader of the group and this relegation to Amy's foil could not have been easy.

She read more, the hours passing by in an enviable kaleidoscope of a dream life, tropical islands, perfect skin, and fantasy-inducing filters, and for those hours Meredith felt she was there with them, not lying on an old mattress in a shared apartment with no air conditioning that stank of the weed being smoked by her younger flatmates.

It was intoxicating and although she could distinguish the dream world presented online from the life that the group actually had, there was also the fact that they did travel to these places, they did stay in the best hotels and eat in the restaurants that Meredith could only dream of eating in, and they were living a lifestyle that placed hers in the shade, not that this was too difficult to achieve. And, all this with no discernible talent – other than posting thousands of images that told you less about their real personalities than a five-minute conversation. Yet Meredith could see why people could become so invested in them. It was the same thing that she felt: this could be her, it should be her... and now she could see a way in which it might be her.

Richard had taken her phone number and promised he would be in touch when Amy arrived in town so that they could all meet up and have 'a wonderful reunion'. She had received a text that morning inviting her to a party at their hotel later that evening and she had decided she would go. It was clear that their life in 'The Squad', as they called themselves on Instagram, was better in every way than hers. They had improved their lives and Meredith admitted to herself that she was envious. This would change.

Amy had liked her once and Meredith had ignored her. This time she wouldn't ignore her. She would become Amy's friend.

Meredith examined herself in the cracked mirror that Inga kept propped up in the corner of her room. She was aware that she was considered attractive and not a day went by without someone, usually a man but not always, going out of their way to strike up a conversation or ask for her cell phone number.

But she did not consider herself pretty. She was conscious of the asymmetry of her nose, caused a long time ago by the flailing hand of her father, which gave her face a look of, to quote one of the kids who had bullied her at school, 'a Picasso painting'.

She was not vain by nature or choice but today was different. Her appearance would require thought. Meredith's normal attire for Barcelona summers was flip-flops, shorts and T-shirt, working on the basis that all of this would be covered in sweat and city grime within an hour of the sun rising. But not tonight. Tonight, she needed to strike a balance, a way of signalling she was wealthy but by wearing clothes that would look, to an observer that she was poor. She had seen this look worn by the people who queued outside the flagship stores of Gucci, Chanel, Fendi, and Valentino, along Passeig de Gràcia, and understood its meaning.

For Meredith, the problem was her lack of such clothes. Which was why she turned to Inga, one of her roommates in the run-down apartment she shared with three others. Inga, five years younger than Meredith, was obsessed with her phone, fashion and money, and was the only person who Meredith knew with access to such clothes. This was, perversely, due to her lack of the third in her triumvirate of obsessions, money. This lack had driven Inga to become adept at shoplifting clothes from the highest of high-end stores in Barcelona and before that, Stockholm, from where she had recently relocated due to 'work issues' – namely, the Swedish police issuing a warrant for her arrest.

'What do you think of this?' Inga held up what looked like a pile of rags.

Meredith shrugged. She was reliant on Inga's expertise in this field. Meredith understood the value of delegating detail to those who lived and breathed such ephemera. It was always the detail where the greatest decisions on trust would be made. This was one of the things that Meredith understood was different in the way she saw other people. She observed such details but immediately distrusted them, seeing them as camouflage disguising an individual's true nature. She tried not to look bored and instead let out a 'wow!' as she could see that it was what Inga was waiting for.

'Ja, I know, right? I got it last week from Stella McCartney. Remember I told you about the security guard and how I flirted with him whilst holding the dress right under his big dumb Spanish eyes?'

Meredith recalled a previous evening when she had forced herself to eat in the lounge, observing the unwritten rules of shared living. She had listened to the various, self-serving stories revolving around travelling and drugs, when people could be bothered glancing up from their phones and talking, and now she did recall Inga mentioning something about stealing a dress, but given all Inga's stories were about stealing a dress she could not say whether it was specific to this dress.

'Oh my gosh yes, that was so cool. Honestly, I don't know how you do it. You're so clever!'

She knew exactly how Inga did it. It was based on low wages and low expectations. Low wages for the guard who couldn't be bothered looking beyond the pretty girl talking to him and breaking the monotony of his day, and low expectations on behalf of Inga, who at twenty-seven should be looking beyond shoplifting as a career. Meredith was aware of the inherent hypocrisy in her view, but in fairness, there were extenuating circumstances in her lifestyle choices, and in any event, consistency of thought and action had always been amongst the most tedious of qualities in her view. Much better to do and think what you want, regardless of external and internal critics.

Meredith raised her slender arms and let Inga drop the rags over her head whereupon something remarkable happened as they floated down and around her body. They transformed into a beautiful dress that clung gently to her hips and waist, accentuating her figure, while seeming to almost hover lightly from the rest of her body. It made Meredith think of Cinderella's dress and struck the perfect balance between wealth and poverty porn. It was perfect.

This time it was Inga that let out the 'wow' and she looked at Meredith with the simpering cow eyes that told her that she would be able to have the dress for free.

'You really are beautiful, M.'

Meredith appraised her reflection critically. There was something missing. She looked at her shoes, scruffy Adidas trainers, and then down at Inga's shoes, which were brand new Dolce and Gabbana pumps. They looked like her size.

She smiled at Inga.

4

Meredith sipped her gin and tonic and tried not to look too bored.

The view from the open-air pool and terrace at Soho House was picture-postcard Barcelona. If she looked to her right there was the statue of Columbus pointing out across the Mediterranean – with the mountain of Montjuïc, the place of civil war torture and atrocities, looming above. To the left, she could see Port Vell with its row upon row of oligarch's taxis moored next to each other. She often speculated what heinous crimes and evil deeds must take place on these yachts but tonight it seemed like a lot of the occupants were sharing this terrace with her.

The cosmopolitan crowd around her were already drunk by the time she arrived. Despite the cooling mist that was pumped from the pipes strung around the terrace perimeter, most of the people here, particularly the *guiris*, were red-faced, and their clothes, Chanel, Gucci and the rest, hung from them like peasant's rags. Barcelona in August could do that to you.

A couple next to her, he a vegan architect, she a vegan media manager (she had heard themselves loudly introduce each other

by declaring these aspects of their identity) were cooing over the
view. Meredith followed their gaze down Moll de la Fusta
towards Montjuïc, seeing things that they did not see. There on
the corner of Carrer Nou de Sant Francesc was the café from
where the Moroccans ran their retail heroin operation, and
opposite on the pavement, the spot where she had seen two
homeless men plunge knives into each other during an argument about a shopping trolley full of plastic.

'You know, it's not called 'the Paris of the South' for nothing.
Just smell that air, straight from the Sahara,' said the architect,
and he breathed in deeply through his nose.

The woman winked at him. 'That reminds me, time for a
cheeky one!' She tapped her nose and wandered off towards the
bathroom.

As soon as she was out of sight the architect turned to
Meredith. 'So–'

Meredith raised her hand to cut him short and walked off
towards the bar. One of the reasons she hated parties, events and
particularly gatherings of those who considered themselves the
elite, was the constant harassment and assumption that she was
lucky to have fallen within the ambit of their charms. So
tedious.

She ordered another gin and tonic and this time asked the
barman to hold the hibiscus flowers. Richard had told her to
arrive at 8pm and she had, making her way up to the terrace as
instructed, but now it was nearly 9pm and of Richard and the
rest of them there was no sign. Meredith's plan seemed ridiculous now. These people, the global elite, the media types, the
self-styled creatives, bored her so much that a numbing pain
was forming behind her eyes just overhearing the self-aggran-
dising talk disguised with a false modesty that passed for their
conversations. It was just one long series of advertisements,
with the question 'So what have you been doing?' being the

big red button that launched a thousand self-promotional missiles.

She had decided to have this one last drink and then leave. She wandered over to an uncrowded part of the terrace and looked out across the port, past the Senegalese selling 'top manta' – counterfeit goods – on their blankets that covered the walkways like a patchwork quilt, and further to the horizon and beyond it, Africa. She wanted to go there one day. Perhaps, once she had finished this drink, she should just pack up, jump on a ferry and head south. It would beat listening to vegans telling each other they were vegans.

Meredith put her glass down and decided to leave. Lying in her single bed listening to an audiobook beat the shit out of this.

She headed towards the exit from the terrace but was suddenly blocked by the architect who she had shown the hand to earlier. His pupils were dilated and he looked angry. Meredith had seen this type of coked-up rejected male before and she knew what was coming. He would have been confused by her rejection of him. Nobody rejected him and even if they did, they would usually have pretended to be interested in his self-serving bullshit, listening long enough for him to believe they found him as fascinating as he did.

He held his palms up, indicating he meant no harm. 'Listen, we got off on the wrong foot. My name is Matt and–'

She tried to step round him but he moved to block her again.

'I'm just trying to have a friendly conversation here. Listen, I'm a nice guy. I'm an architect, I build things, man. Talk to me, yeah?'

He leered at her and leaned in so close that she could smell his expensive cologne that was failing to block the baser notes his body was producing. It was all an act.

'Get out of my way,' she said.

'Just talk to me, yeah, you're being a–' She never got to hear what she was being. Instead, Meredith shoved him hard and his expression changed from one of expectation and assuredness to helplessness as he toppled into the pool.

Other guests cheered and clapped. Meredith didn't look back. She would have been happier if the pool hadn't been there and she could have shoved him right off the terrace to the street below.

As she reached the door that led to the staircase out came Richard. He had bloodshot eyes, a rash-red complexion and it was obvious to Meredith that he had been crying. 'Oh, Nancy! Thank God!'

He threw his arms around her and buried his head into her shoulder. Meredith's instinct was to push him away immediately. She was not comfortable with such an invasion, and still struggled with the customary double kiss on the cheeks she had to put up with in Catalonia, often instinctively jerking her head back when someone she didn't know moved in for the peck.

'Are you okay, Richard?'

He blubbered something she couldn't hear into the fabric of her Stella McCartney dress. She gently pushed him away and looked down at her shoulder. There was the unmistakable outline of a sweaty face on the dress. She resisted the urge to push him down the stairwell.

'It's been so awful, they've been fighting again, I hate it when they fight it's just too much and even Adam can't stop them, it just gets worse and worse. I hate it!' All the words banged into each other and Richard had the look of a plaintive child whose parents have been arguing over the dinner table.

'Calm down, Richard, who is arguing?'

He looked up at her with surprise. 'Amy and Olivia of course.'

Meredith thought about the audiobook and her bed. It would be so easy to just fade into the Barcelona night and wake up tomorrow and sell wine to tourists. But the truth was that even if she didn't like the people on this terrace, she liked this terrace, this dress and even the hibiscus flowers in her gin and tonic hadn't bothered her too much. 'Calm down Richard, it will be fine. I was just leaving, but why don't you take me to them.'

Richard seemed to brighten up but there was no apology for leaving her alone to wait for an hour. 'Come on, maybe they've stopped arguing now.'

Even before Richard pushed open the door of the hotel room, they could hear, above the sound of bass-heavy dub music, the raised voices of a man and a woman shouting at each other and the lower-pitched Australian drawl of a man repeating the phrase, 'Can everyone just chill out!'

Richard produced a key pass and the lock turned green.

They entered the room, a large suite full of people scattered on the various sofas and beanbags. In the centre of the room Meredith recognised Amy. She was older but her skin looked younger than it had ten years before. It was glowing with a chemical urgency, and her body, which had been slim and youthful, was now gym-hardened and enhanced. Her hair and make-up were of a standard that Meredith expected cost more than her monthly rent and she looked like a beautiful picture come to life, an Instagram-filtered vision of herself, which of course, she was. Meredith couldn't help being blown away by the transformation. Equally surprising was that this girl, who had been quiet and reserved, well until the drugs kicked in, was now clearly the centre of attention.

'I will not be talked to in this way and I will not wear this thing!' She threw a pale green shirt on the floor. Amy was shouting at a woman who sat, with her feet tucked under her, in a large green leather armchair. Meredith recognised Olivia.

'No one is suggesting you like this, but it's what has to happen. You have a contract. Adam, will you help us out here?'

A man in his mid to late forties, tanned and wearing a white shirt open at the chest, and sporting a large gold wristwatch, circled Amy. In between taking hits on a vape pen, he shot out staccato phrases in a cockney accent.

'H&M.' He took another hit and let out a cloud of smoke which hung around him like rainclouds around a volcano summit. 'Edwin.' He jabbed the vape pen in the air. 'Carhartt. We've got contracts to consider.'

Amy paid him no attention. Olivia leaned back in her chair. Meredith got the sense that this was not an unusual event and that well-rehearsed roles were being performed.

'Amy, darling, whatever you need, you know we all love you and will make this work.'

'How can it? I can't wear this at all.' Amy threw her head back dramatically and then stormed off into an adjoining bedroom, slamming the door behind her.

'Well, did you try the yellow one? Dylan!' She directed this at a buff young man with blond hair who was sitting on a beanbag looking at his phone. 'Can you fetch Amy the yellow Fendi top.'

Dylan sighed, and muttering, 'Can everyone just chill out,' followed Amy into the other room.

Olivia, who until this point had not acknowledged Richard and Meredith's entrance, now stood up and walked across to them. 'I see you've stopped blubbering, Richard. You really shouldn't take these things personally. You know what she can be like.' She looked Meredith up and down. 'Who's your friend? Nice dress, by the way.'

Seeing Olivia again brought back further memories. Olivia high-handedly ordering drinks from waiters with disdainful waves. Olivia laughing at the Australian tourists for their unsophistication. Olivia constantly mentioning how things had been better years back when she first came to Thailand. Olivia had been a bitch then and it seemed nothing had changed.

Meredith turned up her smile to ten. 'Olivia, you don't remember me, but I remember you. I am so stoked to meet you again. You haven't aged a day.'

Olivia's eyes narrowed: it was clear that she didn't like being at a disadvantage. She put a hand on her hip and then pointed at Meredith. 'Yeah, I remember you, Ko Pha-ngan yeah? Amy had one of her crushes on you. Well, well, well, where did Richard drag you up from?'

Meredith had needed a story to explain her lack of social media presence and she was glad now that she had picked one that had no link to fashion or anything that could be considered a threat to Olivia. She could see that Olivia wouldn't wear competition well. Meredith laughed, 'Well, there was a few more years partying, if I'm honest.' This was true. 'But then I sobered up in China and started doing some NGO work, ended up in South Sudan. And now I'm writing a book about the independence movement here.' All fiction but it would, hopefully, explain her poverty and lack of searchable content.

Olivia nodded approvingly and then smiled back. 'Well, great to see you again and welcome to the madhouse. Come on, let's see if Amy remembers you. Just remind me, what was your name again?'

Meredith held out a hand. 'Nancy.'

Olivia linked her arm with Meredith's. 'Amy has changed a bit. She's a star now, don't you know.' Olivia waved her hand airily and laughed.

'I met her in one of those squares in town, I knew it was her, I remembered,' said Richard.

Olivia turned her back on Richard. 'Fascinating. You can tell us later.' They stepped over some people sharing a spliff. Olivia whispered conspiratorially in Meredith's ear, 'He's such a little bore, always whining. He needs to be careful or Amy will get tired of him.'

They entered the room that Amy had disappeared into.

Amy was on a pile of clothes astride Dylan. She heard them come in, turned to them and winked mischievously, and then without any embarrassment, rolled off Dylan and propped herself up on an elbow.

'Fuck, Amy,' said Dylan, who busied himself trying to cover up his groin as he shuffled off to the bathroom, a task made difficult by his boxers, which were caught around his ankles.

Meredith stared at Amy. She couldn't believe that this was the same girl she had known, briefly, in Thailand. This Amy was confident and controlled and so very different from the shy, gauche girl from her past.

Meredith wondered whether she had changed as much as Amy seemingly had in ten years. She was still scrambling around to find her place in the world, to make a living, find somewhere she fitted in, and here was Amy, with the same friends, but who had somehow transformed herself from a peripheral player to the centre of her galaxy, with a lucrative career, handsome boyfriend, and an enviable identity. Meredith watched, appalled, fascinated and admiring.

'Well, fuck me. If it isn't Nancy from the Full Moon parties!' She spoke with a strange cockney-Jamaican accent which was very different from the public-school accent she had had when Meredith knew her.

'Hi Amy, how are you? I'm so stoked to see you again!'

Amy patted the bed next to her. 'Oh my God! I love your Californian accent! I remember how adorable it was. Get over here and give me a hug right now.'

Meredith obeyed and joined her on the bed. Amy was just in her knickers and a clean white T-shirt, but she glowed. Her skin had the lustre of moonlight and her scent was expensive and made Meredith feel small and weak. She wanted to have that scent more than anything she had ever desired.

How had Amy achieved this transformation?

Amy hugged her and without prompting immediately began to tell her. Everything had been triggered apparently by 'that post' and Amy didn't explain it, assuming Meredith must know. There was before 'that post' and 'after that post' and everything 'after that post' was 'just crazy'. There had been product placements, then sponsorships – only ethical ones, of course. Amy had to watch Adam because he was always trying to get her to sign up for something that wasn't woke, just for the dollars. But her fans trusted her and she wasn't going to sell them out for anything. It was her brand, her trust, and once you lost that you had nothing. Didn't Nancy agree?

Nancy did agree.

Olivia sat in a chair in the corner of the room and observed the conversation. Meredith got the impression that it was a conversation she had heard many times before.

Meredith steered the conversation back to 'that post'.

Amy played with her hair a little. It was as though remembering the time before she became an influencer was remembering something traumatic, the time before fame and success.

'It was kind of weird. At one point I felt strange doing it. It was like almost guilt, you feel me? But he deserved it.'

Meredith nodded. She understood now. She had googled Amy earlier that day and read about an incident when she was a student. A professor, male, white, and stale, had accused her of plagiarism and she was going to be chucked out of university. But it turned out he had also been stalking her on social media and befriending her on Facebook, but using a sock puppet account and a fictional identity. She had posted the messages he had sent her on Instagram and YouTube with a video she had made where she confronted him at his home, in front of his wife and kids, about the messages and the sock puppet account. And although the messages were of the infatuated admirer kind, rather than those of a sexual predator, he had quickly felt the full force of the online mob. He had lost his job and his marriage.

As far as Meredith could work out the claims of plagiarism had never actually been disproven but she thought it importune to mention that now.

'Everything just took off after that. I was asked to do loads of YouTube stuff and my own channels were getting pounded. I started out with the political stuff and transitioned into fashion, both areas which you'll remember I totally love.'

Meredith had a memory of Amy's fat ass hanging out of a too-small bikini at a Full Moon party. 'You betcha I remember.' The smile always accompanied a big lie.

'So, it was a natural progression. Everything is political now anyway, everything. Talking of which, you being a local, you have to tell me all about this independence thing going on. I am just loving the yellow ribbons and the flags. You know yellow is so on-trend. And the guys, oh my God, Catalan guys, dark eyes, dark beards, so romantic.'

She grabbed Meredith's arm and laughed.

Meredith wondered if Amy was still attracted to her, or indeed women at all. Amy had seemed like a lost soul when she knew her, just wanting anyone to pay her attention, for anything, and misinterpreting any attention for sexual interest. It would be useful, though, if Amy was still interested.

Meredith held Amy's gaze and Amy didn't look away. Meredith had the upper hand and then smiled, the smile that always awakened desire. Amy cocked her head to one side and then started laughing. 'Olivia, I knew old Nancy was a dyke. You go, girlfriend. We've all been there. You have to go with what makes your soul sing. Isn't that right, Dylan?'

Dylan, who had come out of the bathroom and plonked

himself down in an armchair, seemed to jerk awake even though he wasn't asleep. 'Sure is, babe!'

Amy smiled kindly. 'Oh, I remember making a pass at you at a party. I was so off my tits! Do you have anyone special here in Barcelona?'

Meredith reeled. Amy had been all over her in Thailand, desperate for her attention, but things had changed even more than Meredith realised. Is this how Olivia felt, watching Amy catch up in confidence, status and *savoir-faire* and then one day having to acknowledge that Amy had surpassed her in all these things? And Amy assumed she was a lesbian and had now placed her in that box. Meredith didn't care whether she was or not. She could choose who she was as and when she felt, but now Amy had categorised her like a bug on a pin. Meredith felt her cheeks redden but she regained her composure.

'Same as you, Amy. I keep it casual. Life is for living.'

Amy rolled a cigarette and asked if Meredith wanted one. She declined, even though she would have liked one. She didn't want Amy to know anything more about her, anything that could be seen as a weakness, right now.

'This place is so boring. You know right, all these Soho Houses, so similar, all these boutique, Instagrammable hotels, Jesus, they make me puke. You must know some cool places living here?'

Meredith thought of the little Chinese bar near Estació de França where she could get a one-euro beer but she didn't think Amy had this in mind. She wanted to avoid anywhere people might know her and call her Meredith. She was just on the cusp of mentioning a bar in Gràcia where tourists didn't often go, but which was full of the same hipster international crowd as surrounded Amy, when Richard said from somewhere behind her, 'Nancy took me to this amazing bar. It was full of Catalans drinking and plotting. What was it called Nance? The Blue Bedroom?'

'La Alcoba Azul,' said Meredith, itching to punch Richard, as the last thing she wanted was to take this group to one of her secret places.

'Oh my God, that sounds right what we need. Get away from all these fucking tourists and their constant posting.'

'Leave it to the professionals,' muttered Olivia.

Amy either didn't hear or pretended that she hadn't.

Meredith smiled. Sure, she could take them there.

TWENTY MINUTES LATER, after navigating the labyrinth of narrow alleys of the Barri Gòtic, they squeezed themselves into La Alcoba Azul.

The narrow bar, no wider than ten feet, was packed, as it always was at this hour, whatever the night, and full of the usual assortment of anonymous lone drinkers, groups of Catalan separatists and a single tourist looking uncomfortable. They formed a dense mass of alcoholic humanity, laughing, carousing and living, into which Meredith, Olivia, Richard, Dylan, Adam and assorted hangers-on squeezed, despite it looking, as it always did, that it couldn't cope with one more person entering.

Meredith shouted across an order to Jordi and told him to send the bill to the short *guiri* with the expensive glasses. He replied, 'The one who looks like a gone-to-seed Tom Cruise?' Meredith looked and now she noticed Adam did bear a resemblance to the actor.

She turned and found herself face-to-face with Olivia. She could see Amy and the others at the far end of the bar already talking with a couple of the local *independentistas* who had taken to using the bar as a place to plot and scheme their next moves against the Madrid regime. Meredith always steered clear of them: they were magnets for the *Mossos*. And to her mind, there was nothing more corrupt than idealism.

'Richard tells me that he saw you selling wine to tourists? How did you get involved in that? I seem to recall you were a law student when we met.'

'Thinking of going to law school' was a phrase that had tripped off Meredith's tongue for many years in answer to the question 'What do you do?' as people never bothered with any tricky follow-up questions to such a mundane reply. But she had neither the means nor the inclination to join that profession. She smiled at Olivia. 'I wanted to do something a little less dishonest.'

Olivia was close to Meredith, the bodies all around them, pressing in, but at the same time oblivious in their loud Catalan conversations. 'God, yeah I know what you mean. And I guess you're a little too old to be a student anymore.'

Meredith laughed. It sounded genuine. It had taken many years before it sounded genuine to her as well, but now, she could not distinguish between the sound of her fake laugh and her genuine laugh. 'Gee, I'm only 28, but I guess that would still make me a mature student.' She was thirty-two and she smiled at Olivia.

Olivia frowned. 'So, you were only eighteen when we met in Thailand?'

She knew she looked at least five years younger than her real age but she wondered why she had felt the need to knock off all those years. The important thing was being below thirty. She wished she had told Olivia she was twenty-nine. She started to smile again at Olivia.

'You smile a lot, Nancy.'

Meredith caught a half-smile from turning into a full smile. What did Olivia know? 'Guess I'm just friendly. I like to put people at ease. It's nice to be nice.' She had seen this written on a T-shirt worn by a tourist surrounded by a large group of friends. She had tried using it on Spider, who sub-let his room to her, a few times. He had just laughed at her.

Now Olivia looked at her as though she had said something strange and pressed closer. 'I googled you when you were talking with Amy. Standard issue people check. I literally couldn't find a single thing about you. No Facebook profile, no Twitter, nothing on Google. Do you know how hard it is to have nothing on the web at all like that? I've never heard of that outside a spy movie.'

Olivia was staring at her with an intensity that made Meredith look away. Towards the rear of the bar, she could see Amy was huddled in deep conversations with the more good-looking of the *independentistas*. Meredith didn't recognise them but she wanted more than anything else to go and join Amy, become her friend and to get away from Olivia and her questions.

'I've never been very active on social media.' She controlled the incipient smile but kept her tone friendly. 'I've always been more of a book girl.'

'Sure, I get it. But nothing, nothing at all. Do you know how hard that is? Where are you, Nancy? It's like you've never existed.'

Meredith shrugged. 'The truth is, I had all my information removed. Here in Europe, we can do that. I had to.'

Olivia toyed with the cocktail stick that held the olive in her vermouth. 'Why?'

This was intolerable and for a moment Meredith thought about walking out. After all, the road to monetising Amy wasn't clear and Olivia's intrusive questioning made Meredith want to throw her drink, a gin and tonic, in Olivia's face. Maybe even follow up with the glass or perhaps a kiss.

'A couple of years after I met you guys, I ended up moving to Australia. I met this guy, Barry. He was lovely, a tree surgeon, and we hit it off, even got a place together but then–' Meredith let her voice catch. 'He started hitting me and it got pretty bad. The usual story, I'm ashamed to say. I tried to leave him but he always promised me he would change, that he loved me. God, I feel stupid saying this, but I believed him. Well, until he put me in hospital with three broken ribs and a fractured eye socket. After that, I walked out. I took everything but when he got out of prison, he started following me online so I disappeared, physically and digitally.'

Meredith surprised herself when a tear welled up in her right eye. This was a skill she didn't know she had. Nothing pleased her more than evidence of improvement.

The tear did it. Olivia put out a hand and took hold of Meredith's wrist. She leaned close in. 'That happened to me too. My ex-husband. Jesus, I married my abuser.' Olivia fixed her with a stare. 'You have to remember it's not your fault.'

Meredith wanted to laugh and although she resisted she still couldn't stop herself smiling. What a stroke of luck. She never would have had Olivia as the type who would let herself be dominated but there it was, and perhaps that explained Olivia's relationship with Amy too. She talked the tough talk but in reality, she was a beta type all along. *This will make things easier,* thought Meredith.

'And sorry for what I said about your smile. It's beautiful, it really is, but ever since Amy jumped the million-followers barrier, we've had all sorts of people coming out of the woodwork trying to use her.'

'I would never do that, Olivia. I'm not even sure what that means. As you have noticed, I don't really do social media.'

Olivia smiled back. 'I know, and I'm sorry for being such a bitch. Come on, let's join the others.'

They pushed through the crowd. Meredith was used to the closeness of people and the need to thrust through regardless of who was in your way. It was what you had to do to make progress in a Barcelona bar but Olivia was full of *sorrys* and *excuse me's* as though these magic words would clear the way. Meredith kept on moving and in her wake, Olivia followed until they reached the back of the bar.

Adam was on his mobile phone and Richard and Dylan were talking to one of the *independentistas*.

'Where's Amy?' said Olivia.

Richard pointed at the tar-stained door that led to the alley at the back of the bar. 'She's gone for a cigarette with that guy, Freddie was it?'

The Spanish guy he was talking with laughed. 'Ferran. It's Catalan.'

'I might join her. Want one?' said Olivia.

Meredith didn't want to smoke but for a bonding ritual she was prepared to give away a few minutes of her life and it would be a relief to leave the cloying heat of the bar.

They stepped outside into the dark alley. The glow of Dylan's cigarette tip made it look like he was on standby waiting for Amy to activate him. It was cooler out here, but not by much. The remains of the day's blistering city heat still hung heavy.

'Where's Amy?' said Olivia.

Meredith looked down the alleyway. It was empty. Amy had gone.

5

They had ghosted her. After the night out at La Alcoba Azul she hadn't heard anything more from The Squad. Now, a week later, and after sending two texts to Richard, without receiving a reply, she had given up on them.

They clearly had seen her as nothing more than a passing interest, a local trinket to be examined and then discarded. It had left Meredith feeling rejected and, worse, it had made her realise how shabby and worthless her life was compared to theirs.

She awoke to the sound of Spider shouting about a wet towel. This was something that Meredith had noticed in the various shared houses, hostels and squats that had formed the bulk of her living accommodation over the last ten years. The more progressive, alternative or different the lifestyle a person claimed to follow, the more likely it was that they were super possessive regarding bourgeois comforts. If you want to see vicious, watch two hippies argue over the last kumquat in the bowl.

She rolled over and put back one of her wax earplugs that had come loose in the night. With it back in, she could sleep a little longer. Meredith had drunk too much the night before. She had made the mistake of joining Spider, Inga and the others in enjoying a couple of litres of Don Simón wine, the kind that came in cartons and cost one euro.

She had done that a lot this week and she was aware that it was because of The Squad's loss of interest in her. The glimpse into their lives had made it inevitable that she would compare it with her own and there was no doubt that her life was but a pale shadow. And so she had drunk to block out the feelings of envy and worthlessness, even to the extent of joining Spider and her other housemates in their boring drinking and smoking sessions during which they talked endlessly and incoherently about the details of their squalid lives and the shows they were watching on Netflix. This only had the consequence of intensifying her feelings of inadequacy. No one was interested in her life, especially herself.

She had analysed the night out with The Squad and couldn't work out why they had just dropped her. After they returned to the bar following a perfunctory search for Amy, who had seemingly gone off for a night of Catalan relaxation with Ferran, she had spent the rest of the night consoling Dylan. They tried to convince him that Ferran was merely showing Amy some of the barrio's magnificent Gothic architecture. It had taken a lot of booze but eventually it had worked and by the time they left the bar at 4am he had seemed accepting of this ludicrous version of events. More importantly, they had stumbled out into the early morning and parted with warm words about meeting up and spending more time together in Barcelona. Dylan and Richard had hugged her and even Olivia had said they would be sure to be in touch. But since that night Meredith hadn't heard anything from any of them. She had been ghosted.

Meredith had also lost her job. The day after the night at La Alcoba Azul she had slept in all day until late afternoon and when she had eventually wandered down Plaça del Pi to see if Alfonso wanted some assistance in selling wine, he had told her to get fucked because he had needed her that morning.

The Amy experiment had been a disaster and it was due to her own inability to connect with people. Her father had been right – she was just a twisted, weird little kid with no friends and it would always be the case. It was with this thought that she drifted back off to sleep in the warm cocoon of her bedroom which was throbbing with the accumulated summer heat.

At first, she ignored her phone but when it rang for the third time in succession, she was surprised to see it was an English number, so she answered it.

'Are you dressed?' It was Olivia and she sounded as sharp as ever. The hard edges of composed professionalism, which Meredith had managed to round off with alcohol and her story about being beaten up by her Australian boyfriend, were back.

Meredith found her tone grating but she focussed on the person she wanted to be, which was calm and helpful, as she guessed that if Olivia was calling her, there might still be something to be gained from the situation. This time she wouldn't fuck it up, she would be more vigilant in what she said and how she acted. She would be normal and they would like her, she would make sure of it. The contrast between Amy and Olivia's life in Soho House versus her existence in this dump listening to stoners arguing over wet towels was uppermost in her mind.

'Morning, Olivia, how are you?' She could hear traffic noise in the background.

'You live in Gràcia. Is that how you say it?'

Meredith had a bad feeling about where Olivia was heading. She sat up in bed. The heat made it feel like pushing against an invisible curtain. There was, of course, no air conditioning in this flat, not like the ice-cold luxury of Soho House. She recalled telling Olivia that she lived in the cool, bohemian area of Gràcia rather than the truth which was that she lived in a seedy apartment in the Raval, a much less salubrious part of town.

'Yeah, where are you, Olivia?'

'I'm on my way, in a taxi. I'll be there in ten minutes. What's your address?'

Meredith stood up and looked around, locating any clothing that wasn't crumpled or dirty.

She gave Olivia an address of a swanky apartment block in Vila de Gràcia and told her she would meet her outside.

'I'll be there in ten minutes. We've got a big problem.'

As soon as she hung up Meredith started working her way through the piles of clothes like a scavenger on the city dump. Once she was dressed, she ran to the Drassanes metro station and hopped on the train to Gràcia with Olivia's *'We've'* still fresh in her mind.

Twenty-five minutes later she strode up to the apartment block address she had given to Olivia. Olivia was standing outside smoking and looking cross. Meredith sipped from a cup of takeaway coffee. 'Hey Olivia, sorry, I just popped out to the local coffee shop, I needed this.' She held up the polystyrene cup of cheap coffee she had bought from the local supermarket by the Fontana metro. 'They make an amazing matcha latte, you should try one.'

Olivia looked up at the lavish balconies festooned with drooping palms. 'Matcha, yeah can't stand it myself, but it photographs nicely for Instagram. Nice place, by the way. Which one is yours? You forgot to give me the number of the apartment and I've been buzzing them all. Does everybody in this country sleep in all morning? Your neighbours will hate you, by the way.'

Meredith noticed that Olivia looked bright and clean, was wearing a white blouse and tan skirt that looked box fresh, and Dior sunglasses. Meredith couldn't help contrasting this with her own hastily-put-together ensemble of creased Uniqlo T-shirt and denim shorts, which had been the only things she could find that were not stained or dirty. To any casual observer, it would look like it was Olivia who was the native to the city and not Meredith.

Meredith held up her Styrofoam cup. 'I can't start the day without a good cup of matcha.'

Olivia eyed the Styrofoam cup with what appeared to be loathing. 'You should buy a reusable cup; those things are lethal to the planet. Amy promotes a good brand of them. You should check them out.'

Meredith smiled and was immediately self-conscious, recalling Olivia's comments about her smiling a lot from their night out a week ago. 'Biodegradable,' she shot back, which was almost certainly untrue.

'No such thing. But listen, we need to talk. Get in.'

In the back of the taxi, Olivia checked her mobile phone and began. 'So, we are on a tight schedule here in Barcelona. We have several shoots lined up and of course, we need to produce content for the 'Gram posts. Everything was booked months ago and now we are all just sitting there twiddling our thumbs whilst we wait to produce content that just isn't there. Adam is tearing his hair out, I've literally never seen him so angry and Dylan... well Dylan, we put him on an electric scooter and sent him out into the city. It's best that he's out of the way. I swear he's so dense light bends around him.'

Olivia smoothed her skirt with an elegantly-manicured hand and turned to Meredith.

Meredith marvelled at what wealth could bring – the clothes, the phone and the assurance that anything could be achieved was insulation against the real world. Meredith wanted that more than anything.

'So, what do you think?'

'About what? Sorry, this is about Amy, yeah?'

Olivia tutted. 'Who else are we talking about? Of course, it's about Amy. She didn't come home after our impromptu night at that bar you took us to last week.'

'What, she's gone missing?'

Olivia sighed. 'No, she's gone off on a jaunt of her own. She does this from time to time. Takes up with a man, a cause or just wants to be alone. It's classic diva behaviour. But the important thing is that she's costing us money. We have sponsors to please and we can't go more than a few days without posts featuring Amy. That will lead to follower fall-off and that, as you probably don't realise, hits our bottom line. We need her back today. She isn't here on fucking holiday.'

Meredith had noticed that Olivia didn't talk this way around Amy when she had met them the week before, although this was more reminiscent of how she had talked to Amy ten years ago in Thailand. It wouldn't be surprising if Olivia was a little resentful of their exchange of roles but did this particular cut run a little deeper, wondered Meredith.

'And how can I help?'

Olivia looked at her with disbelief. 'Well, it's all your fault, yours and Richard's. You took us to that bar. They are your people. You know the language and it will be quicker for you to find her than us. So, that's what we need you to do: find her.'

Meredith sensed an opportunity and although she wanted to tell Olivia to 'get fucked' because of her tone and get out of the taxi, she instead nodded and told her that she would love to help. That was what normal people did, they say they will help even if they don't mean it.

'Won't she just come back at some point?'

'She has form. Last year in Berlin she went missing for over a week. She was shacked up with some Syrian artist. She does this, you see, she is always searching for a new identity; refugees and migration last year, and now I fear you have given her an introduction to another: Catalan independence. Sun, wine, sex and revolutionary politics. Hell, what's not to like?'

To Meredith, this seemed the most indulgent thing she had heard in a while and she appreciated why tight little anger lines were forming around Olivia's eyes.

'How can I help?'

'Do you know this man, Ferran, who she went home with?'

'I've never seen him before in my life.' This was the truth.

'I spoke to the barman two days ago. He was very unhelpful. He said he had never seen him before,' said Olivia.

Meredith doubted that Jordi was telling the truth but she nodded and said, 'It's probably the truth: these bars get a lot of passing customers.'

'We want you to find Amy. Today if possible. She's not answering her phone, ignoring messages from me and Adam, and this is exactly what happened before. I want you to nip it in the bud. We will cover whatever expenses you incur, as long as they are reasonable and you provide receipts. There's a small finder's fee as well, let's say €250. It should cover your travel and coffee expenses and leave you something to compensate you for loss of work, although, if I recall, you mentioned you were self-employed.'

The car was approaching the Moll de la Fusta and Soho House. Meredith looked out of the window and watched pink-faced tourists struggling along in the heat, pulling suitcases behind them. She didn't want to spend any more afternoons rounding them up and sending them to Alfonso's den, if that is, he would ever take her back.

She could negotiate. It was clear that they were desperate and would give her more, but that would make it look like she needed the money and she couldn't let Olivia know that she had nothing.

'I was planning on taking a few days holiday in any event. It's what we do here in August, the city being so hot and full of–' she looked directly at Olivia '– *guiris*, and I'd be delighted to help you guys find Amy.'

The taxi pulled in outside the hotel.

'There's something else as well. Amy has been appearing in some other posts,' said Olivia.

'What do you mean?'

Olivia held her up her iPhone so Meredith could see the screen. It was an image of Amy, but less glamorous, without make-up but looking relaxed. She was standing in front of a flag and smiling broadly. Ferran had his arm around her waist. In Catalan, the word 'llibertat' had been imposed on the photograph.

'So, the barman doesn't know Ferran but it took me around five minutes to find this on Instagram. His name is Ferran Alba and he is ignoring our direct messages. He's big in this independence movement but apart from that, I have drawn a blank. No one will talk to me and I won't lie, my lack of Spanish and Catalan is proving to be a problem.'

'That's the Estelada. It's the flag of Catalan independence. It's kind of controversial, especially if you're not in favour of independence,' said Meredith.

'I know that now, thanks to Google. And do you know what a shitstorm this has provoked from our sponsors already today? Amy's branding contracts are clear: no political or ethical entanglement outside the acceptable topics.'

'What is acceptable?'

'Oh, you know, climate change, as long as it doesn't relate to specific claims against the companies we work for; racism and sexism; but nothing to do with 'difficult' issues like this fucking referendum thing. This all looks a bit Brexity to me. We could lose contracts if she continues to post this sort of nonsense. And that's where you come in.'

'You want me to find her and stop her from posting to social media.'

Olivia rolled her eyes – all the other evening's bonhomie was gone. 'We want you to bring her back to the hotel and fulfil her professional duties. We think you owe us, but we will pay you. Will you do it for us?'

Meredith was going to do it. She would help them out and she would make them like her. She would become part of The Squad.

ADAM WAS SHOUTING at the photographer. 'Make it clean. I want it clean and crisp! Like the crack of a whore's whip on your arse, yeah?'

The Spanish photographer, in ubiquitous Barcelona artist uniform of a black T-shirt, black jeans and black boots, didn't reveal much emotion in his face, hidden as it was behind a thick black beard, but he carried on clicking in much the same fashion as before Adam shouted at him.

'Yeah, that's it, you're feeling me, I can tell!' Adam seemed pleased.

The scene in question was Dylan and Richard sharing a large cocktail with two straws. Both of them were topless, showing off gym-honed physiques. Both were wearing hats: Dylan a straw fedora with 'I Love Barcelona' in a ribbon around the brim and Richard a trucker's baseball cap.

Olivia leaned in closer to Meredith. 'Adam's genius was to build a narrative around the Instagram posts. He's a storyteller, essentially. The pictures on Instagram, while often beautiful, don't usually have a forward-propelling story. So Adam invents one. At the moment this set, of these two losers, will be hash-tagged along the lines of 'What the boys get up to when Amy's away'. The overarching story is that Richard is secretly in love with Amy, although of course, in reality, he's much more likely to be in love with Dylan.'

'Give it some ticket!' roared Adam as the boys pretended to arm wrestle.

'And do people believe this?'

Olivia laughed, 'Oh my goodness, yes! We did some posts last week when we realised Amy wouldn't be returning with the boys riding around Barcelona in a rickshaw looking for her. It has over 100,000 views already. Adam is a genius really: he turned her disappearance into one of the best posts we've ever had that didn't actually feature Amy.'

Meredith noted the 'we' and wondered about Olivia's relationship with Adam both on a personal and legal level. She would do well to find out. She had assumed Olivia's bitterness was due to being in the shade of Amy – but what better way to reassert control than to seduce the Svengali.

'So, Adam set all this up?'

Olivia waved at a waiter in a pressed white uniform. 'Oh, shit yeah. He spotted Amy. She had been annoying the hell out of all of us, well it was just me and Richard back then, by taking photographs of everything we did. She had a reasonable following on social media but nothing spectacular. Then we helped Amy do the video exposing her professor. What a stroke of luck that was. Adam was on the lookout for a vehicle to drive his concept of storytelling, saw her, beautiful, oppressed but defiant, and he contacted her. Next thing it was glamorous locations and product endorsements and here we are.' She threw her arms out wide.

'A gin and tonic, Hendricks gin. Nancy?'

It took Meredith a second to realise that Olivia was talking to her. Becoming Nancy again required concentration. '*Un cortado, por favor.*' She smiled at the waiter who visibly fell a little in love right on the spot.

Olivia yawned and nodded towards Adam. 'I guess he's our Svengali, but he is a genius, he really is. He used to manage that girl band, Liquid Love, back in the noughties, made a fortune and then lost it all in the 2008 crash. But he thinks big and influencers are the new rock and roll.' Olivia laughed. 'He says that a lot. He's so old.'

Adam grabbed a bottle of olive oil from one of the tables and poured a big slug into his hands. He then applied it onto Dylan's exposed biceps. Dylan looked surprised.

'Suck it up, big boy, you've got guns and we are going to fire them. Okay you' – he pointed at the photographer – 'make him look Mercedes or Porsche. Yeah?'

The photographer knelt down and started clicking even more furiously in response. Adam wandered over to them.

He was tanned and he had the sheen of wealth and confidence together with a streetwise swagger that immediately put her on her guard. This was someone who had to work and overcome a poor background, she could tell. He was like her and she should be careful around him.

Full smile.

Adam put his arm around Olivia.

'Sorry, we didn't talk much last week.' He hadn't said a word to her in La Alcoba Azul. 'I had business conversations to work through and that, but it's really pukka to have you on board, Christ she's a one, our Amy, eh? You can't turn your back for a moment. Olivia has told you this happens quite a bit?'

He didn't seem to pause for breath as he talked and Meredith wondered whether he was high.

'She mentioned Berlin.'

Adam slapped his hip and laughed. He leaned in close to them both. 'I know your generation don't like me saying this, but as my old man used to say, you can't trust a spic. A couple of glasses of sangria in they start telling you that you look an "English rose" and then it's a short step from there to swarthy charms back at his *casa*. I've had to tell billy-o over there' – he flicked his eyes to indicate Dylan – 'that I'm sure it's some cultural exchange thing and not "Spanish practices", you know.'

He licked his lips and smiled with his eyes. 'Gin and tonic, yeah,' he shouted to the barman, who was serving another customer.

Olivia tutted. 'Adam, you're so reductive and that is so racist. I apologise, Nancy.'

Meredith smiled and put out her hand. The truth was she was more bored by the authoritarian policing of her generation's language than most although she was acutely aware of the game that must be played to avoid social, and, increasingly possible, criminal sanction.

'It's fine, I can see Adam is only joking. How is Dylan holding up? He seemed quite upset the other night.'

Adam shrugged and waved at the barman again. 'He is like a well-trained dog. He can't focus on two things at once so the key is making sure he has a bone to chew on. Hence this photoshoot. Look at him, I swear if I held out a biscuit, he would sit on his hind legs and beg for it.'

Olivia put a hand on Adam's shoulder. 'Adam is frightfully mean about our Dylan. He takes a wonderful picture and we need some male eye candy on the feed. It keeps those on the more sexual end of the teenage spectrum happy, and what could be more wholesome than our chunk of Australian spunk over there.'

Meredith recalled opening the bathroom door at La Alcoba Azul to be confronted by Dylan looking up with a face full of white powder.

The barman placed a gin and tonic down in front of Adam.

'I love the measures here. Did you see how much gin he put in there? But you know why, yeah? It's because the service is so fucking slow – you'll need it to last until they get round to bringing you another.' He said this deliberately loudly but if the barman heard he gave no sign.

'This business with the Catalan dude... well, it's no secret that Amy likes to sow her wild oats – well maybe a secret to Dylan, but if he paid more attention to her and less to working out then maybe he would have noticed Amy spends a lot of nights 'researching old towns', if you catch my drift. But this time it's different. Has Olivia shown you the Instagram post?'

Meredith had changed her mind: she didn't like Adam. He reminded her of a snake, his eyes fizzing around their sockets looking for prey. 'Yes, I saw. That's very controversial here, at this moment in Catalonia's history. I find the whole thing fascinating, and as I told Olivia, I'm doing some research on it, hopefully for a book.' Meredith was lying. She couldn't care less. Group politics, the search for some identity that transcended your own seemed to her like a fool's errand. Catalonian or Spanish, the people in charge, the elites, would still find a way to screw you. But she knew what Adam wanted to hear.

'That's great, just what we need. I hadn't appreciated the shitstorm that was coming our way on this. Santander is threatening to pull sponsorship. It's one fucked-up paella, let me tell you.'

And he did indeed begin to tell her. As he droned on about clicks, CPCs, followers, loss of revenue and 'opportunities', a word that he used a lot, Meredith looked beyond him and Olivia. Her sunglasses hid the fact that she was looking down the historic Colom to the Columbus monument at the bottom of La Rambla.

Adam, Olivia, Amy and the rest had not mentioned or seemed interested in the architecture, or anything about the history of the city around them, accepting it purely as a back-drop to their lives as if the purpose was for them and only them. A life of foreign holidays, wealth and the ubiquity of beauty and pleasure had made them blind to the beauty of their world. *They don't deserve it,* thought Meredith. If she had their money and opportunity, she would enjoy it properly and use it to see the world properly, with eyes not focussed inward.

'We should be on 'top five destinations in Barcelona' now. We do it everywhere we visit. Amy in the top five sights, perfectly made up, some cool filters, with some discreet product placement, but instead, I've got no Amy and fucking local politics fucking everything up and that, my dear, can't be allowed to carry on.' His voice was thick with cigarette tar, sun, and booze.

Meredith thought she could easily come up with five ways to kill Adam, starting with pushing him off this roof terrace. Maybe he would finally notice the view as he plummeted to his death. 'I can see your dilemma, Adam, and I'm here to help.'

Adam looked at her. It was the first time she thought he was actually listening to her. She knew it was because she was useful to him. He was one of those men who had a filter, hearing women only when they were offering them something they wanted. It wasn't an uncommon trait.

He put his drink down and moved in to kiss Meredith on her cheek.

Meredith smelt tobacco and expensive cologne. His kiss was slightly wet but she smiled throughout.

He pulled away. 'You have a lovely smile, did you know that?'

She shook her head and thought about what she would have for dinner later. There was a pack of instant noodles in the communal kitchen that she could have unless El Spider or one of the other residents had swiped it to fend off the munchies.

'Thank you.' She caught Olivia's eye. 'No one has ever mentioned that before.'

Adam held up a finger. 'Top five smiles?'

'Easy,' said Olivia, 'Barrack Obama, Nelson Mandela, David Bowie, Ava Gardner and Frida Kahlo.'

Adam looked triumphant. 'Wrong! That Frida Kahlo, Christ, she's everywhere these days. You can't wipe your face on a tea towel without seeing her mug. The only smile she's got is the big hairy one above her eyes. The Mona Lisa, Olivia, best smile in the world. Proven.'

He raised both arms in victory.

Olivia shook her head in disgust.

Meredith imagined the top five ways she could kill them both, right here, right now.

1. Smash her cocktail glass and plunge it into their necks, severing their carotid arteries one after the other.

2. Push them both in the pool and then throw in the TV behind the bar and electrocute them.

3. Use the ice pick on the counter and take them both out Trotsky-style; it would be justice for the Frida Kahlo comment.

4. Grab a bottle of Orujo and douse them in it and then throw a match.

5. And the winner, point out the glories of the Moll de la Fusta and, as they lean over to take in the view, send them to their pavement fate with two quick hard shoves.

Meredith flirted with the idea that this was twisted thinking, which is what her father had often accused her of, but instead settled on just having a low tolerance for arseholes. But she would overcome her low tolerance – people were just difficult and she would find a way to deal with this, had to find a way, if she was to improve, and become a better version of herself.

'Yeah, isn't it, Nancy?'

It was Adam. She had been lost in her murderous reverie.

'Sorry, Adam, I didn't catch that.'

'I was saying, it would be a good idea if you got started right away, you know, finding Amy and getting her arse back here toot suite?'

Meredith nodded in agreement but she was thinking and contrasting her life with the glimpse she had been given into their lives. Behind Adam, she could see Richard and Dylan were now wrestling. These were two men in their late twenties, play-fighting. And Amy and Olivia, they didn't seem to do anything that resembled actual work. They lived a life of luxury and privilege that she could only dream of.

Meredith thought finding Amy would be easy. Jordi would never tell her who Ferran was. He prided himself on not revealing anything about his customers: it was the appeal of his place. But she recalled Spider mentioning a bar in Gràcia where all the *independentistas* hung out and she had a hunch that if she turned up there, she would find them, or someone, who for a vermut or beer would know where they were staying. But what she needed to work out was how to permanently make herself part of this world.

'I agree, I'll get on it right away.' Meredith didn't smile this time.

6

The door to Alfonso's cellar was locked.

This was unusual for a Saturday afternoon because this was when he did most of his business selling the cheap wine to tourists usually already half-drunk and so hot from the burning embrace of the city that they would part with dollars just to sit in the cool comfort of the cellar. But not today and this worried Meredith.

She walked to the square and into Bar del Pi. The owner, Ramon, was busy serving a counter full of customers but he acknowledged her with a cheery '*Bon día*' and she took an empty stool at the end of the bar.

The place still maintained its old-world charm and if George Orwell had strolled in, he would have recognised the tobacco-stained walls, shelves full of old bottles and threadbare furniture. But the clientele was standard 'summer Barcelona'. The locals, who refused to acknowledge the existence of the tourists as though ignoring an unpleasant smell, shared the same physical if not psychological space with them. A cortado duly arrived and Meredith asked Ramon why Alfonso's place was closed.

He grunted and then cocked his head back towards the door

where a bunch of tourists where huddled over a bowl of sangria like the witches from *Macbeth*.

'A *guiri* got ill, bad batch apparently. You know Alfonso got his wine from the Albanians? It had antifreeze in it as a fucking preservative. Fucking *cabróns*. If that tourist dies the *Mossos* will be all over the square. It's bad for business.'

Meredith felt her stomach contract as her anxiety relocated from its usual watching brief in her brain to active duty in her core. 'Do you know who the tourists were?'

Ramon shrugged. 'Just some American couple. Apparently, he was ill anyway but he's fucked now. You wouldn't have had anything to do with it, would you?' His eyes narrowed as he looked at her.

Meredith smiled and let her face light up with a joy and innocence she didn't possess. 'Gee, no, I helped him now and again, carrying the stuff, handing out flyers, but I had no idea about the wine being bad.'

Ramon grunted again. 'If you see him tell him to not bother coming back until next summer at the least. And if the American dies then he is better off heading for Venezuela!' He found this funny and laughed loudly.

Meredith wanted to ask him some more questions about where he thought Alfonso may be and whether the tourist may die or was this the usual barroom hyperbole, but he was now shouting in English at a bunch of nervous-looking Japanese students, asking them what they wanted.

She left the bar and wandered through the streets of the Barri Gòtic without any real idea of where she was heading and not sure who she could turn to. This was not an unusual experience for her. Although she had lived in the city for three years, she had few, if any friends. There were plenty of people she knew, who she could rely on to meet for a drink, but these were transactional relationships based on value exchange and loneliness. There was no one she could call and just talk to about her worries, her life, her future. It had always been like this, skipping from city to city, being a visitor to other people's lives and in many ways, she knew herself to be the ultimate tourist.

Her father had realised what she was early on in life and had, from the age of eight, called her a cold fish. But she didn't think this was true: she tried to fit in wherever she ended up. It was just that she hadn't met the right people, the right group into which she fitted. Money was part of the problem, of course. She was so busy scraping a living she never had the time to focus on friends, on living well and allowing herself to become 'part' of a place. She envied Amy and the easy way she had become something and was willing to become part of something else here in Barcelona and elsewhere. It was like Amy was set to receive and to transmit and she, Meredith, was only transmitting.

As she walked the tight alleyways shrouded in golden late afternoon sunshine that cut through the drying clothes on the rails above her, Meredith realised that she could change, she must change, she should become more like Amy.

But first, she had to find her.

THE DOOR to the apartment block was dark green. Well, the remaining flecks of paint that survived the general lack of care and attention were dark green; the rest of it was stripped down to its essence of blackened wood and as usual, the door was open, allowing any intruders easy access to the block.

She had told Spider, Frederick and the rest of their stoner friends to make sure they always closed it but they just laughed in her face and made comments under their breath about what a frigid bitch she was. At one time or the other, when they could be bothered raising themselves from the couch, they had all made a pass at her and had all been rebuffed. The insults followed soon after.

Meredith made her way up the grey concrete stairs, ignoring the ammonia smell of stale piss, which was always so much worse in the summer, until she reached the third floor and the door of apartment thirty-two. This too was slightly ajar and this was unusual. Spider and the rest of them always shut this door: they were paranoid about someone stealing their weed.

She pushed the door open slowly and gingerly stepped into the flat. It was quiet but this wasn't unusual at this time of day, as most of the residents didn't get up until well after lunchtime, but something was different. The hallway was clean. There was an absence of the usual junk, old bikes, electric scooters, skate-boards, and surfboards.

There was a low murmur of hushed voices from the lounge and she headed there, wondering what lay ahead.

The answer was all of her flatmates in various stages of undress like they had only been recently awoken.

Spider, Frederick, and Inga were lined up on the couch like errant schoolchildren and standing in front of them was a small man. She would put him no taller than five foot, dressed in black slacks, a black corduroy jacket, and a black fedora. His skin was the colour of dark mahogany and lined from many Catalonian summers. He turned to face Meredith as she entered the room and smiled at her broadly.

He tapped the floor with the cane he held in his right hand. 'And now we are complete, I believe?'

Spider nodded sullenly.

'Would you like a seat, my darling?' He indicated towards the couch on which there was no room at all.

Meredith knew what must have happened and what must have become of the possessions no longer in the hallway. She did a quick mental inventory of what she owned. Luckily, apart from the clothes and her ancient iPod, which she carried around with her at all times, there was nothing of value in her room. The only thing was her stash of money under the floorboards. She had managed to squirrel away just over €5,000. It was her escape money and all she had to her name in the world.

She remained standing.

'Do you know who I am, dear?' The little man's teeth were yellowed and black and he stank of cigar smoke. His mouth made Meredith think of a sulphurous crater.

'The King of Spain?'

He laughed and at the same time she noticed Spider shake his head and his eyes widen as though imploring her not to provoke the man. Meredith looked at the man again and became aware of how still he was. His black-clothed frame was small of stature but now she was aware of how his presence filled the room as though feeding on the fear, which was tangible.

'Well, there have been worse but alas no, I am Carlos Llul, merely the owner of this, and other properties in Barcelona and I make my humble living by receiving rent. And unfortunately, you lovely people have not been paying the rent and this is unacceptable.'

The others were looking downwards and now Meredith noticed that there was blood dripping from a cut to Frederick's lip. Surely, this little man hadn't done this to him.

As though answering her question there was a noise behind her and she turned as one of the widest men she had ever seen walked into the room. He seemed to be as wide as he was tall, which wasn't very. She put him at no taller than five foot three, but his bulk made him look enormous. He had South American features and his fingers were like plump chorizos. He was clearly behind the removal of the furniture and the injuries to her flatmates.

'Ah Diego, thank you for removing the items. They will go a little way – a very little way – to paying your overdue rent, but only a little way, yes? I need the rest now, if you please.'

Meredith was up to date with her rent. She paid it to Spider, who was the actual leaseholder, and who then subcontracted the rooms to the rest of them.

She turned her back and went to leave the room, but Diego stepped in front of her, blocking her exit.

'Don't, Meredith,' said Inga.

Carlos whirled round, surprisingly lithe on his feet for such an old man, and pointed at Meredith. 'You need to listen to your friend.' He knelt down, bringing his face close to Inga's. The Swedish girl began to shake. He brought his face close so his lips almost touched hers. 'If you all don't bring me my full rent, all of it that is owed, then it will not be your furniture that is taken away. It will be something far more irreplaceable. I trust you all understand.'

Inga nodded quickly, followed by Spider and Frederick.

Carlos stood up and looked at Meredith. 'And you?'

'I've paid him already.' She pointed at Spider.

Carlos cocked his head to one side and studied her for a second. 'You are different than these, yes I see it, but here is a little secret: I don't give a fucking shit. My money is all I want. Until Friday, yes? Here is my card if you need to contact me for' – he looked her up and down salaciously – 'anything, anything at all.'

He held her gaze for a moment and then clicked his fingers. 'Friday.'

He left the room with Diego.

Without looking or speaking to the others Meredith followed him out. She didn't trust herself not to put a fork in Spider's eye.

7

Luckily, they hadn't found the money hidden in a small gym bag under the floorboards, nor had they taken anything else, but that was only because she didn't own anything of value. To be so broke not to even have anything worth stealing did not feel like success at the age of thirty-two. Meredith flopped onto the mattress and inserted her headphones so she couldn't hear her housemates' vicious argument which was raging in the living room. She put on John Coltrane's *Giant Steps* and soon she was sleeping. When she woke, she realised with a curse that she needed something from the last person she wanted to be nice to right now.

Spider looked at her with suspicion but his fingers didn't stop their rolling action as he completed his spliff. Meredith was sure that his fingers performed this action even when he slept. 'Why do you want to know?'

Meredith cursed inwardly. Why did things have to be difficult with the people who had the least to lose? 'I've been asked by a friend who is writing an article on the independence movement and I know that you mentioned a bar in Gràcia where the key players hang out.'

He licked the paper and placed the large joint in his mouth.

Spider in another life could have been a model when heroin chic was in fashion, but he had never had the misfortune to be discovered. Meredith knew from experience that in a few years his face would start to show the ravages of his life of sloth and after that, he would be just another could-have-been.

He lit the joint and fiery embers leapt from its glowing end like lava rocks propelled from a volcano.

He sucked in deeply, held the smoke for what seemed like an age and then breathed it out. Meredith hated the smell, sweet and sickly, and Spider knew it.

She told herself that soon this would be over, and she could move out of this shithole, sharing with Eurotrash, who seemed content to just let their lives fade away in dark apartment rooms whilst listening to the same music and playing the same video games that they had enjoyed in their teenage years.

'Why should I tell you? I told you once already and you didn't listen or care. Now you want something you're interested. It's always the same with you Meredith, you only see people for what they can do for you. You're cold.'

He looked a little scared as he said this, his bloodshot eyes darting from her and then down again.

Meredith tried not to look annoyed. It wasn't true, so why did it bother her? She just liked some people and disliked others, that was perfectly natural and she shouldn't have to apologise for it. Yes, this occasion, she did want something from Spider, but surely that didn't make her manipulative or a cold fish.

She smiled but Spider just laughed. 'Won't work on me. Maybe in the past but not anymore.' He jabbed the joint at her. 'I know that smile.'

Meredith wished she didn't have to deal with the Spiders of this world. She needed a place and it wasn't here or anywhere she had been so far in her life. 'Look, I can help out with your share of the rent this month.'

Spider looked up and a greedy little look appeared on his face. 'Well, well, well, little Miss high-and-mighty really needs my help, eh?'

Meredith stood up. 'I can ask around. I'm sure Cheese will tell me.'

Spider looked panicked and waved for her to sit down. 'No, no, I was joking. Sure, I could do with a little loan, that's all it would be, a loan. Could you give me an advance now on next month's rent? You heard Carlos, I could do with a hand right now.'

'How much?'

'€100?'

Meredith took her purse out of her bag and took out two twenties. She handed them over to Spider, who immediately squirrelled them into his pocket.

'The bar?'

He grinned sheepishly. 'Oh yeah, the bar.'

8

Olivia sipped the wine and Meredith swore she almost purred.

She had ordered two glasses of white Garnatxa, confident that even Olivia with her refined palate wouldn't have tasted this before.

'That is so good, Nancy.'

'People are usually surprised by the white Garnatxa. Everyone knows the Garnacha for its reds but this is quite–'

'Unexpected.' Olivia held the glass up and examined the colour of the wine. 'And the colour. I thought it was off because it's so cloudy, but it's stunning.'

'That's the word, "unexpected", exactly. It's a natural wine so it's produced without any chemical intervention, no pesticides, no external yeast and definitely no sulphites. I'm glad you like it.'

She was glad that Olivia liked the wine, but she hadn't left the selection of the bar to chance. Bar Brutal was close to Soho House but more importantly, it served only the best in viticulture bio wines and was one of the best vinotecas for natural wines in the city. Meredith had spent a few hours the night before looking at Olivia's social media posts. She had the usual passions – photography, and travel, of course, but it was food, wine and the environment that she preached about the most, so Bar Brutal had been an easy choice.

Meredith didn't care for the cloudy, sediment-heavy natural wines and thought them lacking in refinement but they made great Instagram copy and Olivia, Meredith had noted with pleasure, had already taken a few photographs with her phone of the bottle they were drinking and the unfiltered wine sitting heavy in their glasses.

She needed Olivia on her side, that was clear enough, and to do this she needed to assuage her suspicions. Amy, once she found her, should be easy enough to win over – she liked Meredith or rather Nancy already. Olivia was the issue. If only Olivia wasn't around, things would be a lot easier, but she was, so Meredith would have to make her see just what an asset to The Squad she could be. Meredith wanted more than just to be a local fixer and 'person they used to know'. She had already determined that she wanted more of their life and less of her own.

They were sitting, side-by-side, on stools that faced the bar.

'I have to say, Nancy, you have turned out differently from how I expected.'

Meredith didn't appreciate the 'turned out': she was still a work in progress, would be for some time and she was determined to become the person she wanted to be, to improve. Olivia was what, four years her junior and Meredith could tell that she thought she had 'made it', achieved her dreams, was where she wanted to be at this stage in life. Meredith wasn't sure whether she should be jealous of this or infuriated.

'What did you expect?'

Olivia frowned. 'I remember you as somewhat exotic because I couldn't relate to you at all. We weren't sure whether you liked boys or girls, which we all thought was so cool. And you seemed destined for something else, your whole 'being there but not there thing' made me think you knew something the rest of us didn't and would end up as the President or the leader of some apocalyptic cult.'

She didn't need to add the implicit coda. *And look where you ended up and where I ended up.*

Meredith had no idea what 'thing' she had back then or what Olivia was referring to. Was this why she seemed guarded around her? She remembered feeling liberated after escaping the States and just wanting to do all the things that she hadn't been able to do during her teenage years. This may have meant she was a bit wild and reckless but she was entitled to this, surely, after what she had been through.

'We only knew each other for a couple of weeks ten years ago.' Meredith desperately tried to keep any sound of anger or embarrassment out of her voice but she wasn't sure that she succeeded.

'Yeah, but you don't need that long to know the essence of someone, yeah? Look at social media, people are attracted to Amy, to me, to The Squad, because they can see our essence in those images and videos and they empathise with us.'

'They want what you have,' said Meredith rather too quickly.

Olivia didn't seem to notice Meredith's tone. 'That's true but you can look at the same hotels, exotic locations, cars, and restaurants' feeds and sites – but people want to see us. It's the people, it's us they want to be, not the things we have.'

Meredith knew it was true. She had spent the last few evenings browsing Instagram, looking at images of The Squad, and it was intoxicating: they seemed to have everything material. But Olivia was right – it wasn't that that drew you back. It was the story behind the pictures, the beauty and confidence of Amy speaking to younger, insecure girls as an expression of what they could be if only they looked a little bit like her. Perhaps they could achieve this by going to the same places or buying the same make-up which Amy generously listed in the tags below her images. It was pure advertising and advertising worked best when selling a lifestyle, and The Squad's lifestyle, with its pictured camaraderie, and easy-going enjoyment of pleasure, with nods to all the right causes to offset the consumption guilt, was pitch-perfect. And Meredith wanted to buy.

'So, what happened? I know you don't live at that building where I picked you up. I check out everyone we work with and you aren't registered there. What's even odder is that there is nothing about you online at all. I know you explained about your boyfriend in Australia but do you know how weird that is these days? It looks so odd.'

This was good news. It meant they had only searched for 'Nancy Heller'. If they had searched for 'Meredith Weaver' then they may have come up with a little bit more. Meredith had made full use of the privacy laws to clean her online footprint as best she could, but some things would always be there. She could lie about the flat, but Olivia was too shrewd and thorough for that lie to be sustained.

'About the flat in Gràcia, okay, I hold my hands up. I was a little embarrassed. You guys are all staying in Soho House and I'm in a shared flat, more like a squat, actually. And as I told you, for the last ten years I've been travelling and, well, here I am.'

'Some people might consider that a cool way to live and, to be honest, Nancy, with your looks and a good camera you could have monetised your life a long time ago. It's not too late. How old are you? I know you told me last week but I was so drunk I can't remember a thing.'

Meredith had told her she was twenty-eight and regretted it – but she was sure Olivia could remember everything. This was a test. She would need to maintain the lie.

'Twenty-eight,' she lied.

'Same as us. You could easily do it, you know. You just need a bit of patience, and with that face' – she drew a circle with her finger – 'you could still do it. But you need to do it before you're thirty – that's the youth threshold.'

Meredith was acutely aware of her age and its value as the world grew younger. And she was also aware of its limited time value. Her stepmum was a case in point: she had traded her beauty early for the love of her father and it had proved to be the worst bargain she ever made. But by the time she realised it, it was too late and she was old, worn out and terminally ill. Meredith would not make that mistake.

'I appreciate the advice and I think what you guys have done is fantastic and I'm really kind of jealous. I will find Amy. That won't be a problem – but do you think you and Adam would help me, you know, monetise my life, as you say?'

This is why she asked to meet Olivia again. She needed to get it on the table as soon as possible. Finding Amy would be easy and then what? They would drop her as they had after she met them a week ago.

Olivia blinked and didn't reply immediately. When she did, she didn't look directly at Meredith. 'Well, I'm sure we could give you some general tips but we are a pretty close group, you know, and the dynamic as it works at the moment is the secret of our success. That dynamic is our identity and we need to protect that. That's why this Amy business is so frustrating: she plays around with these other identities not realising she is jeopardising the only one that sells.'

Meredith had wanted to ask Olivia if she could come to stay and live with them in Soho House but she could sense that this would also be met with a negative reaction. Olivia was the road-block she would have to deal with in another way.

Olivia must have noticed the disappointment register on

Meredith's face. 'Look, I'll speak to Adam about getting a voucher together for you to take some online social media classes. Given your existing profiles, which is like nil, then I'd advise you start with the basic classes first.'

Meredith flashed her smile to try and disguise the feeling of hatred she had towards Olivia. 'That's very generous of you. I think I have a good lead on Amy, by the way.'

She would let this good lead take a couple of days to pan out as she may as well take those per diem expenses.

Olivia reached out and touched Meredith's arm.

'That's really great, Nancy. I knew you would be able to help us. See, you are good at something, chin up. Once you get her back we can take a look at you' – she looked her up and down – 'and make a decision on what your identity should be.'

Meredith gripped her glass hard and looked straight ahead.

D*rift.* That was the real answer to Olivia's question. Meredith had allowed *drift* to be her identity. With horror, she realised that in the absence of examining and deciding what she should do with her life she had slipped into the coma-like state of the majority of the population, just waiting for someone or something to come along and recognise her talent, for the universe to coalesce around her with benevolent love, and give her purpose. She was in essence no different to Spider, no, scratch that, she was worse because she was aware of her position but had done nothing to change it.

She had drifted whilst a bunch of spoilt, pampered youths had prospered and it wasn't, as much as it may be comforting to think, due to their inherent privilege.

Meredith ignored the catcalls of two young Moroccan teenagers who looked up from their mobile phone screens to shout sexual innuendos at her. The teenagers were wearing the international uniform of the middle-class rebellious, an homage to US rappers, of expensive leisurewear, Gucci trainers and baseball caps that rested on their heads. Wasn't this another sign? The fact that Amy and Olivia had realised the world, which

Meredith explored by foot, was reduced to the size of your phone and you could market your life directly to the masses. Whilst Meredith had been scamming tourists and selling bangles on the beaches of Bali, these girls had been thinking bigger and with more confidence.

She needed to do this, but Olivia would be a problem as it was evident that she saw the group as a closed unit. *Well, we will see about that,* thought Meredith. But first, she needed to find Amy. She checked the address and name on the piece of paper that Spider had given her. It was of a bar in Gràcia that didn't appear in any online guides and wouldn't be popping up on Instagram anytime soon.

It was on a small square, hidden in the barrio, and the approach was down narrow alleys with apartment balconies festooned with Esteladas. Every few yards yellow graffiti was scrawled on the pavement and road declaring '*independència*'. This area of Gràcia was the beating heart of the independence movement in Barcelona.

Eventually, she came to a small square, Plaça del Raspall, in the centre of which was a fountain weakly lit by a cracked streetlight. The square was empty save for the bar in one corner. The bar was called La Barraqueta and there was a hammer and sickle image on the sign above the door. Outside the bar stood a few smokers talking furtively in between drags of their cigarettes or swigs of their bottles of beer.

Meredith walked across the square, and as she did, she could feel the eyes of the smokers on her. When she reached the group, they made no effort to stand aside and let her through to the door.

One of them, a small dark man with a rat's tail haircut said something in Catalan she couldn't quite catch and the others laughed.

'*Què has dit?*'

They looked surprised that she asked them what the man had said.

An older man, maybe in his late thirties, with a dirty grey beard and whose cigarette drooped from his lips like a brown-stained frown, grunted and then stood back, allowing her to pass through and enter the bar.

Meredith walked forward to the door and pushed it open but before she entered the bar she paused and turned to face the group. She smiled as sweetly as she ever had and watched the eyes of the men reappraise her and soften.

'You are all cunts,' she said in Catalan, and before they had a chance to reply she stepped into the bar.

The music was loud, South American rhythms and an electronic drumbeat that suited the atmosphere of shouted conversations and alcohol-fuelled rebellion.

It was dark and packed with the usual *independentista* crowd. Everyone was dressed in dark colours, many with military touches such as caps and fatigues. Che Guevara's spiritual presence was strong here.

She made her way to the bar and waved to the barman, a bearded heavyset guy who nodded almost imperceptibly to indicate that he had seen her.

'A caña,' she said, and he quickly drew and set down a small beer on the bar before her.

'Can I ask you a question?' she said in Catalan.

He shrugged his shoulders.

'Do you know this girl? Has she been in here?' Meredith held up her mobile phone and showed him Amy's Instagram profile picture.

The barman looked at Meredith properly for the first time. 'Who are you? Are you police?'

She smiled sweetly and shook her head. She had a vague awareness that the people just behind her had stopped their conversation and were now listening to what she was saying. 'No, I'm a friend of hers. We are just here visiting and' – Meredith performed a little giggle – 'we are tourists and she met a guy, this Ferran, and I'm just trying to find her.'

The barman looked over Meredith's shoulder as though catching the eye of someone behind her. Meredith turned and came face-to-face with the drooping cigarette man from outside.

'A tourist who speaks Catalan. Most of them can't even say paella properly.'

She went to protest but he took hold of her wrist and gripped it hard. 'Tell me who you really are and what you want with Ferran.'

Meredith looked down at her wrist and then with her free hand she grasped hold of her beer glass and smashed it on the bar before holding the jagged edge up to the man's throat. 'Let go of my fucking hand.'

Everyone in the bar was looking and the place seemed quiet although the music was still playing.

He looked at the glass poised next to his neck and then back at her. 'You haven't got the balls, you little whore.' He tightened his grip on her wrist.

Meredith took a deep breath.

'Let her go, Oriel!' A young man with a wry expression of amusement in his dark eyes placed a hand gently on Oriel's shoulder. Oriel turned and when he saw who it was, he released his grip on Meredith's arm.

The new arrival looked at Meredith and nodded towards the glass.

Meredith put the glass back on the bar. The young man whispered something in Oriel's ear and then joined Meredith.

'Apologies for Oriel. He thought you were an undercover agent for the Guardia Civil. He has a vivid imagination.'

Meredith leant back against the bar and studied the young

man. Closer, she could see he was a little older than she first thought, with laughter lines around his eyes and a touch of grey in the otherwise thick black hair at his temples.

'Thank you. I can't stand violence but no man grabs hold of me like that.'

The young man held his finger up at the barman and another beer was placed in front of her. 'I'm Edu. Nice to meet you, even in these circumstances.' He held out his hand.

Meredith took his hand and then he pecked her twice on the cheeks. 'Is this your bar?'

He laughed and looked almost embarrassed at the question. 'No, this is a cooperative. Everyone owns it, even Oriel. I just manage the place. And I have to say it is very unusual to get tourists in here. Guardia undercover agents would be more likely and as easy to spot. So, if you are not a tourist – and I don't think you are – and you are not an agent, then perhaps you want to tell me exactly how you ended up in my bar.'

Meredith put her mobile phone on the bar and showed him the picture of Amy. 'This is my friend. She has left her job to play fuck buddies with a guy who drinks in this bar, and I want to find her and speak to her before she loses her job.'

Edu picked up the phone and looked at the picture. 'That's the first time I've heard being an influencer described as a job.'

'You know her?'

He looked at the picture again and then smiled at her. 'Maybe, maybe not. If I did, I'd need to talk to them to see if they wanted to speak to you. It's only polite. Give me your number.'

'Nancy, my name is Nancy Heller. Amy knows me from Thailand.'

Edu arched an eyebrow. 'I won't ask now why someone who needs to remind Amy who she is, is looking for her. I'll let you tell me that story over a drink if that is okay with you?'

Meredith wasn't swayed by chat-up lines or confidence but

there was a humorous glint in his eye that made her think he didn't take himself too seriously.

'What's your number, Edu?'

He gave it to her and she sent him her number.

'Get me to Amy and the drink's on me,' she said, and then turned and left the bar.

This time there was no problem with the crowd of smokers outside the door, they just parted and let her through.

10

T he message from Richard was short:

> We need you! Come and meet us and bring your swimming costume

It contained a link to a Google Maps location that Meredith didn't need as she knew the place well.

Meredith cycled down to the coast using one of the city bikes. Along the way she passed the many distractions set out like sticky fly traps to capture tourists before they ever got the chance to reach the more relaxed beach at Bogatell: restaurant hawkers, *manteros* selling counterfeit goods and weed, flew by in a blurred mosaic of colour as she pedalled furiously to get to the beach.

When Meredith arrived at the beach she noted with dismay, but not surprise, that The Squad had secured themselves a volleyball court right by the sea. She hated exercise. To her, it seemed a pointless waste of energy and she would much rather read a book or listen to music than run around like a child. However, her hours of reviewing Amy's profile told her that sporty photographs gave great returns in terms of 'likes'. It was no doubt because it provided an excuse to show more flesh, an opportunity that Adam had seized upon.

A quarter of the beach was sectioned off for volleyball courts. The rest of the beach was filled with sunbathers. Meredith didn't like the beach: the sunbathers reminded her of lounging seals and the volleyball players of eager infants chasing a ball. In her opinion, the beach was a place for juveniles and sloths. She spotted Richard and Dylan first. They were clowning about in one half of the court, with Olivia and Adam on the other side of the net. She took off her sneakers and, holding them in her hand, she hopscotched across the burning sand to join them.

All the boys were topless and although Richard and Dylan fitted in with the general Barcelona beach aesthetic of ripped muscles, golden tans, and laid-back ease, Adam did not. His thin, pale body was beginning to turn pink. His alcohol-bloated, red and blotchy face contrasted sharply with the rest of The Squad's burnished and toned bodies. When he saw Meredith approaching, he ran over to her and threw his arms around her. Even on the beach, he smelt of cologne and tobacco.

'Thank all the fucks! They dragged me in to play and I fucking hate volleyball nearly as much as I hate the beach!' He stood back and appraised her. She was wearing a flowing linen jumpsuit over her bikini. 'But you, Nancy, wow! You are going to fit right in.'

Olivia had wandered over. She was wearing a plain black Chanel swimsuit that was designed for long, athletic bodies like hers.

'Ain't that right, Olly?'

Olivia responded with a flat smile. 'Sure, why not. Are you going to play then? You don't strike me as the sporty type.'

'I'll give it a go,' replied Meredith.

Olivia turned and walked back to the court.

'Don't mind her, she's probably on her period.'

'Every other day,' muttered Meredith so only Adam could hear. He laughed.

'Hey Nancy, are you ready to get thrashed?' shouted Richard. He high-fived Dylan.

'Go on and join them. I need to get some material and we can catch up on your progress in finding Amy later, I'm guessing you haven't tracked her down yet?'

'Soon,' she replied.

Adam sat down by the side of the court and began to unload a backpack, taking out a large camera and lenses. Olivia was standing at the far end of the court, hand on hip, waiting for her.

Instead of joining her straight away Meredith knelt down next to Adam. 'I will find her, you know. It may take a couple more days though. And here' – she took out some factor fifty sunscreen from her bag – 'let me put some of this on you – we don't want you burning and looking like a *guiri*.'

Adam stopped fiddling with the camera equipment and let Meredith apply the sunscreen to his neck and shoulders. 'That's really thoughtful of you.' And then to Richard and Dylan who were closest, 'You could have told me I was turning into a fucking lobster!'

'Sorry, Adam,' said Richard. Dylan seemed distracted by the sight of his own feet and didn't pay any attention to Adam.

As she rubbed the cream into Adam's back, she could feel Olivia's eyes burning into her back and she made sure she did a good job of covering all of Adam's pasty and now slightly-seared flesh. When she was done, she stood up and walked slowly over to join Olivia.

'Nice job,' said Olivia, 'but you should know Adam is all about business, nothing else.'

Meredith was about to object, and she certainly had no interest in Adam sexually, but she wasn't going to rise to Olivia's bait. She figured that Olivia was constantly testing, pushing and then pulling. You just had to go with it and see where it led, and hope that when she did make up her mind, it would be in your favour.

'Now, you better be able to play well, and you can't play in that.' Olivia pointed at Meredith's linen jumpsuit.

Feeling awkward and knowing that the boys' eyes – and those of others on the beach – were on her, she shuffled out of the suit. Wearing just her bikini, another Inga donation, Meredith joined Olivia in the centre of the court.

'You look better than I remember. You had a little bit of puppy fat before. Poverty suits you.'

It was true. Meredith had shifted the additional weight she carried in her younger years because often she couldn't afford more than one meal a day. However, even though the weight had gone she still carried around the self-consciousnesses about her body that went with it and she felt uncomfortable showing so much skin.

'Let's just play,' said Meredith.

'Sure.' Olivia bent down and picked up the ball by her feet and then threw it straight at Meredith who just about managed to catch it before it collided with her head.

'Sorry, I don't know my own strength sometimes. Why don't you serve first?'

Meredith looked across at a nearby court where a young girl popped a smooth serve over the net. It looked easy. She threw the ball up and as it came down, she hit it, caught the top and powered the ball into the sand next to her feet.

'Jesus, you live here. I thought you would be good at this,' said Olivia.

'You can have another go. We won't count that,' shouted Dylan from the other side of the court.

'Patronised by the men, great,' said Olivia. 'You okay with this?'

Meredith nodded. *Christ, I hate sports,* she thought.

She picked the ball up and felt its weight in her hands. It was just a matter of striking it in the centre. *Keep your eye on the ball,* she told herself and then launched it into the air. This time as it descended, she hit it hard and flush in the centre and it flew across the net. Dylan managed to push it back into the air but Richard mistimed his spike and the ball slammed into the net.

'One nil,' called out Dylan with a big grin on his face.

'Better, I was starting to think you couldn't do this either. No luck finding Amy then?'

'I'll find her, don't you worry. I know how important she is to you all.'

Olivia sighed loudly. 'Concentrate now – Dylan is serving and you know these Australians – nothing behind the eyeballs but mighty fine at sports.'

The serve came in fast and hard. Olivia dived and got her hands to it, but the ball bounced straight off them and out of play. Olivia was left lying on the sand.

Meredith looked down at her. 'Hard cheese,' she said.

'What?'

'It's from an old movie.'

Olivia got up and dusted the sand from her body but some of it was stuck in the suntan oil that covered her. Meredith guessed some was stuck to her backside as Adam was kneeling by the edge of the court taking photographs.

'Whatever, let's play. I can't stand being beaten by these boys.'

'Agreed,' said Meredith.

They took the next point with Olivia spiking the ball after Meredith managed to get her hands to a serve from Richard. This time they exchanged a high five.

From then on it was catch up. They kept one point ahead of the boys until the score was 20-19 and Meredith was to serve for match point. She tossed the ball up and hit it. It was the same result as her very first serve: it hit the ground by her feet.

The boys jumped up and Dylan shouted, 'We are not giving you this one. We've got you now!'

Olivia shook her head and muttered something under her breath that sounded like 'useless' to Meredith's ears.

With the game tied Olivia served next to Dylan. He fielded the return easily, sending the ball high and setting it up for Richard, who jumped and then smashed it down into the sand.

'Fuck!'

Olivia stormed over to Meredith. 'Okay listen, Richard is going to serve to you and as you've seen, his serve is shit. He's also a complete flake and will be shitting himself with anxiety right now so he will play it safe and float it over. So move forward, take it early and set me up. We've got this, yeah. Don't fuck it up.'

Adam was still snapping away constantly and now a small crowd had gathered as the games on the courts either side came to an end.

Meredith didn't say anything but just returned to her side of the court.

Olivia stood by the net and then turned to Meredith and nodded to indicate that she should move forward to receive the serve. Sweat was pouring down Olivia's back and Meredith was also feeling the heat and although she was used to it – as much as you could be – she wasn't used to exercising in it. It seemed like a stupid thing to do and she resented being in this situation. *As though it matters an iota who wins this childish game,* she thought.

Meredith took a step forward.

Richard threw the ball up and then on its descent hit it

gently so that it floated, just as Olivia said it would, across the net, and started to drop softly towards the sand. Meredith reached it easily. The correct move was to push the ball back into the air to allow Olivia, who was poised by the net in anticipation of this play, to smash the ball down into the other side of the court but instead, Meredith raised both her palms and hit the ball, hard and fast, towards Olivia. It was too fast for her to react properly and although she tried to get her hands to the ball it slammed into her face.

Olivia fell to the floor clutching her nose.

Dylan, Richard and Adam ran to her aid.

'Oh God, I'm so sorry, are you all right?'

Olivia looked up at her, eyes full of fury. 'You did that on purpose.'

'I'm so sorry, Olivia. It's just that I'm so useless at this game.'

Helped by Richard and Dylan, Olivia got to her feet. There was blood on her chin. 'I'm going to get cleaned up.'

'Hang on, Olivia, just let me get this.' Adam held up his mobile phone and took a picture of Olivia.

'You fucker,' she said.

Richard put an arm out. 'Are you okay, Olivia? That looks bad.'

She knocked his arm away. 'Get off me, I'll be fine. I'm going to get cleaned up in the toilets. You better be buying a good lunch, Adam.'

Olivia traipsed off towards the concrete block of toilets at the other end of the beach.

Adam examined the screen. 'Probably won't use that. Maybe for a private member special,' he said to no one in particular.

Meredith began to walk off the court but Adam grabbed hold of her arm. 'Look at this, by the way.'

He showed her his mobile phone. It was The Squad's Instagram feed and the picture was a heavily-filtered image of

Meredith waiting to receive a serve on the beach volleyball court. Even she had to admit it: she looked amazing, athletic and supple with the afternoon sun at her back accentuating her lithe figure and making the specks of sand on her skin look like golden crystals. The look on her face was one of absolute focus and it made her look like she was a transcendent zen figure of pure flow.

At the time the photograph was taken she had been thinking, *How do I get off this baking, sweaty, sand-filled hellhole?* But the photograph made the experience look like the most fun in the world. Hell, it even made Meredith want to play volleyball again, something she knew she would never do.

> 'That's how you do it. It's a magician's trick. That's not
> really me.'

Adam took this as a compliment. 'I posted this twenty minutes ago. Check out the likes.'

There were over 650 already.

'It doesn't seem that many.'

Adam chuckled. 'You don't get it. At this rate this could end up being one of the most popular posts we have ever done.'

Adam must have seen something in her expression change. 'Are you all right, Nancy? I should have asked you but I can take it down if you want?'

Meredith nodded and looked again at the image. It made her stomach twist with excitement and fear. Her image, and location on Instagram, and seen by God knows how many people by the end of the day. The text accompanying the image stated:

> *The newest member of the gang? We found her after ten
> years! Friends forever and a demon volleyball player,
> Welcome to Nancy!*

Nancy. No one was looking for Nancy. What were the chances that her father's relatives cared one jot? There was no one after her: it was just paranoia that had driven her around the globe. She was safe and now she had the chance to be something, to make something instead of drifting.

'No, that's fine. Keep it there. It's just a bit of fun and I do look pretty good. You are a great photographer, Adam.'

Adam linked his arm with hers. 'Come on. Let's go and get lunch and make the right noises to calm Olivia. Congratulations, Nancy, you're officially "talent" now.'

Olivia would be furious and this made Meredith smile.

11

The bed was nearly as big as her apartment room.

She lay, arms and legs splayed out, enjoying the sensation of comfort, coolness, and the security that only a €750-a-night room at Soho House can bring. It felt right and her mind felt at ease for the first time in months, maybe years. She realised now that this was what had been missing. Here she could focus on what she wanted and not scrabble around looking for scraps to just get by and survive, to pay the rent to buy shitty food. How could you concentrate on your inner well-being and growth as a person if you had no time or space to do it? And now here she was and she knew what she wanted. She wanted to stay here forever.

It was Adam's idea, or so he thought, that she move into Amy's suite: she may as well, as Amy wasn't using it. She had told him all about her landlord problems and how they were distracting her from looking for Amy. When the penny had finally dropped, he had looked triumphant as he suggested it made perfect sense for her to move in as it was all paid for and would give her more time to look for Amy and to help them on the occasional photoshoot. Olivia had been talking to Dylan at the time and when Adam announced the fact that Meredith would be moving into the hotel with them her face had remained impassive but she had stared at Meredith with cool hard fury.

Lying on the bed Meredith determined to work hard on making Olivia like her. There was no reason why she shouldn't – well, apart from the volleyball incident, but she had been provoked and perhaps it had been an accident after all. They were about the same age, were similarly well-read, and liked the same things. There was no reason for Olivia to see her as a threat as she was nothing of the sort. She just wanted to be like them. And if Olivia couldn't or wouldn't accept this then any unpleasantness could hardly be blamed on Meredith.

There was a knock on the door. It was room service. She tipped the porter with one of her last, crumpled five-euro notes and then sat on the bed looking in awe at the silver platter on which was fresh orange juice, a cortado, an egg white omelette, avocado toast and copies of *La Vanguardia*, *El Periódico*, *El País,* and *The New Yorker*.

But before she began to eat, she remembered what Adam had told her. *Document everything: it's all content.* She reached across and picked up her mobile phone from the bedside cabinet and quickly took a bunch of snaps of the breakfast platter and then for good measure she walked to the floor-to-ceiling window that looked out across the Passeig de Colom. She opened it slightly and the heat hit her like a blast wave accompanied by a dry breeze that made the voile curtains twist and turn in a most romantic way. She then took off her robe so that she was just wearing a little silk slip and pants and then balanced the phone on the top of a chair and checked it was focussed on the window. She set the timer for ten seconds and ran over to the curtains.

She raised her right leg slightly and looked out of the

window. *Longingly,* she thought. She knew this was a popular pose of Amy's, looking longingly out of a hotel window. She heard the camera snap away and when it was finished, she checked the photographs. They were the same shots she had seen on Amy's timeline and she knew once Adam had finished applying filters and working on them, they would look even better.

She sent them to Adam and then settled down to enjoy a breakfast she had been waiting for, for a long time.

Leaving her old apartment hadn't been a pleasant experience – but what could you expect from Spider and the rest of them. She had told them she was going on holiday for a while and Spider had told her that he would have to sub-let her room. She had just shrugged as she knew he would say this and there was no use arguing with him. Then she had slapped a big padlock on her door so he couldn't access her room. He called her a 'real shit' and stormed off to the lounge to get furiously high. Inga had seemed upset and had hugged her, which Meredith found strange as she didn't think of herself as friends with the Swedish girl, but she had hugged her back and told her she wouldn't be away for more than a couple of weeks. She had decided to leave her €5,000 under the floorboards and not take it to the hotel. It occurred to her that Olivia could lock her out of the hotel room at any time with a quick word to reception. So, it seemed wiser to leave the money where she could guarantee access. She didn't think Spider and his stoned cronies had it in them to break down her door and search her apartment but she was sure it was safe there even if they did. They hadn't the first idea of how to use the fridge, never mind a screwdriver.

After breakfast, she took the most luxurious shower she had ever had, got dressed and went upstairs to meet Adam. He was waiting for her at a table by the pool. It was shaded by a large canvas umbrella and there were pastries and a coffee pot on the table. He didn't look up from his mobile phone when she sat down.

His thumbs moved quickly, and then when he was satisfied, he looked up.

'Nancy! How was the room? Pretty good, hey?'

She agreed but didn't say that it was the best place she had ever stayed. She had already noticed the habit of Richard, Olivia and Dylan, and the other Instagrammers, which was not to be enthusiastic about material things. Enthusing about the natural world was fine but not cars, hotel room and brands. That was for a sub-set of more vulgar, often Eastern European or Middle Eastern influencers, the kind who posed next to private jets or with their pet cheetahs. The Squad's angle, not unique, was friendship, good times, and authenticity.

'I love the fact that they only use natural, organic materials,' said Meredith.

Adam didn't appear to hear her: he was back looking at his phone. 'So, listen, change of plan today. The photoshoot with Richard and Dylan, I'm sticking you on the back burner for that.'

Meredith felt something in her stomach twist and turn. 'Okay,' she said quietly.

'Here she is,' said Adam.

'Move over, Adski.'

Meredith turned round and saw Olivia approaching.

Adam compliantly moved along to let Olivia squeeze in next to him.

Olivia smiled at Meredith. 'I'm guessing that Adam has mentioned we want you to concentrate on finding Amy and getting her to come back. We thought it made more sense to focus on what we are all here for. So, we will have to stand around all day, in this heat' – she mimed a fan – 'being bloody human mannequins, and you get to have all the fun running around this lovely city looking for Amy. How's that going by the way?'

Meredith glanced out towards the sea and then down to the street. It was maybe seventy feet below them and any fall from here would be fatal.

'Nancy?'

She turned back and smiled at Olivia because she knew that Olivia hated her smile. It was because Olivia's smile fooled no one, not like hers, which had been forged in the harshest of environments. 'Of course, I was just about to tell Adam I couldn't make the shoot as I have to meet a lead who knows Ferran.'

Olivia clapped her hands and then threw an arm around Adam. 'That's great news! We'll have you back in your old life in no time!'

Adam looked a little sheepish. Last night, after a bottle of Rioja, he had been full of promises of sponsorship deals and branding tie-ins, and had said he would spend the day setting up her social media channels. 'Yeah, I think that's a great idea, Olly. It also gives me some time to set up Nancy's social media accounts today.' Adam fiddled with his phone and didn't look directly at Meredith.

Olivia reached in and grabbed a croissant from the table. 'Don't let us hold you up. I know you must be keen to get started,' she said, and then bit into the croissant.

Meredith wanted to reply but the weight of Olivia's words and her triumphant expression crushed her ability to speak as she knew her voice would falter, crack and let her down. She recalled similar occasions as a child when she thought she had ingratiated herself with other children – something would always happen; they would be cruel, mock her thrift-store clothes or the fact that her mother was dead, and each time she never saw the blow coming and the shock rendered her speechless. At school she had recoiled from the insults but never forgave them, planning and then taking revenge, that eventually led to her expulsion after she placed a dead rat in Kristy Nichol's gym bag for saying in front of the whole class that 'Meredith has no friends because Meredith's mother is in hell as are all sinners who violate God's law and kill themselves'. She found herself struck as dumb as she had been back when she was a child, knowing that there was an answer, a form of words that if only she could find them, would make her accepted, would make her right, would make her loved. But the words didn't come. They never came.

Instead, she mumbled something about Edu and the café but Adam was looking at his phone again and Olivia didn't even pretend to listen.

Meredith got up and walked back to her room. What had seemed so exciting and new before, now seemed mocking and cruel, like pressing her nose up against a shop window full of enticing items she would never be able to afford.

Mechanically, she applied sunscreen and then packed her small rucksack with everything she would need for the day. She didn't look back at the room when she left.

Edu had replied immediately to her text and agreed to meet her. She had chosen the café as she didn't want to go back to La Barraqueta and run the risk of bumping into the Gràcia branch of macho socialists again. She chose a square in Gràcia and arrived there early – but he was already there, sitting at one of the café terrace tables with a view of the clock tower in the centre of the plaza.

He looked pleased to see her and stood up and they exchanged greetings and cheek kisses. He offered her a chair and she sat down.

For a second he said nothing, just looked at her, and she realised that he genuinely did like her and that this urbane, confident man was perhaps already a little in lust with her. This sometimes happened but this time she felt pleased about it because it would help her instead of being the hindrance it usually was.

'I was pleased to receive your call. Things have been a little crazy so it's good to take some time out and meet' – he paused – 'a friend for coffee.'

'Is that what we are, friends?' she said.

He laughed and then waved the waiter over. 'Friends have coffee, no?'

They ordered a cortado for her and a café solo for him.

'How is the bar?' she asked him.

'Busier than ever but we are under surveillance the whole time from the National Guard. They think that someone is trying to re-establish the Terra Lliure.'

Meredith shook her head. 'The Terra Lliure? Is that another one of the unions, or co-ops?'

Edu ran a finger around the edge of his coffee cup and didn't reply immediately. He glanced at the tables either side which were occupied by tourists and then he leaned forward and spoke in a hushed tone.

'After the failed independence bid, the jailing and exile of our leaders and the way Madrid has treated us, some people are whispering that the Terra Lliure are coming back. They were a separatist group, from back in the eighties, who advocated more violent methods to achieve independence.'

'A terrorist group?'

Edu made a noise in the back of his throat and shrugged. 'It depends on your viewpoint. Some would call them freedom fighters but the point is the police have got it into their heads that the bar is where some of them meet.'

'Is that true?'

Edu smiled with his eyes. 'If I had a euro for every *independentista* who has a bellyful of drink and then talks about overthrowing the Spanish state and restoring the republic I would be a rich man. But it's all bullshit. Still, the police sit in the square and then send in undercover officers, who although they stand out, put off my customers but' – he threw his hands in the air – 'this is usual for Barcelona, eh?'

A young man sat down in the middle of the square and started to play an electric guitar. It was an ancient Catalan *cancione*. Meredith hated this type of music: it was so clichéd. But Edu closed his eyes and hummed along for a second.

'And you, Edu, would you be violent to achieve independence?'

He shook his head vigorously. 'I want independence of course, but I hope we can achieve it without resorting to those methods. But let's not talk of independence: that's all my friends ever talk about! Tell me, how are you, Nancy?'

Unexpectedly, Meredith found herself telling Edu about the last couple of days and how Olivia had treated her. As she talked, she realised that she didn't have anyone she could tell these things to. Perhaps Inga would have listened if she talked to her but she had no desire to do so. With Edu it was simple. He had an easy-going, non-judgemental manner and things felt less 'weighty' in his presence. Perhaps, Meredith thought, this was his secret power, like her smile, and even as she talked to him freely, she was wondering whether she could somehow learn his trick. It would be so very useful to be liked and for people to want to open up to you.

She noticed that Edu was staring at her as she talked and when she felt herself on the brink of mentioning her father, she controlled herself and stopped.

'What is it?' he said.

'Nothing, it's just I am droning on here, downloading all my crap onto you and I don't even know you.'

'No need to apologise, I like it and' – he leaned in again –

'that's what friends do. So I guess with the coffee and the conversation we could say we are friends, no?'

Without thinking about it she smiled at him.

He slapped his knee in triumph. 'There you are! Shall we get some early lunch?' And he began to turn round to call over the waiter.

But Meredith was thinking about what she had said, and it annoyed her that he seemed to know that the person she presented to the world was different somehow, and she focussed on the reason she was here. 'Edu, you promised to pass on my message to Amy. Did she respond?'

'Oh that, yes, she's fine. She is having some fun with Ferran. He is very handsome and he is the face of Catalan independence for many of the young here. He has a large social media following, which appears to be the measure of success these days.'

She put her hand on his arm. 'Listen, I need to speak to her. Will she see me?'

He looked down at her hand. 'Of course, I have her address here.' He patted his shirt pocket where he had put his phone. 'We can go as soon as you like.'

'I want to go now.'

He looked slightly disappointed but then looked down again at her hand and smiled. 'Sure, I'll get the bill and we go there now.'

He led her through the alleyways of Gràcia and then they crossed Gran de Gràcia and into the more upmarket area of Sarrià-Sant Gervasi. The narrow alleys gave way to broader boulevards and grander apartment buildings.

Eventually, they reached a tall modernist apartment block with an imposing large oak door inscribed with carvings of flowers and grapevines. Edu pressed the bell to the attic apartment. After a couple of seconds, a voice asked them, 'Who is it?'

and Edu identified himself. The buzzer sounded and Edu pushed the door open.

The lobby area was finished with beautifully glazed tiles, the colour of egg white, that gave an atmosphere of stately calm. At the far end of the lobby was an old gated elevator.

'Wow, this is beautiful,' said Meredith.

'Yeah, and we are going to the top.' He pressed the large green button and pulled the cage door open. They stepped inside. The lift space was cramped and there was barely enough room for the two of them. As the lift ascended slowly, she felt her fingers touch his for a second and an almost electrical charge pass between them. She wondered if he felt the same thing. Neither of them spoke and then the lift clanged to a halt and Edu pushed open the gate.

They stepped out directly in front of a wooden door which swung open.

A handsome man, a younger, healthier-looking version of Che Guevara, greeted them. Meredith expected that the physical similarity was something that Ferran worked upon as his long black hair had an expensive sheen and his beard was well-groomed. First, he hugged and kissed Edu and then stood back and appraised Meredith. 'And you must be Nancy. Edu told me all about you. I'm Ferran.' He took hold of Meredith's shoulders and they exchanged cheek kisses.

'Hi, I was at the bar the other night, when you met Amy, but I don't think we spoke.'

He shrugged as though he couldn't be expected to remember such trivial details.

'Sure, it's possible. I go to a lot of bars, meet a lot of people, so maybe we did, maybe we didn't, eh? Come through, Amy is on the terrace.'

She glanced at Edu and caught him staring at her. She smiled and he smiled back. She was now pretty sure that Edu liked her. This could be useful, or it could be problematic. She would need to be careful with him.

Ferran led them into the apartment. It was a fabulous blend of modern and classical. The floor was covered Catalan-style with hydraulic mosaic tiles in black and white. There were large pieces of mahogany furniture and there were grand abstract canvasses dominating the walls and a neon light sculpture on the living room wall that spelt out the phrase 'Life is NOT what THEY make it'. At the far end of the living room was a set of French windows that opened out onto an expansive terrace festooned with wicker furniture and a large bamboo and canvas umbrella. They stepped out onto the terrace and Meredith almost gasped when she saw the view it gave over the city and the Mediterranean in the distance.

'Pretty impressive, hey?' said Edu who was at her side.

'It's wonderful. This must be one of the best views in the city.'

Ferran looked amused as only those who have ever known wealth can do when confronted with their riches. 'I look at the city and I just see a Spanish colony. From here I can see the Spanish flag flying on government buildings across the city. Oppression. That is what this view says to me.'

Before Meredith could think of a suitably profound response the French doors opened and Amy stepped out onto the terrace.

She looked at Meredith and then her mouth formed a small 'Oh' and she rushed forward and threw her arms around Meredith. 'I knew you'd find me!' She held onto Meredith for a few seconds and then let go and stood back to get a good look at her. Meredith remained fascinated with the change in Amy. She looked so different from the young, gauche eighteen-year-old she had known in Thailand. She had filled out in a good way, putting on muscle in her arms and core, and there was little doubt she had surgically enhanced her lips and breasts. Her hair was a thing of resplendent beauty that cascaded in jet black curls onto her shoulders and her make-up was of the expensive kind that made it look as though she wasn't actually wearing any.

In short, she looked like money.

Greetings always made Meredith feel especially awkward. They were so prescribed and she always wondered why didn't people just admit that this was all bullshit and cut to the chase. Meredith did what she always did: she grinned as a placeholder.

'Sorry about running off the other night but you know, sometimes you've just got to be spontaneous. That's what I tell my followers. Olivia needs to realise that they expect authenticity and this is my authenticity and if she doesn't like it then screw her.' She performed a half curtsy and raised a middle finger. Both of them laughed and Meredith decided she liked the new Amy.

'No problem. It was a bit crazy and it was me who took us to that bar so I'm to blame really.'

'Yeah, she can be a bit business-like.' Amy touched Meredith's forearm.

'She can be a total fucking ball-breaker, you mean.'

They both laughed.

'Boys, why don't you go and talk politics for a bit and let me and Nancy catch up?'

Ferran looked pleased with this suggestion, Edu less so, but they excused themselves and went back inside, leaving Meredith and Amy alone on the terrace.

'Isn't he just the best?'

'Ferran? Yeah, he looks like a young Che or Javier Bardem.'

Amy play-swiped at Meredith. 'It's not just that. It's the fact that he has a cause. He believes in something and now I do. It's so romantic and empowering. That's what we all need, something to believe in, something to be passionate about, don't you agree?'

Meredith wondered whether Amy was teasing her. Surely, she could see that this was just political tourism?

'I know what you mean but I always looked at it more from an academic perspective. I felt I didn't have skin in the game to really understand it like a native, but I know it gets passions high here.'

Amy pouted and clinked the ice cubes in her gin and tonic.

'To me it's the most authentic thing in the world. They believe it so fervently. Can you imagine what it's like to just live and breathe a cause? I think it's just about the best thing you can possibly be as a person.'

There was a momentary silence between them. Meredith hated this. It happened to her a lot as though she was always misjudging things by the smallest but most important margin. She did what she often did in these situations and lied. 'I agree, and I support them, obviously. What I meant is that sometimes it's hard to actually fit into such a close-knit world and group – but you seem to have managed where most people don't.'

This appeared to please Amy and she perked up immediately. 'Yes, and you know why? Social media. I have a confession to make. You did take us to the bar last week but I told Ferran to meet me there. You see, I connected with Ferran through Instagram before we landed in Barcelona and of course, I wanted to meet him, I mean look at him!' She laughed, making a sound that seemed as well trained as a pet poodle. 'But once I got involved – I went to a meeting with their march committee yesterday – I knew I had found something really important that I can focus on instead of just selling clothes and make-up, you know?'

'I totally get it, Amy.' Meredith didn't. 'By "march committee" do you mean *Diada*?'

'Yeah, the Catalan national day of independence, *Diada,* that's it. It's in a few weeks and I knew that I wanted to do everything I could to help these people and the cause. I can really make a difference with my social media skills.'

Meredith thought back to the conversation she had had with Adam when he showed her various images of Amy from around the globe embracing eco-warriors, gender campaigners and social justice activists of all stripes. She had form, but this did seem different. She had been gone for over a week now and perhaps Ferran with his well-funded revolutionary lifestyle was the missing ingredient that allowed her to embrace this cause so wholeheartedly. A perfect mix of cause and wealth. Meredith looked out over the terrace and the view across the city and down to the Mediterranean and was tempted to say she would be on board with any cause that afforded her a lifestyle like this.

'Olivia is really annoyed that you are not answering her messages.'

Amy rolled her eyes. 'I know! I bet she couldn't believe her luck when you fell into her lap. I told her I wanted some time out but she's so focussed on money, she's lost track of what's important.'

'What is important? Isn't your following important?'

'You sound like Adam or Olivia now. Of course they have importance, but compared to a people's struggle for independence?'

Her eyes took on a dreamy look. Meredith had seen the same look on clubbers in Ibiza as the first wave of ecstasy rolled in, and on the parishioners at her father's church when they began to speak in tongues.

'I suppose you're right. But I need to tell Olivia something. Her and Adam are paying me to get you to come back to The Squad.'

Amy laughed and then placed her hand on Meredith's forearm.

'He is so predictable. Well you can tell him that I intend on seeing this through, however long that may take. I'm helping Ferran with the social media campaign and it's vital work that actually means something to me. Olivia and the rest of them can keep things ticking over. I saw that you had done a post as well. It looked amazing. You've got a great figure. If you like it, you should do some more. They can be fun for a while.'

Meredith was hoping this would be Amy's reply. It meant she didn't need to move out of the hotel and it gave her a chance to win Olivia over and cement her position within The Squad.

'And what about Dylan?'

Amy sucked in her bottom lip.

'I do feel kind of guilty but you have to be true to your heart and I'll let him down gently at some point. To be truthful, as long as he's well fed, watered and has access to sex he's happy. Given how you look Nancy, I'm surprised he hasn't made a move on you yet.'

Amy's eyes flickered downwards and was it only Meredith's imagination but could it be that Amy was still a little in lust with her? Meredith beamed at Amy to make sure, but Amy didn't show any further signs of taking the bait.

'Now, tell me all about how you became such a success as an influencer. I can't believe all that you've done since we were dancing on that beach in Ko Pha-ngan.'

Amy was more than happy to tell her everything and they spent the rest of the afternoon talking about Amy's 'journey'.

Later, outside the apartment, Edu took Meredith's arm as they walked along the street, and she let him. 'Did you have a good conversation with your friend?' he asked her.

'Yes, it was very useful.'

He stopped walking and looked at her. 'Useful?'

She realised she had picked the wrong word. 'I meant it was good for us to catch up. We are going to have a coffee tomorrow as well. Thank you for helping me, Edu.'

He looked a little crestfallen. 'Does this mean you don't need me anymore?'

She smiled at him.

'You know, Nancy, you are very beautiful.' And then he leant in to kiss her and she let him do that as well.

12

It had been Meredith's idea to go to the Carmel bunkers and take photographs.

The site was an old, abandoned, civil war anti-aircraft position on a small hilltop in the Carmel district to the east of Park Güell. Meredith knew that the views of the city were unsurpassed from up there and reckoned that only local stoners and some of the more determined tourists who were happy climbing up the hill in the middle of the summer heat would be up there.

Adam had seemed pleased as he had been complaining that a lot of the shots they were getting were too clichéd, a bit touristy. When he had asked her for ideas she had been happy to be able to suggest a location she thought would be off the beaten track.

However, when they arrived at the top of the hill, albeit deposited by taxis not too far away, there had still been some walking in the ferocious heat that accompanied the late August afternoon. Even worse, when they arrived, they found the bunkers full of millennials posing for photographs in the same places that Meredith had thought would make good spots for their images. Adam did a quick check on his phone, swiped a few times, frowned, swiped a few more times and then smiled.

Olivia, hand on hip, shot him a questioning look. 'Well?'

He grinned. 'It's not been compromised. Lots of small fry with tiny followings, but that's good.'

Olivia clapped his back and they walked off towards the highest gun emplacement.

Meredith followed with Richard and Dylan.

'Why is it good that this place is already well known? I thought the point was to find somewhere unique,' Meredith asked Richard.

Richard, dressed head to toe in fluorescent Ralph Lauren like an escapee from a nineties *Vanity Fair* advert, stepped carefully to avoid throwing up any dust that would cover his deck shoes.

'We love first adopters of a place. It shows that there is an appetite for the images here. That the tastemakers have got here first is fine. What we need to avoid is any of the big hitters with huge followings making it here before us. Then we'd be seen as just copying another influencer. This' – he pointed up at the ruined gun emplacement – 'is just perfect, darling. It shows we know what's hot. Adam is going to love you for this.'

They reached the top of the gun emplacement. The floor of the emplacement was made up of old, faded and cracked tiles, that still retained their beauty. There was a large, faint circle described on the tiles showing the circumference of the base of the AA gun which had covered the approaches to the city over the mountains and across the city to the sea. The view was stunning, one of the best in Barcelona, taking in the mountains, the city and the sea.

A couple of young Swedish girls were at the top posing for photographs and when they saw Richard and Dylan they began to giggle and then ran over to ask for selfies. Dylan and Richard duly obliged.

Adam hugged Meredith. 'This is the fucking mother lode! Look at that vista! I fucking love you, Nancy!' He lifted her in the air and spun her around.

It was Olivia who brought them down to earth. 'We will have to be quick, look.' She nodded at the Swedish girls whose thumbs were moving quickly over the surfaces of their phones. 'The word has gone out.'

Adam put Meredith down, placed his camera bag on the floor and began to pull out his camera equipment. 'Dylan,' he shouted, 'I want handstands' – he waved towards the view of the city – 'at the edge of the emplacement. Come on, let's go.'

'One thing which is important,' whispered Richard, 'is that the shots look like we are the only people here. I don't know why but despite the fact it's about sharing photographs amongst millions of people, photographs of lots of people don't do well.'

'Probably because looking at them is a solo pastime,' replied Meredith.

Richard laughed. 'Like all the best ones, darling. Come on, it's showtime.'

Dylan was performing a one-handed handstand and Adam was on his knees clicking away on his single-lens reflex camera.

The Swedish girls were behind Adam and were taking pictures on their mobile phones.

'Richard, you're on!'

Olivia had joined them. 'Run along, Dickie, time for your jester routine.' She handed him a small bottle of water.

Richard grimaced but accepted the bottle. He walked into the shot and then with an exaggerated run and jump, started throwing water over Dylan. Adam kept snapping away.

'Dickie applied for RADA, you know. Got turned down. Who would have thought that, given his obvious talent.'

Richard and Dylan were play-fighting now.

'Their shots are always the same: fast shutter speeds capturing the water droplets going over each other. Consistently gets high "likeage".'

'And what about us?'

Olivia applied some lipstick and looked down the hill. A small crowd of teenagers and millennials was making their way up with their phones held aloft.

'We need to hurry: they are coming.'

Adam didn't stop shooting, just waved Meredith and Olivia forward. 'Dylan, Richard, fuck off. Olivia and Nancy, you're on.'

'We do pathos and sexy and that is all. Hurrah for gender stereotypes, hey.'

Dylan and Richard moved back behind Adam. There was a largish crowd forming there and they started posing for more selfies with them.

'I don't know how long they will be able to hold them back. We are going to have to work quickly here. Sit at the edge, arms around each other, looking into the distance. Think...' Adam paused for a moment. 'Think sadness and that.'

Olivia rolled her eyes at Meredith. 'Told you, but it works. Come on, sit down here.' She sat at the edge of the gun emplacement and Meredith joined her. She noted that there was a drop of around thirty feet beneath their dangling legs. *If we fell from here, we would very likely die,* she thought.

Adam moved around behind them but kept shooting. 'Keep looking out to the sea. Sadness! This is our "looking for Amy" shot!'

'How is Amy's hunk, by the way?'

'He's very good-looking and she seemed quite settled there.'

'Put your arm around her, Olivia!'

Olivia slung her right arm over Meredith's shoulders and shuffled up closer so their thighs were touching.

'She does this everywhere we go. She will be bored soon and then come back and after that–' Olivia made a forward movement with her arm and for a second Meredith thought she was going to push her off the platform.

'Be careful!'

'Only messing around: "saved your life" as we used to say at school.'

There was the sound of many footsteps.

'Shit,' said Adam.

Three girls sat down next to Meredith.

'This is so cool, ja,' said the one nearest to her in a German accent.

'Game over,' said Olivia, 'come on, let's go.'

They stood up and their places were immediately taken by a Korean couple.

Everywhere she looked Meredith could see a phone screen pointing in her direction. It was disorientating and unnerving. Richard appeared by her side and took hold of her elbow. 'It's a bit weird at first, but you will get used to it. We have to go: they can get a little strange when their numbers get this big.'

They shuffled through the throng, fixed grins in place, and made their way down the steps to the bottom of the emplacement. The top was swarming with people now all taking pictures, some replicating Dylan's acrobatic pose, most trying to sit on the edge in the same place where Olivia and Meredith had been a moment before.

'That's really scary. Someone could get hurt,' said Meredith. It was true, thought Meredith, people wanted the experience, or rather a photograph of the experience, so much that they seemed oblivious to the precipitous drop. They would risk their lives and those of the people around them for so little. What would people do for something more deserving, she thought? What would she do?

Richard didn't stop walking down the path towards the road where the taxis would be waiting. 'People do, all the time, but the key is to make sure you get the photograph if they do.'

They reached the taxi and Adam was standing outside the cab waiting for them. 'Great work guys. You okay?'

He didn't wait for an answer and got in the cab. They joined him and headed back down into the city.

13

Maria stood back and admired the results of her work. She was pleased and so was Meredith.

'You look so different but still so, so beautiful!'

Meredith would have blushed but that was something that seemed to happen to other people. 'Why thank you. It is quite striking but I love it.'

She examined herself in the mirror. It was strange seeing her reflection with electric blue hair. It was her, but a reinvented version. This was an odd thing to think as it was only her hair that had changed colour – but it did seem to be more fundamental than that. She smiled at her reflection. She liked it, and in Barcelona, it wouldn't stand out.

One lesson her father had given her, however unintentionally, was the best way to hide was out in the open. If the police were investigating the cause of 'Tom from Milwaukee's poisoning', it wouldn't hurt to change her appearance.

This also applied, of course, to her increasing Instagram appearances. The risk was vanishingly small that someone from Seneca, Oregon, would be checking Instagram and recognise Nancy as the sixteen-year-old Meredith Weaver who had run away from home following the death of her father. But the blue hair would make her feel more secure.

And what was more, she was positive it would get her more views and likes. Adam would be pleased.

'You will break hearts with this hair, *guapa*,' said Maria.

Meredith thought of Edu but just as quickly forced herself to focus on the prize, which was the life that Amy and The Squad led.

ADAM CLAPPED his hands when she entered the rooftop pool area. 'Out-fucking-standing. I fucking love it. I'm getting my camera.'

Dylan, who was swimming lengths in the pool, popped his head out of the water. 'Nice hair,' he said and then submerged himself and continued on his way. It was the longest conversation they had had to this point.

Olivia was sitting at a table sipping on a gin and tonic and she waved Meredith over and smiled at her.

Be on guard, Meredith told herself. She joined Olivia at the table and Olivia leant forward and pecked her on the cheek. 'You not joining them for a swim?' asked Meredith.

Olivia pulled a horrified face. 'Absolutely not, I hate it and, to be honest, I can barely swim. Just enough to save my life. Oh, and I adore the hair. Adam is right: we can use this right away. Hair changes are a big thing. You're not super well known yet but we have to tell you that our post, 'Looking for Amy' has hit nearly 100,000 likes in twenty-four hours. That's huge!'

Meredith looked for any sign of irony or teasing but there was none. Olivia may be suspicious of her, may not like her, but one thing she did value was the business of The Squad, and

Meredith had scored well here. There was hope she may join them yet. 'Thanks. The hair was an impulse thing, you know.'

She didn't add that it was the kind of thing Amy would have done.

'And what a great impulse! It's a whole new you and on the subject of "new", I wanted to "reset" our relationship. I feel I've been less than welcoming when, after all, we dragged you into our world, not the other way round. Will you forgive me, Nancy?'

Meredith didn't smile but instead, she put out her hands across the table and Olivia took hold of them. 'There really is nothing to forgive.'

'Love it! Hold it there!' Adam took a bunch of shots. 'Okay, you can let go now. I got that.'

Olivia raised an eyebrow. 'What's the phrase, Adam? "You know the price of everything and the value of nothing."'

'This is great content and now, if you wouldn't mind, Olivia, I need to get some solo shots of Nancy's new hair. We are going big on this.'

Olivia shifted along and stood up. 'I'm glad we had this little chat, Nancy.'

'Me too,' said Meredith.

'Come on, Nancy! Give me that legendary smile!' said Adam.

She twisted her head to one side and smiled her most innocent smile, but even though Olivia had her back to her as she walked off, Meredith was sure that she heard her snigger.

LATER THAT EVENING, as she sat waiting for Edu to arrive, she saw something puzzling. They had arranged to meet in Plaça de la Virreina and she had arrived, as was her habit, early. As she sat drinking her cortado and watching the people who passed by and stopped in the square, she saw Edu enter the plaza from the opposite corner from where she sat in the Café Virreina.

He stopped briefly to speak to a group of men who were drinking at a terrace table in another café. He hadn't seen her yet, she was sure, and more to the point he didn't seem to have noticed the small, middle-aged man who had followed him into the square but who had now stopped by one of the trees. He was pretending to look at his phone but his eyes never left Edu.

Why would Edu be followed? Was he married? Could this be a private detective? But this didn't fit: she had done a cross-check against social media sources and there didn't seem to be any suggestion of a wife or significant other.

Edu had spotted her now and he waved to her as he crossed the square. She waved back but she was watching the small man who was now, she was sure, using his phone to take a picture of the group he had just been talking to and would, she was sure, soon take a picture of her when Edu arrived.

She got up and shoved a five-euro note in the hand of the surprised waiter and then walked down Carrer de l'Or which ran adjacent to the square. Edu had watched her do this and he followed her. She ducked into a doorway and when he half-jogged past, she stepped out and joined him.

'Hi! I thought we were having a drink there!'

She linked her arm in his. 'You are being followed. Don't look back and walk quickly with me.'

He looked back. '*Hijo de puta!* Okay, let's just go into the next bar. He won't follow us in there.'

Meredith shook her head. 'No, keep walking. We need to shake him off.' She picked up the pace and they ducked into the next alley and then sprinted along it, jinking down another side passage and eventually emerging in Travessera de Gràcia, one of the main thoroughfares that ran northeast to southwest across the barrio.

Meredith risked a look behind and couldn't see the small man. 'Come on, down here.'

They walked quickly down another alleyway and then cut down an even narrower street that was strung with washing drying on lines so low that they had to move through them like palm leaves in a jungle. They heard a woman shout some abuse in Catalan and when they reached the end of the alley Edu grabbed hold of Meredith's shoulders. 'Stop, we've lost him.'

Suddenly it was quiet, save for the barking of a lone dog from the open window of one of the apartments above them.

Meredith shook loose of his grip. She was angry with him: the last thing she needed now was the police becoming interested in her, not when there was a possibility of becoming a more permanent fixture in The Squad. She pushed him back. 'Who is following you? Government or gangs, which is it?'

He looked startled and began to speak. 'I don't know.'

'You're a liar.' She turned and began to walk off. Edu ran and caught hold of her. 'Look, I'm sorry, it's the Guardia, the National Guard. They think I'm part of something a bit more extreme in the independence movement but it's paranoia, I just let those guys use my bar to meet up.'

Meredith started to walk off again but stopped. 'No, most people here are part of the independence movement. There is more to it than that. What do they think you are involved in?'

He shook his head slowly and then closed his eyes for a second. When he reopened them, he nodded. 'Look, they think I've got something to do with Terra Lliure, the freedom-fighter group I told you about. It's total bullshit but everyone is panicked and one rumour can get you arrested. Some of the guys who meet at the bar, they say things when drunk, make big talk about "taking the struggle violent", but it's nothing more than that, talk. The Spanish government is so paranoid they spy on everyone. It doesn't mean anything.'

Meredith looked at him. He was almost pleading with her and she could see that he was telling her the truth or at least something very close to it. 'Okay, I believe you.'

The lines around his eyes softened and the faint inklings of a smile appeared.

Meredith realised just how hot it was and how the exertion and stress of getting away from the man following them had made her sweat. They both looked like they had been caught in a downpour.

He stepped closer. 'But can I ask you a question?'

She stood her ground as he closed the distance between them. 'Sure.'

'Why did you run when you saw someone following me? What's your secret, Nancy?'

There it was again, his superpower. She wanted to tell him everything. Or maybe it wasn't a superpower. Perhaps she did have some feelings for him? Meredith wasn't sure but something was different and she felt it.

Trust. It was a valuable commodity and Meredith decided to buy.

'My name isn't Nancy. It's Meredith.'

And this time she kissed him first.

14

'He really likes you, you know?' said Amy.

Meredith stretched out and let the sand run between her fingers. She didn't particularly like the beach. There was a vulnerability about lying down amongst strangers whilst wearing a bikini that made it less relaxing than she knew it was meant to be. Barceloneta beach had added dangers, such as hawkers, thieves and drunken, leering *guiris,* that meant she was never off her guard. She remained vigilant so that she didn't become prey to the many predators that stalked the beach.

Amy, on the other hand, seemed chilled to the point of dreamy oblivion. Behind her Gucci shades, Meredith could see that her eyelids were heavy, which may also have something to do with the weed she had been vaping since they met a couple of hours earlier. She had offered the vape pen to Meredith, who had declined. She didn't trust anything that interfered with her thought processes and she was surprised and slightly disappointed with Amy.

Meredith made unfriendly eye contact with a Senegalese man with large green sunglasses and a bag full of trinkets who was approaching them, and he diverted his course towards a group of Dutch girls sharing a large blanket next to them.

'Edu? He seems nice enough, I suppose. How is your romance with Ferran going?'

Amy rolled onto her back so she could see Meredith, who was sitting cross-legged next to her. 'I feel like I could be in Cuba in the fifties. He reminds me of Che Guevara.'

'But without the cold-blooded executions?'

Amy sat up and fiddled with her bikini top which was threatening to rebel and fall down her body. 'It's the belief I love. The strength it gives him and his friends. You must see it in Edu as well. They know who they are and what they want. I want that.'

Meredith tried to understand but couldn't. Amy had everything, that rationally, you needed for a happy life. She had financial independence, worked with her friends, was not subject to performance appraisals or worrying where the next month's rent was coming from. She had the freedom to read, relax, and enjoy the world, but she somehow wanted to give this all up, or threaten to give it up, for some parochial ancient argument between strangers about who taxed them. Ultimately, wasn't that all the difference amounted to, who you paid?

'I totally get it,' she said, 'we all need to be part of something bigger than ourselves. If we don't have God, we will believe in anything.'

It was clear that Amy didn't know or understand the pejorative nature of the G. K. Chesterton quote and nodded along enthusiastically. 'That's so right, Nancy.' She reached across and held Meredith's hand. 'I'm so glad you are back in our lives.'

Meredith couldn't see Amy's eyes behind her sunglasses but she had the feeling that Amy was looking at her figure. Meredith straightened her spine a little and pushed out her chest. 'But what about Ferran himself, apart from the cause?'

Amy let go of Meredith's arm. 'He's handsome and rich. These aren't negative qualities, you know.'

They both laughed.

Meredith watched a sweat bead roll down Amy's chest and slowly ground her hands in the sand. 'Adam is pressuring me to get you to come back this weekend, if possible. You know there is the sponsored gallery-opening thing.'

Amy rolled back onto her front. 'He can get stuffed. I'm helping prepare for the march in a few weeks.'

The march on the National Day of Catalonia, the *Diada,* was something that Meredith had only been distantly aware of in the three years she had been living in the city. She had found it a pain in the past as a million Catalans effectively brought the city to a standstill and things had got much worse since the failed independence referendum.

'I'll tell him you said no.' Meredith was already thinking of what she would wear for the opening that weekend and Amy's answer was exactly what she had been hoping for.

Meredith tasted salt on her lips and licked them before taking a cold can of Estrella from the cool bag at their feet.

'Want one?'

'No, I'm low-carbing this month. I've eaten my body weight in patatas bravas these last two weeks. I don't want Ferran slipping off with one of these Penelope Cruz look-a-likees.'

Meredith opened the can and savoured the sweet bitterness of the beer. She noticed a group of four pale-skinned *guiris*, English or German boys, staring at them both, so she gave them the finger and they all started roaring with laughter. Christ, she hated the beach. She had only come here because Amy wanted to meet here and spend some time together because, as she put it, 'We are both dating revolutionaries'.

From what Edu had told her 'a revolutionary' was the last thing that Ferran was. He was a rich dilettante surfing on the cause for amusement and attention. He Instagrammed the protests, and now Amy was part of this. She had just swapped timelines and feeds about luxury hotels and holidays for ones about protests and marches.

Of course, she said none of this. She didn't want Amy returning too soon to The Squad's fold. Although Olivia had appeared to make peace, Meredith didn't trust her and she needed more time to make Olivia and Adam see how much they needed her.

'I saw that you've been appearing in some more Squad posts. I loved them. You are a natural, Nancy, and that blue hair is a real USP.'

Meredith studied Amy's face and decided that she was being genuine. 'I've really enjoyed doing them. I'd love to carry on, but I'm not sure Olivia is a fan.'

Amy stretched out her legs. 'Be a doll and put some cream on for me, would you. I love this heat but goddamn, it's boiling!'

Meredith took out the sunscreen from her bag and squirted a large dollop out into her palms. She leant over Amy and began to work the cream into her long slim legs.

Amy purred with pleasure as Meredith massaged the sunscreen into her and she went slower and leant in further, so close she could smell Amy's skin.

She noticed the boys, pointing and gawping open-mouthed. One of them was holding up his mobile phone.

'Mmmm, that's nice, it's giving me goosebumps. Well, the key to Olivia is that she needs to feel she is in charge. She always was at school and you probably remember from Thailand. She's absolutely brilliant, of course. What she doesn't know about marketing isn't worth knowing but it's been a challenge for her, acknowledging that she isn't number one. You are prettier, and she will see you as a threat but remember she's just protecting The Squad. Give her time, she will come round. You'll see, she always does. Her heart is in the right place.'

Meredith wasn't convinced and if Olivia wasn't happy with Amy being The Squad's focus then she couldn't see a situation where she would accept Meredith as a substitute or, when Amy returned, as an addition to the team. Meredith would just have to think of some other way of dealing with Olivia.

She finished Amy's legs and started applying suncream to her back.

From the group of boys, there was a murmur and then one of them shouted out, 'Use your tongue!' which was met with much guffawing.

Meredith tensed up and Amy sensed this. 'Ignore them. They are just perving.'

She tried to ignore them and went back to applying the sun cream. 'You know when you come back, I'd love to stick around and help you guys out with your work.'

Amy made a soft moan in the back of her throat as Meredith kneaded her skin. 'That's a great idea. We always need to keep things fresh, but I'm not sure I am going to come back.'

Meredith tensed up again and stopped applying the cream. 'What do you mean?'

A thought occurred to her. What if Amy meant it and never came back. Surely, that would mean that Meredith would be her natural replacement. But Meredith dismissed the thought – there was no way that Amy would give up her life for a cause. It was idle chatter, the kind that made rich people feel good about themselves. The only way that Amy would not return to The Squad would be if she was incapable of returning.

'Well, seeing what Ferran does, it's real, you know. It has real meaning, and it makes brand sponsorship seem so shallow and... meaningless. I've been thinking I may try to dedicate my life to something a bit worthier, you know. Maybe the Catalan independence thing, but other causes as well, you know, like the environment.'

Meredith wondered if Amy would think the same if she lived in the shitty shared apartment she did, sleeping on a mattress and eking out a living selling dodgy wine. 'Bit tricky with all those international flights you guys take.'

Amy play-slapped her. 'Don't be such a cynic, Nancy!'

The play-slap elicited an excited whooping from the group of boys and Meredith turned in their direction and noticed that one of them was holding up his phone, filming them. 'Hang on,' she said.

She pulled out another beer can from the cool bag and shook it violently before standing up and walking towards the boys.

As she approached, they made beckoning gestures, and the one filming her, a short, fat ginger-haired boy, held his phone at arm's length, making no pretence at disguising what he was doing.

'Come on, love! We're only having a larf!'

'Why don't you go back to rubbing off your girlfriend.'

'This is going straight on Pornhub!'

She ignored them and when she got close, she gave the can one last shake and then tugged the ring pull. The beer shot out under pressure and she directed it straight at the iPhone held up by the fat kid, drenching it completely.

He started to complain but Meredith knocked the phone out of his hand and it fell into the sand.

'You stupid fucking bitch, you've broken my phone!'

Meredith sprayed the other boys with the beer and they acted as though it was acid, jumping around and screaming.

From all around her Meredith could hear people clapping and cheering.

She threw the can at them and walked back over to Amy

who was sitting on her haunches watching with wide-eyed admiration. 'Oh my God, Nancy, you are so hardcore!'

Meredith didn't look behind but she picked up her bag. 'Come on, I think we better leave. In my experience boys don't like being humiliated.'

Amy gathered up her stuff and followed Meredith off the beach.

15

M eredith had found her groove.

Adam had perfected two identities for her.

The first was 'the old friend from Thailand who is helping The Squad find Amy'. This, admittedly, was wearing a little thin, given Amy had been popping up on Ferran's timeline on various protests and demos, but they were still going with it as it allowed moody images of Meredith walking down the narrow Gothic alleys of the old town.

The second was 'old friends become new friends'. It consisted of shots of Meredith and Olivia laughing while drinking cocktails on a glamorous roof terrace or dancing at a beach bar.

Olivia was still maintaining the apparent rapprochement and Meredith even enjoyed her company, albeit she didn't trust her at all.

The 'new friends' hashtag had proved popular, particularly with the demographic of lonely teenage girls in the age group of twelve to fifteen. This meant they had to wear some fast fashion by Desigual who were targeting this market. Olivia didn't like the clothes and expressed her opinion loudly and often to Adam but he seemed used to it and just shrugged. Meredith found the experience thrilling, however, and tried not to show how excited she was to be given free clothes for just going to a party and having her photograph taken.

There were only two issues that were bothering her. The first was her fear that Amy may become bored of Ferran and return to The Squad, rendering her position questionable.

The second was the matter of money. It was fantastic being dressed and receiving complimentary food and drink but she was not being paid and Adam had not made any attempt to discuss this with her. She had skirted around the topic with Richard, telling him that she had given up her job to join The Squad. He had reassured her that she would earn far more money with them but he hadn't said when or how.

The first fear she couldn't do anything about. The second she decided to speak to Adam about at the first opportunity.

That opportunity would have to come later as this evening was the opening of a new contemporary art exhibition at MACBA, Barcelona's modern art gallery in the heart of the Raval. Meredith loved this building, a white pearl of modernist concrete and glass that sat incongruously in Plaça dels Àngels amongst the old Gothic streets. She had dressed in a new outfit supplied by Desigual. She couldn't help but feel pleased that the last time she had worn a dress it had been the dress that Inga had stolen for her.

The MACBA building was four storeys high with gallery spaces on each floor that were accessed by a narrow, open staircase that zigzagged through the large open space like that of an Escher painting. The whole west side of the building was glazed so the white cavernous interior space glowed with golden light from the setting sun. Meredith saw that Olivia was holding onto the balustrade and assumed she must be feeling slightly vertiginous as they climbed up the exposed staircase. From outside came the constant thrum of skateboards from the dozens of kids who used the MACBA courtyard as a skatepark.

At the top, they were met by waitresses with glasses of cava and Meredith noticed Olivia grabbed one and downed it straight away.

Adam led them into the fourth-floor gallery space where he introduced them to various local branding, content and marketing managers who all looked alike to Meredith, with their designer glasses, manicured beards and expensive suits. Then he went to mingle and 'see what else we can squeeze from these fuckers,' in his own words.

He left her with Olivia, Richard and Dylan, standing by a table sipping their drinks. Nobody said anything for an awkward moment and then Olivia picked up her glass. 'Right, I'm off to circulate, too. Let's remember this is work. And you two' – she looked at Dylan and Richard – 'don't get wasted.'

As she walked off Richard whispered under his breath, 'Controlling bitch.'

Once she had disappeared into the crowd Dylan raised his eyebrows to Richard who nodded. 'Hey Nancy, we are just going to the bathroom for, you know…'

'Whatever guys.' She waved them off.

Meredith sipped her cava and looked out across the room where Barcelona's hippest and richest gathered. She should join them and try and network. She knew that this was part of the deal, how things worked, but this was something she did not want to do. It offended her sensibilities and temperament in a way that made her feel inauthentic. She could lie to others: she had to do so to survive on occasion, but she found it hard to lie to herself. Even to pretend was almost impossible and making small talk with people she didn't know was high on her list of inauthenticity. What she did like was art, though, and she picked up her glass and, avoiding the crowd by keeping to the side of the room, she began to look at the pictures.

The first was an Antoni Tàpies. It was a piece of sackcloth with a large wooden beam nailed to it. There was a daub of red paint in one corner. Meredith liked it. It seemed rooted to the earth and pain and this she could understand. She was aware that this might not be what the artist intended but it didn't matter to her what the artist thought, it was what it provoked in her that mattered.

Then she came to a canvas that reduced her to a statue, struck so still was she by its beauty and its depth. She recognised it immediately. It was a modern homage to a Cezanne work, *The Grounds of the Château Noir*. She knew the painting well: a reproduction had hung in their family living room at home when she was growing up, a memento from her stepmum's college years. This was the same scene, dark trees blocking the whole picture save for a small clearing in the canopy in the top left corner where the light came in.

But the artist here hadn't used oil paints for this work. It was composed of iron, old nails and brick, but she recognised it, nevertheless.

'You like it?' The voice belonged to a slightly built dark-haired woman in her late thirties. She was wearing a black silk jumpsuit and had her dark hair in a coquettish French bob.

'It's the Château Noir,' said Meredith.

The woman looked at Meredith with interest. 'It's the view from my home in Tangiers.'

Meredith was crestfallen. She was sure it had been the garden at Château Noir. Both pictures had cast the same spell over her. It was a spell that made her feel that even though she wasn't able to participate in most of the world, there was a part, a speck of light, that could be hers, a place she could go. 'Oh, it reminded me of something else.'

The woman stuck out her hand. 'But I love Cezanne and the sentiment is the same, I think? Hi, I'm Annik.'

'Hi, I'm–' She nearly said 'Meredith' but stopped herself just in time. 'Nancy.' She shook the proffered hand.

Annik spoke English with a Scandinavian accent and the handshake instead of the cheek kiss was strangely formal but Meredith appreciated its lack of presumption.

Annik looked at Meredith in a way that made her feel at once uncomfortable and privileged, as though Annik was examining her essence before painting her.

Meredith broke the spell and turned back towards the painting. 'I like it very much. You have a lot of talent but I guess you know that already. All these people wouldn't be here if not.'

Annik looked amused, as though she knew that this was small talk and she was deciding whether to play along. 'These people are here because there is money disguised as culture and that allows them to wallow in the money side without feeling too dirty. Very few of them will look at the work, truly look at it, unless it is to be used as talking points for a conversation that will somehow lead to more money. And you, Nancy, why are you here?'

Meredith wanted to be part of the life that Amy had, so why did she suddenly feel ashamed of telling this woman she had never met before that she was an 'influencer'? Wasn't this as noble and true a profession as some middle-class Nordic who was paid obscene amounts just because she had been trained to paint?

As she mentally floundered for a reply a man in a dinner jacket approached and gently took Annik's elbow in his hand and then whispered in her ear.

Annik nodded. 'I'm sorry, Nancy, it seems I have to give my

little speech now. But I would very much like to continue our conversation later if this is possible?'

Meredith pulled herself together again and gave her biggest and brightest smile, the one closest to the truth, to Annik.

Annik didn't seem to melt in front of her the way others did when she deployed this smile. Meredith had that unsettling feeling again that Annik had seen inside her.

She watched Annik move into the crowd and head towards the podium but rather than listen to her speech Meredith decided to go for a cigarette.

Smoking was not allowed in the museum, but this was Barcelona, after dark in a private function, so she followed the smell of tobacco smoke down one level to an empty gallery space. As she entered the room two men were leaving and they grinned and pointed her in the direction of a table in the middle of the space with an ashtray sat on top. It was so incongruous that for a second Meredith wondered if she might be about to use an expensive modern artwork as an ashtray but she rolled a cigarette and lit up anyway.

She could still hear a muted hum of noise from the party in the gallery above but she couldn't make out Annik's speech and she wondered why she hadn't stayed to hear it. The truth was she hadn't liked the way Annik had seemed to see her, really see her, and this had left her feeling anxious.

She sucked deep on the cigarette and looked around. The room she was in was a large space and apart from the table and ashtray there was no other furniture and nothing hung on the walls. Presumably, it was waiting for pictures, a bride without a groom.

In the gloom she thought she saw something move in the corner of the room, and then again, movement. She watched as a mouse ran along the floor before disappearing into the shadows.

'Mind if I join you?' Meredith saw Olivia standing at the doorway.

'Sure' – she looked around at the vacant space – 'I think we've got room.'

Olivia joined her at the table and produced a packet of cigarettes from her bag. 'Is this a piece of art?'

Meredith laughed. 'I thought the same thing, but I don't think so.'

Olivia lit her cigarette. 'It's hard to tell these days, isn't it? Between what's real and what's fake. I mean this table, if someone told us it was a post-modern take on easy twenty-first century capitalism and was worth 10 million dollars we wouldn't be too surprised, would we?'

'I guess not,' said Meredith. 'How's the party?'

Olivia shrugged and leaned back against the table in the same way that Meredith was leaning. 'How I hate these things. I'm a natural introvert so these things bring me out in hives. Most of us are you know, introverts. The people who succeed on social media are those who traditionally would struggle in the mainstream entertainment routes to success. The internet allowed us to be extroverts in our bedrooms or on holiday with our friends and connect with other introverts... which is a long-winded way of saying "I don't like crowds".'

'Me neither,' said Meredith, although that wasn't strictly true. What she didn't like was tedious conversations over canapés and drunken attempts by men double her age to flirt with her. But she needed to bond with Olivia if she was ever going to be accepted into The Squad on a long-term basis.

Olivia took a few more fierce drags of her cigarette and then stubbed it out. 'Yeah. It explains your complete lack of social media presence, well, until now. You've gone from zero to hero there and one of the downsides is some of the unwanted attention that comes along with having hundreds of thousands of people view your content.'

Olivia was still talking in a relaxed, conversational tone but Meredith's stomach had contracted a little and she suddenly felt on edge.

'Well, did you take a look at some of the comments about you on the last picture uploaded by Adam?'

She had and, frankly, they had been a joy to read. Overwhelmingly positive, congratulating The Squad on finding a long-lost member and complimenting her on her looks, make-up and clothes. There had been one or two bemoaning the lack of Amy but that was to be expected. There had been nothing that she would have deemed offensive, which was the constant fear word Adam bandied around when discussing their content. Giving offence that led to an online vendetta was one of Adam's biggest fears in life as it could destroy The Squad's business model in one fell swoop.

'I saw a few, yeah. Are you referring to any in particular?'

Olivia slipped off the side of the table and stood in front of Meredith. 'Funny you should ask as I am. Part of my remit is troll alert and clean up. We can't have the number one comment on a Nike promotional post being about sweatshops.' She started swiping on her phone screen.

Meredith wanted to leave the room now, but she tried focussing on appearing normal. She had spent her teenage years doing this and, although she hated it, it was a skill she had never forgotten. 'The ones I looked at seemed good.'

Olivia didn't look up from the screen. 'Here we go. Take a look at this. Any idea what this is about?' Olivia held up her phone so Meredith could see the screen. The post was from the volleyball game and showed Meredith posing with the ball whilst the sun dipped behind the Hotel Arts on the Port Olímpic.

The comment Olivia had highlighted was from a user called 'Steel83' and reading it caused Meredith to grip hold of the edge of the table.

Steel83: Meredith – is that you? I've sent you a message.
Where u been?!

She knew who Steel was but she tried to compose herself. 'No idea what that is all about. I guess you guys get this a lot of the time.'

'It happens but normally it's a lot darker than this and I only mention this because this Steel83 has posted the same thing on all the posts featuring you and, as we manage The Squad's accounts, I wanted to know, do you want to read the message? We get thousands as you expect and have a bounceback standard message that goes out to the fans. It gets them to sign up to our mail list. We never miss an opportunity! So, do you want me to send you her message?'

Meredith jumped down from the table. She wanted to run from the room, go back to her old apartment, take the money she had stashed there and leave Barcelona but instead, she smiled sweetly at Olivia. 'No, just delete it. Shall we go and rejoin the party? The art is better than this after all.' She tapped the table.

Olivia looked at her curiously for a second and then pocketed the phone. 'Of course. It's what we're here for, after all. Let's go.'

They went back up to the gallery. Annik must have finished her speech as the podium was empty and the place seemed louder, as though the drink and drugs were beginning to kick in amongst the crowd.

Olivia spotted Dylan standing on his own holding two glasses of cava. 'Where is Richard?'

Dylan looked as though he had been asked to solve a complex mathematical equation and his eyes rolled as he struggled to come up with an answer. 'Well, it's a difficult one. Last time I saw him he was near the dunnie.'

Olivia's face flushed with anger and she stormed off towards the bathrooms.

'What's the matter?' Meredith asked Dylan.

'Ah, well, you see Olivia, she worries too much that someone will pap Richard or me having a bit of fun.' He tapped his nose. 'Not good for the sponsors, you know, hypocritical bastards.'

Meredith went after Olivia and caught her at the entrance to the *hombres*.

'If Richard is doing coke, do you care?'

Olivia spun round. 'I don't give a shit. He can shove half of Bolivia up his nostril as far as I care but brands, they do care and one photo could destroy all of us.'

A man exited the bathroom and pushed past them.

'Listen, Nancy, you go in there and get him out. I'll stand guard here and won't let anyone else in. I'll say something about your period: that normally shuts them up.'

Meredith didn't hesitate. She needed Olivia onside. She pushed open the door and peeked inside. There was no one by the urinals so she quickly stepped in and shut the door behind her.

'Richard?'

She thought she heard a low groan come from one of the stalls at the end. It was locked. 'Richard?'

Again, a low groan.

She went into the unoccupied cubicle next door, climbed on the toilet seat and looked down to see Richard curled up in a foetal position on the floor.

'Richard, are you okay?'

He looked up, his skin was pale and clammy, his eyes glazed and there was vomit on his chin.

'Jesus,' she said and then pushed herself up and over the cubicle wall and slid down into his cubicle.

'Hello, Nancy,' he said.

There was vomit in the toilet and splattered about the floor of the cubicle.

'Oh Christ, Richard, are you all right?'

'Just had a dicky stomach. Dicky had a dicky stomach, ha!'

Meredith remembered when she had first arrived thinking how slim Richard was compared to when she had known him in Thailand. Social media was an unforgiving place for people who did not fit the regulation body size requirements of thin and fit.

Meredith helped Richard stand up. 'Come on, let's get you cleaned up.' She spooled off reams of toilet paper and handed it to him so he could wipe himself down and then she opened the cubicle door.

'Come on, it's all right, Olivia is guarding the door.'

'Oh fuck, she knows, fuck, fuck, fuck.'

'How long have you been doing this?'

'Doing what?'

'Oh, please Richard, the bulimia thing.'

He ran the tap and threw water on his face. 'About ten years. You can't tell Olivia. I know what she will do. She will make me post about it. Mental illness is so in fashion. I just fucking know it. I don't want people knowing everything.'

Meredith put an arm around Richard. 'Don't worry I won't say anything. Let's take a look at you.' He still looked ghastly but the vomit was gone and in the dim lighting of the gallery he would just pass for another guest who had drunk a little too much cava. 'Okay, you'll pass. Let's go.'

They left the bathroom together. Olivia was remonstrating

with an elderly Spanish man who was swearing at her in words that made it better that Olivia did not understand Spanish.

On seeing them Olivia let the man pass. He pushed past them.

Olivia looked Richard up and down. 'What have I told you about taking coke whilst we are at sponsor functions? For fuck's sake, you know you could ruin us all.' She pulled back. 'Jesus, you smell awful.'

'He wasn't taking coke. He was puking up. I reckon it's those prawn canapés, I had one and feel really bad too.'

Olivia's eyes narrowed. 'Okay,' she said slowly. 'Well let's get back to it, hey. We are here to mingle and to be photographed, so let's do it, yeah?'

They both agreed and together headed back into the throng.

Meredith found the rest of the evening a struggle and it took her a huge effort to perform the social niceties that seemed to come so easily to others.

She was relieved when, after what felt like an age of repeating the same banal phrases over and over again, Olivia and Adam signalled that it was time to leave and as a group they headed for the stairs.

As they were leaving Meredith felt a hand on her arm and turned to see Annik.

'We didn't get time to finish our conversation. Here, let me give you my number. This may seem presumptuous but I return to Morocco tomorrow and I wondered whether you wanted to come back to my hotel and perhaps get a drink.'

She looked directly at Meredith with no embarrassment.

Meredith sensed the others looking at them. She couldn't see what this would gain her at this point, although she was tempted. She leaned in closer to Annik and said, 'I have a boyfriend and I never cheat, but the future isn't mapped out so I will take your number if you want to give it to me.'

Annik pulled out a pen from her bag and then picked up a drinks mat from one of the nearby tables. She tore the printed front from it and on the cardboard underneath she wrote down a number and then handed the mat to Meredith.

'Call me,' she said, maintaining eye contact with Meredith.

When she caught up with The Squad, Adam asked her what Annik had wanted and Meredith had said she wanted advice on her social media presences and had asked for their details. Adam seemed pleased with this, but Olivia gave her a look that Meredith did not like at all. Not at all.

Meredith had never been on a protest march before. She had never had enough passion to make her waste time on what she rather thought was an exercise of posturing for the benefit of attracting mates.

And yet here she was with Edu, Amy and Ferran, and to her mind, it rather proved her point. At the head of a crowd of around three or four hundred, Amy, with Catalan flags painted on both her cheeks, looked as though she may burst with sexual excitement at the frenzy and repressed violence.

Ferran, a veteran of protests, even seemed to have a protest outfit, which was all black, naturally. Meredith had noticed that the labels on his jeans and T-shirt were designer and he wore a grey check Burberry scarf around his neck. Every now and then, he checked himself out as they passed a shop window as they made their way down Via Laietana, one of the busiest, and now blocked to traffic, thoroughfares of central Barcelona.

Edu had been full of speeches about safety and how he would be there to look after her if things became dangerous. His act of being her great defender she had found slightly nauseating. She had smiled sweetly as she didn't want to embarrass him in front of Amy and Ferran although the younger, vainer man did defer to Edu.

On the march she had noticed many of the other protestors greeted both Ferran and Edu but it was Edu they kept their eyes on.

It had been Amy's idea to attend the demonstration. It was a warm-up before the main event of the *Diada* exactly three weeks later. The protest was against the Spanish cabinet's decision to meet in Barcelona. They did this in cities across Spain, but to many this was seen as deliberately provocative so close to the *Diada*.

They had all stayed at Ferran's apartment the night before. Meredith had spent the day shooting content with The Squad. Then she told them she was going to see Amy and that she thought that one more push may get Amy across the line and back to The Squad. What she wanted was to keep Amy in the bosom of the independence movement and keep her enthusiasm levels high.

Her own 'likes' were getting higher every day and if she could approach the levels of the rest of The Squad, and even, in time, hit Amy levels, then they would surely have to keep her as a member. The key was to make sure her likes kept rising and for that she needed time. Time was dependent on Amy not returning for a little while longer.

At Ferran's flat, they had relaxed over Jané Ventura Cava, bellota ham and cheeses. Amy, who had previously made a big deal about being vegan online, seemed to be quite comfortable eating the ham and cheese, Meredith had noticed, although she hadn't said anything. *Perhaps this is part of the attraction of her new identity,* the meaner side of Meredith thought.

Edu and Ferran had talked war stories about previous marches and how they fought the fascists and they had all got a little drunk. If this was revolution then Meredith was all for it.

But today, today was different.

'This is amazing isn't it?' said Amy, with whom she had linked arms as they marched.

Meredith could smell the rank body odour of the overweight man directly in front of her and it was so hot that she was sweating heavily, as was Amy, and their sweat mingled on their intertwined arms. 'Yeah, it's really great. It kinda makes you realise what's important in life.'

She was thinking about the pool at Soho House which was only 500 or so yards away from where they currently were. It was funny, but if Adam and Olivia decided to leave their air-conditioned rooms they could have come down and talked directly to Amy. Not that it would have made any difference to Amy.

Edu, who had been discussing tactics with another demonstrator further back in the crowd, appeared at Meredith's elbow. 'Are you *chicas* okay?'

Meredith and Amy exchanged an amused look. 'We are, Edu, but thanks for checking on us. It all seems fun but I only know the Catalan national anthem so I don't understand all the chants,' said Amy.

Edu grinned widely. 'It's a good job you don't speak Catalan as most of them are very profane.'

'Those are the ones we want to sing,' said Amy.

He grinned and put his arm around both of them.

Meredith noticed that they were starting to move more slowly and she could see why. Ahead of them, blocking the government building at the bottom of the street, which was their target, was a line of armoured police officers.

She was used to seeing the *Mossos* dressed in their fatigues and carrying weapons for sure, but now they were sporting black Kevlar armour and helmets that made them look like stormtroopers. They were carrying shields and batons and suddenly the atmosphere changed from one of joyous, almost juvenile rebellion, to something altogether more serious.

Behind the line of the *Mossos* was another crowd of demonstrators, maybe one hundred in number, and in contrast to the yellow colours worn by the *independentistas,* these counter demonstrators were wearing the red colours of the Ciudadanos party, the unionists.

Slowly the *independentistas* ground to a halt a yard or so in front of the ranks of *Mossos*.

'What now?' asked Amy of Ferran.

'Now? Now we show them why we came. Here...' He held up his mobile phone and took a selfie of him and Amy. Amy held up her fingers in a V for victory symbol.

He held up his phone again to take a picture of Edu and Meredith.

Edu held up his hand in a mock attempt to stop Ferran taking the picture. But Meredith wasn't so sure it was in jest, though she did wonder what the use would be, given that she could see a police cameraman taking pictures of the demonstrators.

At that moment the crowd broke into a rendition of the Catalan national anthem, *The Reapers*. Meredith watched a little in admiration as Amy joined in, appearing to know all the words to the rousing, bloodthirsty hymn.

'Impressive,' said Meredith.

Amy smiled sheepishly. 'I learnt it from YouTube.'

'What now?' said Meredith to Edu.

He looked a little surprised by the question as though he was disappointed that Meredith didn't think this was enough. 'We sing, we protest, we let the *cabróns* in that building know that we are here.'

'And then what?'

'Then we go home and drink and make love.' He was trying

to be romantic and dangerous, and maybe he was, but Meredith winced inwardly. Perhaps it was cultural: the southern Mediterranean cliché rubbing up against her northern Californian Baptist upbringing, but she found it faintly ridiculous so she didn't reply, but instead she hugged him so he couldn't see her expression.

Nothing much happened for the next half an hour as both sides sang and threw insults at each other whilst the cops looked bored and occasionally one of the stormtroopers would nip off for a cigarette. Amongst the *independentistas* there was a party atmosphere, and beer, joints, ham and cheese were passed back and forth.

Meredith spent the time glancing upwards at the glint of sunlight as it cut across the glass windows at the top of the hotel directly to their left. At one point a middle-aged man stood in his striped boxer shorts and business shirt looking down at the separated groups. *It must be a strange sight from up there,* she thought. But at least he could go and watch TV or relax by the pool. Meredith was stuck here, bored, keeping Amy company.

Even as she thought this, the first missile was thrown. It was a beer bottle. She watched it describe a perfect parabolic arc over the police lines and the vans parked behind them and then land somewhere amongst the unionist supporters. A policeman who had been sneaking a cigarette ran back to his lines and the cops visibly straightened their backs in tense expectation.

The reply took a few seconds and came in the form of a fusillade of beer bottles. They exploded all around them. Meredith saw that one was about to hit Amy and she shoved her out of its path and it exploded into splinters at her feet.

Amy looked shaken. 'Thanks!'

'No worries, pretty intense, hey!' Meredith suddenly found that she was enjoying herself. The *independentistas* strained against the police lines, wanting to push through and get at the unionists.

Edu had disappeared as soon as the first missiles began to land but Ferran was still with them and he pushed forward, camera phone held aloft as he live-Facebooked the experience.

Meredith and Amy found themselves carried by the weight of the mob so they were pressed up against the police lines. Meredith could see the face of the nearest *Mossos* stormtrooper and she saw he was sweating. This was not unexpected in the heat – but there was something else. He looked anxious and frightened and his armoured fist was clenched tight around his baton as though he couldn't wait to start swinging it to dissipate the crowd and his fear.

'I think this could go bad,' whispered Meredith to Amy. She was excited as she knew violence was now a real possibility.

Occasionally, a protestor would push a stormtrooper and the response would be a swift violent pushback with a gloved fist or shield. Meredith saw a young girl hit in the nose and she started bleeding heavily.

From somewhere in the crowd a beer bottle was thrown at the *Mossos* policeman who had hit the girl and it shattered against his visor. His colleague next to him swung his baton and brought it down hard on the shoulder of a middle-aged man with a placard. He screamed in agony and sank to the floor.

Meredith waited for what she now thought would be a full-scale riot but instead the protestors dragged the injured man to safety.

She was rammed close to Amy now and could feel her shaking.

Ferran was still filming and had a manic grin – she could see that to him this was sport and he was thoroughly enjoying it. Meredith couldn't criticise this because, to her surprise, so was she.

They remained like this for a few minutes, pressed up against the police line. Amy began to visibly relax and even managed a weak smile when Meredith said that it was lunchtime soon and there was no way the Catalans would miss a meal to protest. She noticed that Ferran was no longer with them.

But nothing stopped. More missiles were going both ways and then just as she wondered where Ferran had disappeared to, she saw him emerge behind the police lines together with five or six other *independentistas*. They had taken a back alley and now they were in the middle of the enemy and raring to fight.

Edu, who had rejoined them without explaining where he had been, saw Ferran at the same time. 'Meredith, Amy, I think you should leave,' he said, and Meredith saw that he was worried.

Amy turned to Meredith. 'I think we should go.'

But Meredith was watching now as the unionists reacted to the sudden presence of yellow in their massed red ranks. It was a fast, violent reaction. Fists began to fly and she could see now that Ferran and his group were armed with clubs and they began to swing them. The *Mossos* ran to the scene but left the lines in front of them thinner and at the same time both sides pressed forward and the police line broke.

The weight of the mob at their backs thrust them forward again and then they were through the police lines. And all around Meredith was pure kinetic force; bones cracked, kicks landed, as the maelstrom whirled around them.

Edu was holding her hand but then she saw a police baton raise and crash against his arm, and he collapsed in a heap. The policeman raised his baton again but Meredith ran at him and pushed him backwards.

He fell to the floor and Meredith knelt and picked up a smashed beer bottle. She held it firmly around the neck of the bottle and realised that she could plunge it into the area where the policeman's chest armour had ridden up as he fell. She could murder him right here and in this chaos she might even get away with it. *Why shouldn't I just do it?* she thought.

Maybe he saw something in her eyes but he started to scramble backwards using his elbows. Meredith stepped forward but then a young *independentista* with rat-tail hair tripped over the policeman and they both started to scuffle.

'Meredith!' It was Edu.

Meredith knelt next to him. 'Are you okay?'

He looked shaken but otherwise not seriously hurt. 'I'll be fine. What were you going to do to that policeman?'

She grinned at him. 'Nothing, I was just saving you.'

'Nancy!'

Meredith looked back and saw Amy was on her knees with her hands over her ears and she was screaming. All around her people were fighting, forming one big roiling mass of violence.

'Come on,' she said to Edu, and she ran back to Amy.

'Amy, it's me.'

Amy opened her eyes which she had squeezed tightly shut. 'Make it stop! Why are they doing this?'

A unionist with a cut so deep in his temple that a flap of skin hung down over his eye stumbled past them, blood dripping onto them both.

'We have to go, Amy. Can you walk?'

Her skin looked pale and was clammy to the touch even in the concrete heat of the battle and Meredith knew that Amy was panicking. This was not in her playbook at all. This should have sealed Amy's integration into a new world and not terrified her.

Amy stood up.

Edu was wrestling with another unionist, a fat man with a skinhead and mottled face, but he looked like he had the better of it.

'Follow me,' she said to Amy and, ducking and weaving through the brawl, crunching broken glass underfoot, she led Amy by the hand out of the riot.

It was surreal. One metre took them from a full-scale riot with broken bones, armoured police and weapons and into a street that was empty – save for the hundreds of tourists, some eating ice creams, but nearly all with phones pointed at the rioting groups as though this were a stop on the regular Barcelona tourist trail.

'All good?'

Amy seemed to be physically fine but she was shaking a little. She nodded.

'We need a drink,' said Meredith, 'I know a place near here. Let's leave them to it.'

They walked across the patch of empty road and into the throng of tourists who parted and let them through, but took plenty of pictures of them as they did so.

Twenty more yards and it was as though there wasn't a riot taking place just down the road even though they could still hear the screams and shouting.

Amy stopped walking and hugged Meredith. 'That was awful. I never imagined it would be like that. Did you see that man's face? It was all torn up. People could die.' She burst into tears and hugged Meredith tighter. 'It was so horrible. I hated it.'

Meredith hugged her back. 'Oh I know. It was the worst.' But she was lying: she had loved every moment.

17

Olivia had said she had some errands to run so had not joined the rest of The Squad for the afternoon's activities.

Meredith was pleased about this as she had felt that Olivia's new air of courteousness was concealing something else. She told herself that this was probably just paranoia but she couldn't help but feel that Olivia was watching her, and the Instagram comment from Steel had spooked her.

She had gone online and looked up Steel, but apart from the Instagram profile there was no information, and the profile itself carried no pictures of the user nor did the feed show the identity. Meredith had a good idea who it could be based on the pictures that were on there. There were not many images, and no comments or likes, just pictures of a strip of stores, Douglas firs, redwoods surrounding the remains of a campfire and a bunch of trailer homes all from a small town on the North Pacific Coast that Meredith recognised well.

It didn't matter though: so what if they thought they recognised her? It meant nothing, signified nothing and they couldn't do her any harm. But it annoyed her that someone could reach out, over thousands of miles and from many years in the past, and place a cold finger of doubt on her.

She consoled herself by looking out at the magnificent view from Sant Jeroni, the peak of the mountain of Montserrat. They had taken an early morning train from Barcelona to the abbey and then climbed up the trails to the highest point which gave unrivalled views across the plain, back towards Barcelona and the Mediterranean. Adam had wanted a place to shoot some images outside the city and Meredith had known he would love the otherworldly atmosphere of the saw-backed mountain. Once you were up here amongst the towering granite formations and ancient hermitages and caves of long dead monks it was easy to see why many had thought it was the resting place of the Holy Grail.

Adam had loved it but this initial enthusiasm had begun to pale when he was forced to walk up the steep paths that led from the monastery to this vantage point. As Dylan and Richard raced ahead, she had accompanied him and been subject to his smoker wheeze as they climbed.

She had used the opportunity to broach the subject of her future with The Squad and the possibility of being paid, not just for finding Amy, but for her work with them.

He had paused and lit up a cigarette in the same way that a mountaineer might reach for an oxygen tank and it had seemed to alleviate his immediate breathing difficulties. 'I hear you, I really do. And your posts, well, you know they've been amazing. Great results and, fuck me, that last one, through the fucking roof. But I've been good, yeah. That hotel room doesn't come free, you know.'

She had declined to say that he had already paid for it for Amy.

He continued, accompanying each point with a little jab of his cigarette. 'But here's the thing. The Squad has been successful so far and most of that is down to Amy. We need her back. If it was up to me, I'd say yeah, it's a no-brainer, and I like you, I really do, darling. You get her back and then we talk, yeah? And it will be Amy's decision ultimately as she is the creative, you know, the talent. If she thinks it's a good idea then let's do it. But first, let's get her back, yeah?'

Meredith had agreed. What else could she do? And although she had spent the rest of the climb chatting with Adam about the mountain she had been thinking about Amy. After the riot, they had retired to a bar and had a couple of glasses of wine to relax, but the riot had disturbed Amy. She had settled after the second glass of wine but she had told Meredith that she had never expected it to be like that – blood, broken bones and cracked heads.

She was also mad at Ferran. He hadn't made sure she was okay and had remained in the maelstrom of the riot. They had later learned that he had been arrested and released, a fairly common experience for the *independentistas*. But the fact that he had stayed to 'enjoy the fighting', in Amy's words, hadn't boded well for the survival of their relationship. Not that Meredith had been under any illusion as to the expected longevity of Ferran and Amy's relationship, but she had thought it had some more time to run. She had hoped to use that time to consolidate her position within The Squad. But she suspected Amy would be returning sooner rather than later and Adam had made it clear that it was Amy who would call the shots. She would need to speak to her.

Meredith thought she had bonded well enough with Amy and she was thinking that Amy may welcome a counterweight to Olivia. Perhaps that was the way to proceed: to convince Amy that Olivia had been plotting against her. She busied herself with such thoughts as they slowly followed Dylan and Richard up the mountain.

Eventually, the path narrowed and steepened as it left the trees and wound over the crests of huge outcrops of rock that gave views to the horizon in every direction.

'Fuck me, this is amazing,' said Adam in between crusty-sounding breaths.

At the very top, a bored-looking Dylan was sitting on a plinth and texting. He didn't look up as they arrived.

Richard was doing press-ups and grinned at Meredith. 'Wow, this is something else. It's like being on another planet. We will get some amazing shots up here.'

Adam lit another cigarette and began to unload his camera gear.

'You, my little cockfoster, are not wrong. Dylan, put that phone away!' It was a cardinal rule of Adam's that a phone should never appear in their pictures. "The medium must appear separate from the messenger" was his motto.

Dylan rolled his eyes but put the phone in his pocket and then quickly pushed himself up into a handstand on the plinth.

'You are a natural, son!' Adam began to take shots of Dylan performing his handstand with the sublime beauty of the plain that swept thousands of feet below them, all the way to Barcelona thirty miles away.

Meredith and Richard hung back by the railings and watched as Dylan struck more acrobatic poses and then at Adam's suggestion removed his T-shirt to get the same shots but with more flesh on show.

'He is brilliant, you know.'

Meredith wasn't sure whether Richard meant Dylan or Adam. 'Adam?'

'Yeah, not Dylan, Christ, no offence' – he dropped his voice to a whisper – 'he is eminently replaceable and I'm not being too bitchy when I tell you that before Dylan, we had a Troy before Amy got bored of him. Do you think she will be bringing this Frank on board?'

'Ferran, it's a Catalan name. And no, I don't she will be bringing him on board. I think Dylan's place is safe.'

Richard arched an eyebrow. 'For now. And maybe, we will have a new member anyway.'

Meredith did her shucks face and tried to look coy. 'What would you think about that?'

Richard waved his hand airily. 'Well, it's not up to me but if you do want my opinion, I think you would be an excellent addition to The Squad.'

Meredith gave him her smile and then he hugged her.

'What about Olivia? I get the feeling she doesn't really like me.'

'Olivia is just protective of The Squad, that's all. She knows how quickly we can lose all of this.' He held his arms up to indicate their job.

The best job in the world, thought Meredith, *living in luxury and being paid to do so.*

Richard continued, 'And she gets a little too protective sometimes.'

Meredith thought about Olivia's absence and Steel83's comments and she came to a decision she had been pondering on the climb up. 'Adam, guys, can I have a word?'

BACK AT SOHO HOUSE, after they had showered and changed, The Squad met for an early evening sundowner around the pool.

Meredith loved it up here. The sun was just beginning to dip behind Montjuïc. The old fortress atop the mountain, a place of many deaths and torture during the civil war, became suffused with blood-red light and dark shadows. For a moment her many worries were extinguished as she gazed out at its dark beauty.

Adam appeared at her side holding two impossibly large globes of gin and tonic.

She took one and they clinked glasses.

'Today was a fucking good day,' he said.

He showed them the pictures on the train back to the city and they were some of the best she had seen him do. The ones without Dylan performing gymnastics or the guys clowning around, a cut above his usual fare because they captured the essence of Montserrat. She had been impressed and told him so. 'You have real talent, Adam.'

'I always wanted to shoot for the National Geographic, you know, but it doesn't pay the bills.'

For a moment they looked out over the harbour and the Colom where hordes of tourists were making their way to the restaurants over at Maremagnum.

'Beauty doesn't pay. Look down there. What pays is other people, and the trick is making sure you are the payee,' she said.

Adam snorted. 'Cynical but true, I'm afraid. Come and join us. We've got a table and Olivia says she has some good news.'

The rest of The Squad were at a table and Richard and Dylan were busy ordering food from one of the waiters. Olivia was sat, cool and elegant, swiping at her phone.

The waiter, an overqualified engineer who had told Meredith he couldn't get a job so had been forced to serve tables, asked Meredith in perfect English whether she would like to order some food. She asked for tuna tartar and some bread.

Olivia smiled sweetly at Meredith as she took a seat next to Richard. 'I saw the photos from today, they are simply wonderful, some of your best, Adam,' she said.

'I try, you know.'

'Don't be so modest. Didn't you think they were wonderful, Nancy?' Olivia placed additional emphasis on 'Nancy' and Meredith began to get a sick feeling in her stomach.

She took a large gulp from her gin and tonic. 'Yeah, I just told Adam I thought they were fantastic. How was your day?'

Olivia's eyes sparkled with delight and she clapped her hands. 'I am so glad you asked. I had such an interesting day. I had to talk to Adidas and they want us to drop their new city Gazelle range in a series of urban shoots. The shoes are being delivered tomorrow. I had all your sizes apart from yours, Nancy, but I guessed that you are a five, same as Amy. Anyway, the other piece of good news: well you may not be needing them, Nancy, because Amy has texted me today and I get the feeling that she may be rejoining us tomorrow.'

Dylan punched the air. 'Yes!'

Richard reached across the table and high-fived Olivia.

'That is fucking brilliant news,' said Adam. He consulted his phone. 'We have more than half the shoots left and thanks to Nancy here, we haven't had as bad a drop-off in views and likes as we may have expected. Remember Budapest? Now, that was a fucking nightmare.'

'She ran off to a bear sanctuary on that occasion,' explained Richard to Meredith.

Meredith wasn't listening. She was focussing on what Olivia had just told them. Amy was returning and Olivia had made a point of saying she might not be needed. She was out.

Would they kick her out of the room tomorrow? She couldn't go back to the shared flat with Spider and the others. She just couldn't. It was too unfair. She was good at this! She fitted into this world better than the one she had come from, and she would do anything to stay in it.

She would just have to make Amy agree to her joining The

Squad, and as she thought this Meredith began to feel better. After all she had done for Amy, she would have to agree.

Meredith looked around the terrace, at the infinity pool and the discreet white-suited waiters, and felt the warm, Mediterranean breeze on her face. She wasn't going anywhere just yet.

'And there's another thing, Nancy, or should I say *Meredith*?' Olivia was looking at her triumphantly. Meredith exchanged a glance with Adam.

She met Olivia's eyes and then nodded slowly, maintaining a solemn expression she had practised in the mirror over the last few nights since the Steel83 comments.

'You should: it's my real name after all.'

Olivia looked at the others, expecting them to be shocked, but they weren't. Richard looked down at the table, Dylan didn't look up from his phone and Adam just shook his head.

'I got in touch with Steel83, you see, and she told me something very interesting. Nancy isn't who she appears to be. Her real name is Meredith Weaver and she is a murderer.'

Adam placed his hand over Olivia's. 'Olivia, it's okay, we know. Meredith told us everything today. Steel83 is her aunt and she even showed us the news reports from the local paper that I can see you have on your phone there.'

Meredith could see the news report on Olivia's iPhone Xs which was laid flat on the table. She could have recited every word of the article published on October 23, 2001.

'She's a murderer.' Olivia pointed at Meredith.

Meredith sighed and looked at Olivia with what she hoped was sympathy and understanding. That is what she wanted to project. 'I'm not a murderer, Olivia. As you well know from reading the article.'

'You killed your father.'

'It was an accident. He had been beating me on and off for years. It probably explains why I ended up being with men who did the same thing. One night, when he was drunk, I set fire to his collection of old porno mags in the living room of our house and the fire got out of hand and he was so blind drunk' – she let her voice crack at this point – 'he didn't wake up.' Meredith let her head sink to her hands as though she was reliving the moment. She was, but the truth was that if she showed her real emotions to them, she would be smiling, because killing that cruel bastard had been the best thing she had ever done.

'You went to prison.'

'They put me into care, not prison. I didn't murder my father. It was an accident and that article' – she pointed at the phone – 'tells you exactly that.'

'And you lied to us about your name.'

'To be fair, Olivia, I never lied. I started using the name Nancy after I was released because people' – she looked directly at Olivia – 'can be so judgemental and I wanted a fresh start. It didn't seem too much to ask and I never lied. If you had ever asked me about it, I would have told you everything but we are entitled to a past, aren't we?'

'You put us, The Squad, in jeopardy.'

Richard perked up. 'Actually, I don't think so. She was beaten by her dad and traumatised. A horrible accident resulted in his death, sure, but think how that would play if we decided to go with it? We can campaign on it, link it to Trump and #MeToo. I think it could be a winner.'

Adam was nodding in agreement. 'Damn right, Amy's independence cause is too hot, too controversial and nuanced, but Meredith here was beaten by her old, white father and stood up for herself burning his pornographic material. Jesus H, she could be a poster girl for the abused, a strong woman fighting back. You're not seeing the bigger picture here, Olivia, assuming of course, that Amy would be cool with that when she returns.'

Olivia's cheeks reddened and her eyes were blazing.

Dylan looked up from his phone. 'Yeah, and my real name is Dave, by the way. I just thought Dylan sounded cooler. I guess I should tell Amy sometime.' And then he went back to playing with his phone.

'Well, I'm meeting Amy tomorrow and we can let her decide,' said Olivia, simmering with fury.

18

Meredith used her knuckle to ring the bell.

As she waited, she told herself that if there was no reply then she would just turn around and leave the matter to fate. Olivia was due to meet Amy at 2pm for lunch and who knew what they would decide. If there was no reply then the dice would fall where they may.

'Hello?'

Meredith recognised the bright and cheery tone of Amy. Of course, that didn't mean that Ferran wasn't at home. 'Hi Amy, it's me, Nancy.'

Amy giggled. 'You mean Meredith! No worries, I'll buzz you in.'

The door unlocked and Meredith pushed it open with her shoulder and entered the building. As she walked in an elderly woman was descending the marble stairs. She didn't seem to pay any attention to Meredith and even if she did what would she see? A young, slim woman in jogging tights, with a baseball cap covering her hair and sunglasses covering her eyes.

Meredith passed her as she had decided not to take the lift.

The old woman smelt of lavender and antiseptic soap, the disguise of illness and death, thought Meredith.

When she stepped out onto the top floor the door to the apartment was already open and Amy was standing there grinning.

'This is an unexpected pleasure! Come on in. Olivia is coming over at two as well so maybe we can all do lunch together?'

They exchanged cheek kisses and Meredith followed her into the apartment.

'That would be lovely. I just thought I'd drop round and tell you about the whole "Meredith-Nancy" thing but I guess Olivia beat me to it.'

'She called me last night. She's really pissed at you, you know?'

'And you?'

'I get it. Identity is what you want it to be, not what others tell you it should be.'

It was hot in the apartment but there was a warm breeze that made it just about bearable.

As if she read her mind Amy explained she didn't like putting on the air conditioning because it was bad for the environment. Meredith nodded along in all the right places as Amy went on a rant about climate change. There was no sign of Ferran and she couldn't hear anyone else in the apartment.

'Is Ferran around?'

Amy shook her head. She talked as she opened the patio doors and led them out onto the terrace.

'No, he's gone to another meeting. You must have noticed with Edu that they are always at bloody meetings? Anyway, to be honest I don't care. I'm moving out today. I've decided to come back and rejoin The Squad. To be truthful, I didn't realise how violent these guys can get and it's all a bit' – she lowered her voice – 'nationalistic and I'm not sure that's my thing.'

Meredith had suspected this was the case but she had planned for this eventuality and Amy would only have herself to blame. *It was her choice,* that was the thing that Amy would have to see. 'Do you think you are making the right decision? I thought you and Ferran were pretty tight?'

Amy looked at Meredith with curiosity. 'Making the right decision. Well, thanks for your interest Nancy, I mean Meredith, but yes, I think I am. Why don't you take a seat and I'll fix us a couple of drinks. Is it too early for a cocktail?'

Meredith walked to the balcony. The view was as amazing as she remembered. 'In a moment, and no, it's not too early. Listen, there is something I wanted to ask you.'

Amy flopped into one of the loungers. 'Christ, it's hot. Come over here and tell me.' She patted the sunlounger next to hers.

Meredith hesitated for a second and then joined her.

'Before you tell me can you do me a favour and do me?' She picked up a bottle of Hawaiian Tropic sunscreen and passed it to Meredith.

Amy turned on her front and loosened the shoulder straps of her top.

Meredith pressed the tube and poured a generous measure of white cream into her hands. She rubbed her palms together, warming the cream, and then gently but firmly applied it to Amy's back. Amy squirmed at first and then as Meredith rubbed the cream into her skin began to make little moaning sounds. 'So, what is it you wanted to ask me?'

It could still work out well. All Amy needed to do was agree. But even as she talked Meredith was looking out, over the balcony, to the city and the sea beyond.

'I think it's great that you are returning to The Squad. I know the guys have really missed you. The thing is, I think I know what I want to do with my life now. I want to be like you.'

Meredith kept working in the cream and Amy wriggled with pleasure. 'It's funny,' she said, 'when we met in Thailand all those years ago, I wanted to be like you. You seemed so confident and full of life. Like you knew what you were about at an early age. Life is full of surprises. Like your real name being Meredith!' She giggled. 'Not that that bothers me. Olivia told me what they did to you. It's really bloody awful and I can give you some great advice on how to play that on social media.'

'As part of The Squad?'

Amy propped herself up on an elbow. 'Here's the thing, Meredith, God it feels weird to call you that! But you are a little bit old. I don't blame you for knocking a few years off but over thirty isn't good for our demographic and your backstory is a bit macabre. I know Adam thinks we can spin it, but I agree with Olivia. We are lighter and breezier, you know. But also – and this is a great tip – we can't change the balance. There's me and then the others sort of support me, like Messi and the other Barcelona players. You can't have two Messis and I think you deserve to be a star of your own. You strike me more as the loner type, to be honest, and I think you know that as well.'

'I thought I could be like you guys?'

'But you're not, are you? And don't take this the wrong way but there's just something a little "off" about you. Maybe that could be your selling point, rather than the blue hair.' She laughed. 'Once you work out what it is.' She smiled sweetly at Meredith.

Meredith said nothing. She wondered should she lean in and kiss Amy but she knew that Amy would just laugh at her.

Meredith dried her hands on the towel she was lying on. She took the sunscreen tube and placed that on top of the towel. The sick anxious feeling she had been carrying around all morning was gone. Amy had confirmed her worst fears and now she was left with no choice. It wasn't her fault: she had given her every chance.

Amy was still talking. Meredith wasn't listening, but she forced herself to tune into what Amy was saying. 'I saw your photos, some of them are really quite good. And you know, feel free to tag me into any you do yourself. I'll always give you a like: that's what friends are for. Do you want that drink now?'

Meredith nodded and Amy disappeared into the apartment to fetch them some drinks.

Meredith stood up and walked across to the balcony. Looking out, she could see a few other terraces below them in other buildings and some of these had people in them but mainly they were covered in parasols and awnings to protect the occupants of the terraces from the remorseless midday sun.

Amy reappeared holding two glasses of gin and tonic.

'You can put mine on the table and come and look at this,' said Meredith.

Amy placed one of the drinks on the table by the side of Meredith's lounger and then joined Meredith at the balcony.

'It's too damned hot to be standing in the sun, Meredith.'

Meredith stood at the right of the terrace balcony and leaned out.

'Be careful, it's a long way down,' said Amy, laughing as she did so.

'You can see the Sagrada Família if you lean out a little.'

Amy feigned a mock yawn. 'I've only been here a few weeks and even I'm bored of seeing that bloody church.'

Meredith stepped back from the balcony. 'It's a basilica, but I know, it drives me mad that it's all the tourists want to see. Listen, I wanted to thank you for offering to help me out. I've got a new mobile phone by the way. Can I give you my number?'

Amy smiled, pleased probably that there had been no

unpleasantness in what could have been an awkward situation. 'Sure, what is it?'

Meredith held out her hand. 'It's a long one, let me enter it for you. I've left my phone in the hotel.'

For a second Amy paused and then she unlocked her phone and handed it to Meredith.

Meredith quickly opened the settings on Amy's phone and switched the lock time to 'never'.

'Come on, let's get a selfie with the Sagrada Família in the background: it will be the ultimate in cheese.'

Amy looked uncertain and then nodded. 'Sure, why not, and then I better get the rest of my stuff together before Olivia comes round.'

Meredith positioned herself at the far end of the balcony. From here, if you stood on your toes you could just about strain your neck and see the famous basilica of the Sagrada. Amy joined her, standing at her side.

'Okay, let's do this quickly. I'm not a fan of heights.' Amy giggled nervously.

Meredith placed her left arm around Amy and they pressed their backs against the balcony at hip level. Meredith held out Amy's mobile phone in her outstretched right hand. 'That's it: I can nearly see it.'

She changed the angle of the phone slightly and the top of the Sagrada appeared in the right-hand corner of the screen.

Meredith stood on the bottom rung of the iron balustrade.

'Just step on there, Amy, and we've got the perfect selfie,' she said cheerfully.

Amy placed first one heel and then another on the railing.

'That's perfect!'

In the screen of the iPhone Amy and Meredith were pictured with the Sagrada forming the perfect backdrop. Meredith didn't take a picture.

'You're not smiling, Meredith!'

With her left hand, Meredith grabbed hold of Amy's hair and pulled with all her strength and at the same time she jumped off the bottom railing.

Amy pivoted on the small of her back and toppled backwards but managed to grab hold of the top of the balustrade.

'What are you doing! That is so dangerous!'

Meredith dropped to her knees and shoved as hard as she could against Amy's legs at the same time, letting go of her hair. Amy's legs swung upwards and Amy's swinging body weight broke her grip on the railing.

She fell and plummeted towards the pavement far below.

Meredith watched Amy's mouth open but she couldn't tell, and later wouldn't be able to recall, whether Amy screamed or not as she fell. She didn't think so, and then in less time than it would take for her to post a picture to Instagram, Amy hit the ground below with a distinct wet thud and her limbs were rearranged to form a pattern that from where Meredith stood looked like a swastika. She had to move quickly.

Amy's phone was still unlocked and she navigated to Instagram. She took a picture of the skyline, the same scene that would have been the background to their selfie and then she published it on Amy's personal account with the hashtag #ImSorry #Dontignoredepression.

Amy put on the plastic gloves she had brought with her and began to wipe down any surface she had touched with the towel she had been lying on. Part of the reason she had struggled to follow some of Amy's conversation was that she had been mentally ticking off everything she touched.

She had been assiduous in touching as little as possible so it only took a few seconds. But there was the question of the sunscreen on Amy's body: could the police get fingerprints from that? Meredith didn't know, but it was pointless worrying: it was out of her control.

When she was finished, she threw the towel in her tote bag and then after a moment's hesitation she wiped down the tube of lotion. She had been mindful to take it as well but if Amy's body was covered in lotion then its absence would be suspicious. The towel had to come with her as she had been lying on it and there was the possibility that she had left fibres or traces of DNA on there.

Once she was satisfied that she had cleaned the surfaces, a process that took less than two minutes, she prepared to leave the flat. She was tempted to look over the balcony but there would be people there by now and they would be looking up at where Amy had come from. So far, there were no police or ambulance sirens.

Meredith took one last look at the balcony and the terrace and then she let herself out of the apartment.

She ignored the temptation to run down the stairs and instead pressed the button to call the lift. Above her, the ancient mechanism cranked into life and with much banging and grinding of gears, the lift began to rise from the floors below and slowly make its way to the top floor.

If she was seen by anyone it would be too bad. But she was wearing sunglasses and her cap and if that happened it happened. She was lucky, though. The lift arrived and descended without anyone else calling it and when it arrived in the lobby it was cool and empty.

Meredith pulled open the cage door and stepped out of the lift.

She walked to the front entrance of the apartment block and shouldered open the heavy doors. And then she paused. She was still wearing the blue plastic gloves. What if someone had seen her in the lobby, that wasn't the type of thing people forgot. She stepped back into the lobby and slid them off and put them in the tote bag. *You got this* she told herself and it was true, it had all gone to plan, she didn't feel nervous or constrained any longer and she didn't need to be a person who panicked and made mistakes. That was not the new Meredith. She opened the doors once more. The heat hit her hard as it always does when you stepped from the cool of an air-conditioned marble lobby into a Barcelona summer afternoon, but she maintained a steady, normal walking pace and although there were some passers-by, no one seemed to give her a second glance.

In the distance, she could hear the first sounds of sirens heading for the back of the building but sirens in the city were not unusual. She had left her phone in the room at Soho House so it would show her location as there all morning.

Meredith walked briskly now that she was a block away from the apartment. She didn't feel as bad as she had expected to feel. Amy had every chance to help her, to welcome her to The Squad but she had treated Meredith's friendship as if it were as disposable as a post on Instagram.

Meredith even found herself smiling as she moved through the unsuspecting pedestrians going about their business. Nobody could identify her. It would look like an accident: a rich, spoilt girl got depressed and threw herself off a balcony. She probably thought she wouldn't fall, was larking around for attention and then, a slip, and it happened. No harm no foul, just part of a first worlder's life, the trials and tribulations of a millennial. *The type of thing that could happen to anyone,* thought Meredith as she descended the steps into the cool, dark air of the metro station at Sarrià-Sant Gervasi.

19

Meredith was confident no one had seen her leave Soho House early that morning. She had slipped out just as a coachload of American TV executives had arrived with their multiple suitcases, weight and demands, and even if someone noticed her what would anyone remember? A girl in sports gear leaving the hotel, so what?

It did not matter of course if she was seen returning as this would fit in with her plan but first, she had to stash the towel until she could get rid of it safely and that meant she had to return to her apartment. It was the middle of the day but that didn't guarantee that nobody would be at home as none of her flatmates had jobs.

She let herself into the apartment block front door and was immediately assailed by the usual smell of stale piss stewing in the morning heat. She tried to ignore it as she climbed the narrow filthy stairs. By the time she reached the apartment door, she was sweating profusely and her previous calm demeanour had changed to one of anxiety.

She put the key in the lock and turned it slowly. It clicked open and she pushed open the door. The air was rank, heavy and still. There was no air conditioning in here and as she moved through the flat she was glad of that fact because it meant that, as usual, everyone was still asleep after the late, sleepless, suffocating night before. The sound of snoring came from the living room. She risked a brief look round the door and saw Spider slumped in the tatty armchair, and two other figures covered by a blanket on the couch. The table in the middle of the room was covered in beer cans, cigarette papers and a large bong filled with filthy brown water. No one stirred.

Quietly, Meredith made her way to her bedroom. Amazingly, the padlock was still in place. She had assumed Spider or one of the others would have at some point made an attempt to break it but that would require some effort and they had, she was sure, already been through her things many times before and seen that there was nothing of value there.

She unlocked the padlock and stepped into her bedroom.

The contrast with her current living arrangements at Soho House was stark. She looked in disgust at the single mattress in the corner of the room and the rail on which hung her cheap clothes. She looked at herself in the mirror propped against one wall and was satisfied. Beads of perspiration ran down her face – but who didn't look like that after climbing flights of stairs in the summertime in a non-air-conditioned building in Barcelona? What she was pleased about was that there was no visible sign of any change. No new wrinkle or strand of grey hair that had popped up following the incident at Ferran's apartment. And why should there be? Life was just a series of events, one flowing from another. If this was anyone's fault, it was Richard's for recognising her in Plaça del Pi. She hadn't asked to be introduced to The Squad.

Meredith moved her mattress to one side and used a flat

edge screwdriver to lever out the floorboard. Her money, the €5,000, was still there in its little backpack. She took off the sports gear, shoved it and the towel from Ferran's apartment into the backpack, and then replaced the board. She owned a pitiful collection of clothes but she selected the best garment – a blue Uniqlo linen jumpsuit – and slipped it on. She took a last look around and then she left her room and as quietly as she could clicked the lock back into place.

There was the sound of movement from the living room. She hesitated for a second but nothing else happened. No one emerged from there.

Meredith delicately walked across the hallway and placed her hand on the front door handle. She turned it and opened the door.

To be faced by Inga.

Inga's expression went from surprise to happiness in an instant and as her mouth began to open Meredith pushed forward, shoving her out of the doorway, and closed the door behind her. She raised an index finger to her lips. 'Shush, they are all sleeping in there.'

Inga was carrying two plastic bags full of clothes. 'Well fuck them, I've been at work all morning and I don't care about their beauty sleep.'

Meredith took Inga by the arm and took a few steps away from the door. 'I don't want to see them. I owe rent.'

Inga nodded. 'I know, Spider has been talking about busting down your door for the last week.'

Meredith pulled out her purse and took out €100. 'Give this to Spider, my share of the rent. I'll be back in a week and will pay next month's then before I move out permanently, but can you do me a huge favour and don't tell Spider – or anyone else – I was here today. I don't want them knowing I occasionally slip back.' She laughed and although it didn't sound genuine in Meredith's ears Inga laughed too – a sign that she could still convince others with her learned mannerisms.

'Of course, I won't tell him. I don't tell them anything.'

Meredith would be back, but only to clear out her room and pick up her money and the towel. She would burn it somewhere outside the city.

Inga took the money and then threw her arms around Meredith. 'I've missed you. How's the high life? I did follow your Squad on Instagram and sent you a message but I guess you've been very busy.'

Meredith was somewhat surprised by the hug. She didn't think they had that sort of relationship. 'You know how it is. It's just work, really. And we don't answer our own messages: Olivia does that and most of them never get through to me.'

She looked again at Inga with her two sad little plastic bags full of pilfered clothes. She was standing at the top of the stairs. It struck Meredith that if Inga slipped or was pushed she wouldn't be able to stop herself from falling backwards.

Inga smiled broadly. 'I can't imagine. I'm so pleased for you, Meredith, I know how hard you found it living here and I decided I'm going to follow your example. I want to be a success like you. I've started a blog on fashion and the best shops to buy from in Barcelona. I should know, ja?' She held up the two bags of stolen clothes.

And isn't she right, thought Meredith. She had improved her position but she was wise enough to know how much luck played a part. Inga was lucky too because Meredith believed her when she said she wouldn't say anything to Spider. Meredith was sure of that, and if she did, well she was a thief and occasional hard drug user, and who could trust the word of someone like that?

'I think that's a great idea and I'm sure you'll be a huge

success. Drop me a message sometime and we can meet for coffee.'

Meredith didn't return straight to Soho House. First, she stopped off at a designer clothes store in El Born, on Passeig del Born, just around the corner from the hotel, and spent some time browsing the expensive racks of clothes. The shop wasn't busy and she asked the sales assistant to provide her with different sizes of a few pieces which she tried on until she could see the sales assistant was starting to get exasperated as nothing was quite right. Eventually, she left, having bought the cheapest thing in the shop, a small leather bracelet for €20. She made sure she kept her receipt and then walked round the corner to Soho House.

When she entered, she made a point of waving at the young Polish receptionist, Janek, who waved back, and then she made her way up to her room. The 'Do Not Disturb' sign was still in place.

It was just past 2pm. She had left Ferran's apartment just after midday. She was unsure of police procedure but assumed that it wouldn't be long before the news arrived at Soho House. Meredith undressed and took a shower. When she was done, she lay down on the bed and shortly thereafter felt herself drifting off, and soon she was sleeping soundly, dreaming of the Pacific coast and deep blue breakers.

She was woken by urgent banging on the door of her room. She jumped off the bed and quickly put on a pair of shorts and a cotton T-shirt. 'I'm coming!'

She opened the door to a red-faced and distraught Richard. 'You've got to come with me to Olivia's room.'

'What's the matter?' She found it easy to act as though she

didn't know what was happening and although she had suspected that she would not be troubled with the amount of skill required to convince others, she was surprised that she was almost able to convince herself that she knew nothing. This, she decided, was a higher-level skill indeed.

She followed him along the corridor and then up the stairs to the next floor. As they reached Olivia's door she pulled him back and he turned to face her. 'What's this about Richard?'

It was apparent that he had been crying as his eyes were red and began to fill up once again. 'They said not to tell you until you got to the room.'

'Who?'

He started to sob.

'Who, Richard?'

Through sobs, he spluttered, 'The police. Amy, she's...' He couldn't finish what he was trying to say.

'What about Amy? Is she okay?'

'Oh, Meredith' – he flung his arms around her – 'she's dead!'

'Oh my God,' said Meredith, but all she was thinking was that the police had told Richard not to tell her Amy was dead, and why would they do that?

Adam, Olivia and Dylan were all there in Olivia's room. Dylan was standing by the window and staring out with a blank look on his face and as usual, Meredith had little idea what, if anything, he was thinking. Olivia and Adam were seated, Adam on the couch, and Olivia cross-legged in a chair by the writing desk.

Standing in the middle of the room was a middle-aged woman with long grey hair. She looked slightly dishevelled to Meredith's eye. And there was a good-looking younger man, late twenties perhaps, dressed sharply in a well-fitted dark blue suit and white shirt.

It was the woman who spoke. 'Ah, and you must be' – she glanced down at her notepad – 'Nancy Heller, or is it Meredith Weaver?'

Meredith offered her hand and the woman looked at it for a millisecond and then took it and shook it. 'It's Meredith.'

The woman let go of Meredith's hand. 'Two names, interesting, I have three, though. Let me introduce myself and my colleague. I am Inspector Diana-Uria Fernández, and this is Sergeant Miguel Garcia. I have just informed your colleagues that there has been a terrible event.'

Meredith winced at 'event'. Fernández's English was far too good for this to be a slip of the tongue. 'So I gather,' said Meredith, and Fernández's eyes flicked towards Richard.

'Unfortunately, your friend, Señorita Banks, is dead.'

Meredith sucked in a sharp breath and put her hand to her forehead as though she had just been floored by the news. She hoped it wasn't too melodramatic. 'Jesus Christ. How is this even possible? I just saw her yesterday.'

'She fell from the penthouse terrace of her boyfriend's flat,' said Fernández who looked directly at Meredith as though waiting to gauge her reaction.

'Hang on! I'm her bloody boyfriend!' Dylan stepped towards Fernández, who stood her ground but she nodded at Miguel, who gently took hold of Dylan's arm.

'Mr Harrop, could I have a word over here?' He guided Dylan to a corner of the suite.

Adam hadn't said anything yet, but Meredith could see he was upset, hunched over and gripping his chin with his right hand.

Olivia seemed calm and composed but there was a slight tremble in her hands, which she was trying to cover by keeping them folded in her lap. Meredith was pleased to notice that her own hands exhibited no such tremble. She had half expected to be let down by her sympathetic nervous system and to find herself betrayed by uncontrollable tics and tremors, but so far there was nothing.

Fernández produced her notebook and took a moment to read it. 'Señorita Weaver, your friends, they tell me that you were helping them to find Señorita Banks' – she stole a glance towards Dylan and Garcia and lowered her voice – 'after Señorita Banks became involved in a relationship with Ferran Alba.'

Meredith felt uncomfortable and exposed standing there and she sat down next to Adam. She assumed that the others had answered some questions before she entered the room, but this didn't seem right, being questioned in front of them all. 'I'm sorry, all this is a bit much to take in.'

'Please, take your time. I appreciate this is shocking for all of you.'

Olivia, pale and visibly in shock, looked straight ahead. 'Meredith, or Nancy as we thought she was called until recently, was engaged due to her local knowledge to find Amy and bring her back. But it wasn't working out and Amy had reached out to me and was, I am sure, about to rejoin the fold,' said Olivia.

'That's right,' said Meredith, 'Amy seemed very keen to come back to work and Dylan. This is beyond awful. I just don't understand how this could happen. Is there anything we can do to help?'

Fernández didn't miss a beat. 'At the moment we cannot track down Ferran Alba. At this time our priority is to do so. If you have any knowledge of his whereabouts then please do tell us now.'

Meredith pretended to rack her brains but even if she wanted to tell her, she didn't have any idea where Ferran was, and the more time he was out of contact the better as far as

Meredith was concerned. If she was lucky, he would be spooked enough into thinking it was some sort of police conspiracy to frame him due to his involvement in the independence movement. It was possible given his level of narcissism. 'I'm sorry I don't. He will be devastated. I think he really loved her.'

Olivia and Adam exchanged a glance and Richard let out a strangled sob.

Fernández stared at Meredith for a moment as though seeing her for the first time. *Surely, this is the type of question you would ask,* thought Meredith, but for a horrifying second, she wondered if she had misjudged it. Maybe her intonation, the timing or the timbre of her voice – it was the same imperceptible and to her, unknown, observance of unwritten social rules that had made life so difficult for her for as long as she could remember. Her stomach contracted.

'He didn't tell you?' Fernández dipped her head towards Richard.

'No.'

Adam reached out and put an arm around Meredith. 'It's fucking awful. They think she was murdered.'

Meredith let out a gasp that to her ears seemed appropriate and she buried her face in Adam's chest. When she looked back up Fernández was standing over her.

'Murdered. You don't think Ferran had anything to do with it, do you?'

'I'm sorry, but this is true, we do think Señorita Banks' death is suspicious and we need to ask you a question that we have asked all your colleagues. Can you tell me where you were this morning between 10am and 12.30pm?'

Meredith put her face in her hands and rubbed her eyes as though clearing tears. 'I don't believe it. Why would anyone do that?'

Dylan slammed his fist down on the console table next to

him. 'I know who would do it! That slimeball Ferran, I'm going to rip his head off!' He stormed out of the room, slamming the door behind him. Miguel looked at Fernández, who nodded almost imperceptibly, and Miguel followed Dylan out of the room.

Fernández's pen hovered over her pad. 'Señorita Weaver?'

'Sorry, my whereabouts, yeah sure. I was here at the hotel. We had a late night last night and I slept in.'

Fernández paused and then wrote this down on her pad. 'Any witnesses?'

'I went to bed alone and woke up alone. Oh, I did shoot out and buy this' – she held up her arm to show off her new bracelet – 'around twelve and got back about 2pm. It's from one of those small designer shops in El Born. I think the sales assistant may have been pissed at me: I was in there for a while.'

Meredith thought she saw something in Fernández's eyes, a light coming on. Had she said too much? She was saved by Olivia who gently coughed and then stood up.

'Miss or is it Mrs Fernández?' She didn't wait for an answer. 'We are all shocked and upset as you can see and I want to thank you for coming over but we really do need some time, to... to... process all of this and, well, grieve.'

Fernández snapped her notebook shut and smiled at them. 'Of course. I want to again express to you my sorrow for your loss. You are checked in here for another two weeks, yes?'

Adam shrugged and then nodded.

'Please let me know if you intend to leave the city before then. And I will be in touch, no?'

Olivia walked her to the door and as soon as she had left the room turned to them and burst into tears. Adam and Richard led her to the sofa. She sat down next to Meredith.

Meredith tentatively put an arm out and rested her hand on Olivia's knee. Meredith looked at her hand lying there like an alien spacecraft on a distant planet, but Olivia didn't seem to mind.

Adam brought her some tissues and Richard, in his very English way, said he would make them all a cup of tea.

'I just can't believe she's gone, and to think they think she was murdered. I mean, what the fuck!' Adam was pacing the room. 'And to question us like that, the silly bitch. I mean, turns out apart from Dylan and Richard out on their morning run, we were all in bed, I mean, Christ, who does mornings in Spain? I know this might be too early, but we are going to have to post something.'

'Adam, for Christ's sake, how can you think about posting at a time like this?' said Olivia.

'We need to think about The Squad. It's what Amy would want, you know it.'

'Holy fuck!' It was Richard and he was looking at his phone.

'What is it?' said Olivia.

'Amy posted something before she died. Take a look.'

He showed Adam the phone and then he passed it to Olivia who held it up for her and Meredith to read. It was the 'Sorry' picture Meredith had posted.

'Depression? Amy? I don't think so. She was...' Olivia gulped hard but carried on, 'Always so upbeat. It was infuriating sometimes.'

Adam scratched his head and his expression was one of confusion and grief. 'But they always say that, don't they? After the event, people always say, she was never like that, never depressed, we never saw the signs. Maybe we just didn't see the signs.'

'Bullshit,' said Olivia. 'You heard that Fernández woman. They think she was killed, pushed off the balcony.'

'What are you saying, Olivia?' asked Meredith, keeping as blank an expression on her face as she could.

Olivia bit her bottom lip and then looked at them both in turn. 'What if the killer sent that message and not Amy?'

Meredith nodded slowly – the worst thing would be to argue the point with Olivia, but all she was thinking was that her carefully laid plan hadn't survived the day. She felt sick but she was clear on what she had to do next.

20

S he couldn't tell what Edu was thinking behind the tortoiseshell Ray-Bans. After the violent independence riot, they had only seen each once more. It wasn't because she was squeamish or put off by the violence, far from it. She found it one of the most interesting things about Edu, this hidden side. It was because she had wrapped herself up with The Squad as they came together in the face of Amy's death. The shock was still reverberating within the group and online there had been an outpouring of emoji grief the like of which Adam had said he had never seen before. As a consequence, although they had mainly remained confined to the hotel, they had never been busier posting and getting out 'grief content,' as Adam termed it.

She had a feeling that Amy would have approved.

She hadn't intended on contacting Edu again. His fascination with a cause, Catalonian independence, frankly bored her, and in this respect she differed from Amy.

But yet, here she was, meeting Edu again. Despite the boring political talk and his purpose, there was just something about his childlike innocence that drew her in and made her want to spend time with him. She could be as close to herself with Edu as it was possible for her to be with someone else, and this was a feeling that she enjoyed. And of course, she assumed he was still in contact with Ferran who had yet to turn himself in.

Maybe he was upset that she had ignored some of his messages. But he had agreed to meet for a coffee at a bar below the W hotel at the far end of the Barceloneta beach, Platja de Sant Sebastià. She had arrived early and sat watching the broad expanse of beach filled with more tourists than she thought humanly possible. They were being preyed upon by the mojito, beer and trinket sellers from all points south. She had chosen this spot because she knew it afforded her, and Edu, a perfect view from the terrace bar of all comers along the esplanade.

She had just told him everything that she was supposed to know about Amy's death and the visit from the police. He had expressed sympathy and nodded along as she told him how they were all devastated and how it was imperative that Ferran come in for questioning.

But now he was silent and looking at her through those damned Ray-Bans that made it impossible for her to calibrate his responses. 'You must be very sad, Meredith,' he said in a flat tone.

Was he mocking her, being serious, or was this one of those conversational placeholders that she always struggled to understand? 'We are all devastated. It's been an awful couple of days.'

'I can't imagine how you must be feeling. It just seems so crazy to me and now the police are looking for Ferran. But I can tell you this: he would never kill anyone and never Amy. It's such bullshit.'

'Do you know where Ferran is?' She hoped he didn't. She hoped that Ferran had fallen off the face of the earth. It would make everything so much easier.

'I may and I may not. The political situation is so delicate that he is, and I do not blame him for this, he is frightened that the National Guard may want to say this is terrorist-related. He only wants to talk to the Catalonian force, the *Mossos*. Once he has guarantees that this will take place, then he will hand himself in. But don't worry: this should happen today or tomorrow. He's not stupid – he knows how this looks.'

This is bad news, thought Meredith. She had hoped he would go on the run to South America. 'That's great news. He needs to clear things up. This police officer, Fernández, she thinks that Amy was murdered and I'm sure you've seen the news.'

The local and national news channels had gone big on the death of an Instagram influencer in the city and someone had leaked the fact that the police thought that it wasn't an accident. Ferran's photograph had followed soon after.

'The media is always sensationalising things. I don't know what happened to your friend and I'm very sorry about what happened. But there is one thing I can tell you: Ferran had nothing to do with her death.'

Behind Edu on the beach, she could see two heavyset men with red faces. *Too much drink and too much sun,* she thought. They were arguing with a scrawny elderly man who was trying to sell them pieces of coconut. They were getting right into his face and laughing. Edu's words brought her attention back.

'How do you know that?'

Those Ray-Bans! He was smiling now but she couldn't see his eyes, and he wasn't even facing the sun.

'Because I was with him all that morning.'

Meredith cursed silently. This was not what she hoped for, not at all.

'And you won't go to the police because you think they are after you and Ferran because you are separatists. And you think the National Guard will insist the *Mossos* hand the case over if it is linked to any suggestion of sedition or' – she lowered her voice – 'terrorism. Isn't that a bit far-fetched?'

'Pah! The Spanish government thinks the *Mossos* won't investigate their own, that they let the votes take place, that they won't deal properly with *independentistas*. We need to make some arrangements to make sure we don't end up as more victims of this fascist government.'

If Ferran had an alibi then this left her more exposed. She had hoped Ferran wouldn't come forward for another few weeks. They could have all have left the country by then and it might all just be seen as another unfortunate holiday death plunge. Christ, the Spanish even had an 'anglo-saxismo' word for such deaths: 'balconing'.

One of the tourists shoved the coconut seller hard in the chest.

'Jesus,' said Meredith.

Edu turned round and took in the scene.

'Aren't you going to do anything?' His fucking sunglasses were driving her wild. Was he happy, upset or angry? Did he believe what she was saying?

He shrugged his shoulders. 'It's not my fight.'

Meredith pushed back her chair and strode across the pavement to the beach. She walked up to the taller and broader of the two young men. He had curly black hair and stank of alcohol and cigarettes. He was wearing baggy blue shorts and a vest that showed off plump, steroid bubbles of muscle and fat.

She prodded him hard in the chest with her index finger and a look of confusion came over his face. 'What do you' – another prod – 'think you are' – another prod – 'doing?'

He held his hands up and leered at her. 'A fucking yank!'

'Fuck off, yank. This is none of your business,' shouted his friend.

She took a step forward so she was in the big guy's personal space and thrust her face upwards towards his. He took a step back.

'This man' – she pointed behind her at the coconut seller – 'is just trying to earn a fricking living and you two jerks think it's funny to push him around? What's wrong with you?'

She was vaguely aware that a crowd had gathered, eager to watch a bit of beach drama.

'He's a fucking Muslim cunt, innit, trying to flog us shitty coconut for €5,' said the big guy.

'Even a Bounty is only €1,' said the smaller guy.

She bit down on an urge to punch him and part of her hoped that he would punch her. The red rage in his face made her think that this could happen. It would open up so many more possibilities to her. *It will justify anything,* she thought. *If only he would hit me, I could kill him.*

'Listen you *guiri* fuckfaces, this man is earning a living, probably supporting a family and you can just say no, you know. So why don't you just get out of his and my face and go play on the metro line.'

This drew a loud cheer and some applause from the people who were watching the fracas. She closed her eyes and waited for a blow to land but it didn't come. Instead, the two guys looked around, saw that it didn't look good for them, and slunk off.

Someone touched her arm. It was Edu. 'That was very brave and noble of you. I was watching just to be sure. If anything had happened you know I would have intervened.'

She nearly laughed in his face but managed to just about suppress this urge. He looked confused and she wondered how confused he would be if she told him that the only reason she had got involved was because his stupid fucking Ray-Bans had driven her to it. That she had wanted to punch him as much as she had wanted to punch the *guiris* and that, frankly, she did not care much about the coconut seller who was probably selling out-of-date coconut at severely inflated prices to unsuspecting tourists on behalf of one of the local gangs.

'Sure, Edu.' And she gave her sweetest of smiles by way of recompense.

This seemed to please him and he leaned in close. 'Maybe you should come back to mine? We could relax over a vermouth.'

She looked at him. She still found him attractive, that much was true. 'Okay, but on one condition?'

'Sure, name it.'

'You have to take those Ray-Bans off right now.'

HE HAD, eventually, taken the glasses off and she had enjoyed a pleasant afternoon with Edu but she had been eager to return to Soho House and meet up with The Squad.

Over the last few days, they had bonded over the death of Amy. Meredith realised that she laughed more with them as they drank and remembered Amy than they ever had before her death. It was as though a blockage to her becoming part of The Squad had been removed. Amy's death had fast-tracked her acceptance by the group as though one death counted for ten years of shared holidays, parties and experiences.

Even Olivia had begun to come round. She had invited Meredith for drinks that evening and Meredith was determined to make this a stepping stone to a better relationship. They had shared a drunken group hug the night before when they all became teary whilst remembering Amy and she wanted to build upon that. With Amy out of the way it was Olivia who was the key to her remaining in The Squad.

When she entered the reception of Soho House Janek called her to the desk. He leaned in and whispered, 'There is a police-woman waiting for you in the bar. She asked that I send you in as soon as you arrive. She's been here for forty minutes already, waiting for you.' Janek raised his eyebrows and stressed the 'you' in much the same way he did when telling minor celebrities that a producer was waiting for them in the bar.

Meredith looked back towards the door. She could leave right away, get the €5,000 from under the floorboards of her flat and catch the afternoon ferry to Tangiers. Maybe she could stay with the artist she had met at the MACBA. There had been a connection with Annik. She had felt it. You didn't need small talk with a connection like that: it just existed. She should run, leave all this behind. It made sense. The door swung open, allowing in the crystal-clear early evening sunshine which was pouring directly along the Passeig de Colom before the sun dipped behind Montjuïc. She should run, that was the answer.

'Señorita Weaver.' It was Fernández. One of the staff must have notified her that Meredith had returned. She was standing at the door of the bar. 'Will you join me for a drink? I would like to make a quick talk with you.' Fernández held open the door to the bar.

'Inspector Fernández. Of course, anything I can do to help.' Meredith led them to a quiet corner of the bar and they sat down in two sumptuous green velvet armchairs that faced each other across a small table.

The waiter approached them and took their order. A cortado for Meredith and a small beer for Fernández.

Meredith braced herself for small talk and tried to think of some banal topics they could skirt around before discussing business.

But Fernández didn't make any attempt at small talk or any kind of talk. She sat back in her armchair and brought her fingertips together as though in prayer.

She was watching Meredith. Suddenly, the absence of small talk made Meredith's skin itch and even in the air-conditioned bar she felt herself begin to sweat. *This,* she thought, *is ridiculous.* She knew what Fernández was doing so she decided to end it. 'So, can I help you, inspector?'

Fernández still didn't speak and Meredith wondered was it possible that the woman had had a stroke. She was in her late forties at least and stank of cigarettes so it was possible she supposed – but then Fernández seemed to spark into life and she leaned forward. 'Yes, you can but first I have some good news for you.'

Meredith expected she knew what that was. 'What is it?'

'Ferran Alba has handed himself in.' She looked at Meredith, waiting for a reaction. Meredith, unsure of the correct reaction in these circumstances, kept her expression blank and serious. This was murder they were talking about after all. 'That is good news. Do you think he did it?'

Fernández's eyes twinkled with mischief. 'You know my ex-husband, he always used to sneak cakes and biscuits. One of the reasons I left him was he got so damned fat. Who heard of a fat Barcelonés, eh? I always knew whether he had been taking them because when I asked him if he had, there was something in his voice that just told me when he was lying. I hear that in other voices too. I spoke to Ferran earlier and I didn't hear that in his voice.'

Meredith wondered whether she was being serious and if so, what did she hear in Meredith's voice? 'I'm sorry but that doesn't sound the most scientific way of investigating a crime.'

Fernández patted the arm of her chair in merriment. 'Indeed, it is not! And you are right, I am a foolish woman sometimes. But still I've been catching murderers for some time and I do always rely on this feeling. My male colleagues are horribly sexist about this but they are old, impotent bores so what do I care?'

She laughed out loud again, drawing some glances from other patrons. Meredith wondered if she had been drinking whilst she waited for her.

But Fernández's expression suddenly became serious and she leaned forward and put her hand on Meredith's wrist. Meredith desperately tried not to show that this had totally freaked her out.

'Of course, Ferran gave me an alibi and we are checking it out but I think it will check out okay, and if it does, it means we need another suspect. And I wanted to talk to you about that, Meredith. Who do you think that should be?'

Meredith blew out her cheeks and slowly shook her head. In the corner of the bar, she noticed that Jude Law had walked in and taken a seat. It added a surreal tone to their conversation. 'I couldn't possibly think of anyone who wanted her dead. I can't help wondering whether this is an Occam's razor situation where the most obvious solution is the truth of the matter.'

'Which would be?' The merriment in Fernández's eyes seemed to grow.

'That Amy killed herself. There was the text and I hear it's quite a common way for people to go.'

'People to go,' repeated Fernández as though savouring a new delicacy. 'That is an English phrase I have just learned from you. Thank you. Yes, it does happen, people do go that way, but we have a witness in a room in the opposing block who said he saw some sort of struggle between two women on the balcony and then one fell. He was too far away to identify anyone but he is sure of what he saw. And you mention the text, but no one mentions any sign of depression, not her friends, not you, and there are no medical notes of any mental illness.'

Meredith immediately felt paranoid. Why had Fernández separated her from Amy's friends? She was as much one of her friends as any of The Squad. Had Olivia been saying something to Fernández?

'Well, I'm no expert, but people who suffer from depression often don't mention it, or we miss the signs.'

Fernández nodded along vigorously. 'So true, so true, did you see any signs, with hindsight?'

Meredith sucked in her bottom lip and pretended she was trying to remember.

'Maybe, she was a little sad last time I saw her, I don't know.'

'A little sad, a moment, *por favor*.' She leaned down and dug around in her handbag which she had placed by her feet. Meredith could see two cartons of cigarettes and a vape pen in the bag. Fernández produced her notepad. 'Here it is! I am such a bad police person, no?' She began to write. 'A little bit sad was what you said. This is correct?'

Meredith nodded.

'So, she was a little bit sad. Maybe her time with Ferran was coming to an end? Olivia, Señorita Lowe, told me that Señorita Banks was planning on leaving Ferran. It was a summer fling, she tells me, and Señorita Banks was returning to... what you call it again, the team?'

'The Squad,' said Meredith, feeling vaguely ridiculous.

'Ah yes.' Fernández jabbed her pencil at the pad. 'It says it right here, The Squad. But she was returning. It was no big love affair and Señorita Lowe, who has known Señorita Banks for many years, said she was happy and looking forward to coming back to work.'

'That's probably right then,' said Meredith.

'Assuming it was not Ferran, and we know there was no

forced entry, then we are left with a presumption it was someone the deceased knew.'

'Or suicide, if this witness is mistaken about seeing a struggle.'

'Exactly!' said Fernández, and she jabbed her pencil in the air triumphantly. 'Were it not for the other matters.'

Meredith's stomach performed a barrel roll. 'Other matters?'

'Precisely, and forgive my English at all times, please. These are two things. One of the neighbours reported a young woman in the lobby of Ferran's building at approximately 11.30am which is the time when we could expect perhaps the killer to have arrived. And there is a missing item from the apartment.'

Meredith shrugged as though neither of these things meant anything to her. 'There are like, twenty apartments in that building. It could have been another resident or guest?'

Fernández thrust the pencil forward. 'Again, you are right. But let me tell you there are actually twenty-eight apartments, I know because'– she began to chuckle – 'I sent my man, Miguel, you met him, no? I sent him to every one of them to ask if it was them or if they had a guest at that time. He was not happy to do this, I think he thinks it is beneath him... is that how you say it? But he did it and no one could say it was them or that they had a guest at that time. I know what you are thinking, I am too: it can't be all of them, some must have been out so could have had a guest call unannounced and this is true. There were twelve apartments like that but all the owners insisted they had no one scheduled to visit. This is not proof, but interesting, no? And interesting, too, that nobody reported letting someone into the building at that time. So, who is this mystery woman?'

She held up her palms as though seeking some form of divine response to her question.

'Interesting, that's for sure.' Meredith glanced at her watch.

Fernández relaxed back in her chair. 'I am so rude, you must

forgive me. Señorita Lowe said you had a dinner date with her. It
is good that you two are more friends now. I understand that this
was not always the case.'

She paused and waited for Meredith to talk. Meredith had a
curious feeling as though she were submerged and the words of
Fernández were travelling slowly to her through the water. She
felt unsure whether, had she wanted to speak, the words would
actually come out of her mouth. She remembered something
her son-of-a-bitch father had once told her: 'If you don't open
your mouth you can't prove you are an idiot.'

Luckily, Fernández didn't appear to have noticed. Or didn't
show that she had noticed.

'I heard that you may, in Amy's absence, become part of this
"Squad," so this is a good thing that comes from this bad
thing, no?'

Meredith mentally kicked herself and forced her conscious
brain to take over. 'I'm just trying to help out when I can.'

'Yes, of course, it's very kind of you, as I understand from
Señorita Lowe again.'

She had thought Olivia was coming round but what had she
said to the inspector? Meredith didn't say anything and
Fernández smiled at her.

'Yes, this is good and oh, I nearly forgot! It's my age or' – she
held up her glass of beer – 'or this,' and chuckled before taking a
deep sip and then setting her empty glass on the table.

Meredith glanced at her watch once more. She wanted to lie
on her bed, feel cool sheets and breathe purified air. 'Forgot
what?'

Fernández grinned, revealing nicotine-stained teeth. 'The
last clue.'

Meredith already knew what she was going to say. 'What
is it?'

'A towel or rather a missing towel. We thought it strange that there was only one on the sunbeds when we inspected the scene and now we have searched the apartment it is clear that the towel that should have been there is not in the apartment.'

Meredith sighed. 'I don't mean to be negative, Inspector Fernández, but this seems a bit thin? Maybe there was only one towel. Maybe the other was used to mop up spilt wine and thrown away or a million other scenarios.'

'Exactly what I said!' A jab of the pencil again. 'But I asked Ferran this morning and he said that there was one there the day before, on the lounger, so unless the towel went missing between him leaving the apartment and Amy's death then there is only one explanation–'

'Someone took it,' said Meredith, finishing Fernández's sentence.

'*Exactamente!* That's right. And who would take it? Why, someone who had been lying on it, and that means someone comfortable enough to relax around Amy. Find that towel and, mark these words, Señorita Weaver, we will find the killer.' Fernández relaxed back into her armchair.

Meredith tried to do the same but every muscle fibre felt like it was twitching in the hope of being able to sprint away from this place. 'Well, that sounds just great, but how can I help you with this investigation?'

Fernández frowned. 'Well you know I have to look at people who Amy would be relaxed enough to spend time with taking the sun. The autopsy showed she had sun lotion on her back, and we suppose this was put on her by someone else, although unfortunately, we could not obtain any fingerprints from the body. And she perhaps knew, outside the "Squad" just a few people in Barcelona and they were Ferran, the maid to the flat and two or three of Ferran's acquaintances. And they all have perfect alibis.'

'I still don't see how I can help?'

'Ah yes, I just wanted to check the timings, on the day of the killing.' She fiddled with her notepad, trying to find the right page and then gave a little cry of glee when she located it. 'Here yes. You told us that you were in your room all morning and left, around midday, to go and buy a bracelet from this shop, the Born Design Collective, at around 1pm, returning about 2pm? This is correct, no?'

Meredith hated Fernández's chirpiness and hated having to indulge it. She wanted to grip hold tightly to the armchair but she couldn't. She had to maintain the appearance of being in control, of being calm, of being innocent. She had to be charming, of all things she had to be charming. The world rewarded those with charm and was blind to other virtues. This she knew to be the truest thing of all.

She smiled sweetly at the inspector.

'Yes, although it's all a bit finger in the air. I could well have been in the design shop before 1pm.'

'I have good news about that, Señorita Weaver. Although we don't maintain routine government CCTV here in Barcelona like in some other countries, often private businesses do, and we have you there at the Born Design Collective at 1.44pm. It is you, clear as the day. I find this CCTV a bit... how do you say... creepy, personally, but it can be useful. This means we can discount this as the time we are concerned with is 11.30am to 12.30pm. See, I have managed to help you here.'

Meredith wanted to lean forward and poke Fernández hard in the eye just to burst her relentlessly upbeat bubble. But as a native of California she could pretend to be as upbeat and ebulliently positive as any Catalan. 'That is super! Like I mentioned, I wasn't sure of the time. I just drifted around the various shops and boutiques. You know how amazing they are here. As to the times in each... well, gee, I just couldn't tell you precisely.'

'I totally understand, Señorita Weaver. My ex-husband, *hijo de puta*, was constantly moaning at me, saying how could I spend so much time in a shop, but we lose the time there, no? It is meditative but still, it would be very helpful for me if you could write down here all of the places you visited. If we are lucky, we will be able to place you in one and then I can leave you alone and concentrate on catching the killer!' She tore off a piece of paper from the notepad and placed it on the table together with her pen.

Meredith looked at it. 'Now?'

'That would be so very helpful. *Gracias.*'

Meredith picked up the pen. 'Of course, but, again, this is my best guess. I usually just drift from shop to shop and I don't know the names of half of them.'

'I totally understand, Señorita Weaver. If you can't recall the name an approximate location is fine.'

Meredith wrote a list of all the shops she could think of in El Born and then jotted down some vague notes such as 'shop next to an ice cream parlour', 'boutique place near Santa Maria' and other such descriptions which she hoped would keep Fernández busy on a wild goose chase.

When she was finished, she handed the now full piece of paper back to the inspector.

'*Gracias.*' If Fernández was disturbed by the sheer number of locations, she didn't show it.

'May I go now? I have an appointment with Olivia... Miss Lowe.'

Fernández shuffled forward in her chair and beckoned that Meredith should move in closer to hear what she had to say.

This is it, thought Meredith, *this is when she will tell me that she suspects me and will stop at nothing to prove that I am the murderer.*

'Listen, don't look round, but Jude Law is sitting at the bar. Do you think it would be uncool to ask him for his autograph? I could arrest him for being such a *guapo*!' Fernández laughed uproariously at her own joke, making everyone, including Jude Law, look at them both.

Meredith was appalled. Was this the woman who would arrest her?

21

'Can you be more sad?'

Adam was taking pictures of Dylan on a quiet part of the beach close to the Forum building. On the boulders of the breakwater, he had positioned Dylan looking out to sea and now he was snapping away.

Dylan stuck out his bottom lip a little more which presumably was his attempt at looking "more sad".

Meredith sat with Richard on the sand watching proceedings. 'I'm not sure what I think about this,' she said.

'Too soon, you think?'

'Maybe it would be better to wait until the funeral?'

Richard didn't look up from checking his phone and Instagram. 'We can't let up. You know that. And the police aren't releasing her body, so what else can we do? Without Amy we could be sunk, but doing this, you know' – he looked up from his phone as though he had just had an idea – 'is actually improving our numbers. With all the press coverage, it's been good for the likes and follower rate. And you know what, Amy would have wanted this. The Squad was her baby.'

She won't have any children now. Meredith immediately

quashed this nascent thought. 'You're probably right. I think you're up.'

Adam turned his head. 'Come on, Dickie! It's you next! Let's be having you, and remember, be sad!'

'I am sad,' said Richard quietly and then he stood up slowly and walked over to join Dylan on the rocks. He put his arm around Dylan and then from the movement from their shoulders Meredith suspected that they were both crying. She wondered whether it was real or Instagram-required emotion and then decided it didn't matter either way.

She lay back in the sand and looked along the beach. Olivia was standing around fifty yards away, talking on the phone. Olivia had cancelled their dinner the night before, telling Meredith that she was too exhausted after her interviews with Inspector Fernández. Meredith had sensed a coldness in the text that Olivia had sent her, but she was aware that this could be her paranoia. Nevertheless, she was keen to speak to Olivia. She saw that Olivia's call had ended and waved her over.

Olivia acknowledged her and walked towards her. 'Are they crying?'

Dylan and Richard were both sobbing now and Adam was in a frenzy of picture-taking.

'Yeah, Richard seemed really upset.'

Olivia frowned. 'It's been nearly a week. Oh well, it will make a great post.'

'Why don't you join me?' Meredith tapped the blanket.

Olivia looked at the blanket but didn't sit down. She pulled out her vape pen and took a few deep lungfuls and then blew out some great plumes of blueberry-scented smoke. 'You know Fernández was talking to me about a young woman, mid to late twenties, who they are looking for. Apparently, she was spotted visiting the apartment block and no one knows who she was.'

Meredith stretched as though she were the most relaxed

person on the beach. She was glad she was wearing her sunglasses as the sun was directly behind Olivia, who was almost in silhouette. 'Yeah, she mentioned that to me as well. Didn't seem to amount to much really.'

'Hmmm, maybe, but it fits one of two profiles that I know. Me and you.'

Meredith laughed. 'That's what I thought and that's why she came to speak to us but we both know that it wasn't us, so I think it's just checking the boxes.'

'I know it wasn't me,' said Olivia.

Meredith squinted but couldn't make out the look on Olivia's face because of the sun behind her.

Adam shouted something.

'Does he want us to join them?'

Olivia turned her head slightly to catch what Adam was saying. 'Yeah, but perhaps it's better if you sit this one out, Meredith, just until we've cleared everything up. Oh, and after tonight it might be better if you moved out of the hotel. I hope you understand. I think it's better, just until this is all cleared up and we decide on how to move forward.'

'Does Adam know about this?'

'Adam?' said Olivia with surprise. 'Oh God, Adam just does what I tell him but since you ask, yes, he's totally on board with it. As you know, we need to protect the brand at all costs.'

Meredith tried to sound normal as she said, 'Of course, no problem.' But there was a catch in her throat and she was sure that Olivia would have noticed that.

She watched Olivia walk over to the boys and she contemplated staying, aiming for the relaxed look, maybe joining them for a drink after the shoot. But what if Olivia told her not to join them? She couldn't bear that. When she was sure they weren't looking she packed her things into her bag and then walked off the beach without looking behind her. She knew, though, that they were watching her go.

MEREDITH WALKED ALONG THE PROMENADE, ignoring the skate-boarders, rollerbladers, electric bikers and Segway users that swerved and dodged around her. She was deep in thought and she simply didn't see them. It seemed clear what she had to do. Firstly, the most important thing was to do deal with the towel. This was the only piece of physical evidence, assuming nothing else was found and she didn't think anything would be, that linked her to Ferran's flat and the sunlounger. She had to return to her old flat and retrieve it. Her next move she was more uncertain about. One thing she knew she could never do was to return to her old life and go back to living in her old flat. That was out of the question.

Meredith headed to the metro and caught a train to Drassanes. From there she entered the narrow, dark alleys of the Raval that spread through the barrio like capillaries bringing fresh blood to the hawkers, prostitutes and drug dealers who hungrily eyed everyone who entered.

Eventually, she reached her apartment block on Carrer de la Riereta. The door to the apartment block, as usual, wasn't locked, and she climbed the gloomy, damp stairs towards her third-floor flat.

She let herself in and this time was not as lucky as before. A loud reggae beat greeted her together with the heavy, sweet smell of strong weed.

As soon as she stepped through the front door a young man who she didn't know, all skater-boy hoodie and neck tattoos, walked past her from the kitchen carrying a large bag of chips.

His eyes were red and he drawled a low, stoned 'hey' at her. Canadian, she guessed.

She followed him into the living room. On the couch was Spider and draped over him was Inga.

Inga jumped up when she saw Meredith. 'M!' She threw her arms around her.

Meredith hugged her back, pleased to see someone who was glad to see her.

'Yo, Meredith,' said Spider in his usual slurred, dopamine-infused way.

'Are you two...?' Meredith nodded towards Spider.

Inga blushed. 'Yeah, I've been lonely without you around and you know he's not so bad. You're not so bad, are you, Spider?'

Spider leered at her. 'You better believe it, honey,' and then he pulled her back to the couch where she fell on top of him. They both giggled.

'So, are you back for good now?' Inga asked.

'Maybe, I just need a few things from my room.'

'About that,' said Spider, and both he and Inga stood up and followed her as she left the room.

Meredith thought she would collapse on the floor.

The lock to her room was gone.

'It was the landlord. You know we owed him rent.'

Meredith spun round and faced Inga. 'I gave you money to cover the rent!'

Inga looked at her shoes.

'Oi, don't speak to her like that,' said Spider.

'Let me guess: you spent it on drugs.' She didn't wait for an answer and opened the door.

Straight away she saw that the floorboard was loose. She put her hands on her mouth to stifle a scream.

Spider chuckled behind her back. 'Did you have anything

hidden? They pulled up the boards in my room, too, but I haven't got anything worth anything, save for my album collection, and they left that, the cultural barbarians.'

Meredith dropped to her knees and used her fingertips to lift the edge of the floorboard. She looked in the space beneath. The bag containing her money, the towel and her sports gear was gone. 'When did this happen?'

'Last night. The landlord's big thug came and made us stay in the living room whilst he checked our rooms. We told him that we had nothing, but I guess you did. How much were you squirrelling away from us, then?' Spider asked.

It didn't matter now. '€5,000.'

'What the fuck! You were holding out on us all this time,' said Spider.

'Oh M...' Inga put a hand on her arm.

Last night... there was still time. If they took the money it was possible they would just throw the bag containing the towel and the clothes away. She pushed past Spider and Inga and stormed out of the apartment, taking the stairs two at a time. When she reached the street, she turned left and there, just yards away from the house, was the large plastic rubbish cart that served the street. She pressed down on the lever with her foot and the cover lifted open.

She almost retched at the hot fetid smell that hit her from the mass of fermenting food, waste and filth that filled the bin. She had seen the poor and dispossessed scouring the city bins for scraps of metal or anything of value. She had always judged them the most blighted and tenacious of the city's underclass but she had never understood how they could bring themselves to climb in and immerse themselves in such a putrid environment. Now she did understand. It was survival.

Meredith pressed with both hands and then pushed herself

forward and into the bin. The lid slammed shut as she tumbled over and inside.

At first, she thought she would die. There seemed to be no air, but she tried gulping and realised that there was, though it was heavy, hot and wet. It was the smell of baking excrement, grease and every bodily fluid and waste product you didn't want to imagine. Meredith breathed this air and began to sort through the piles of rubbish. She thought she had the bag, but it was a stinking wet nappy that she triumphantly brought to the surface. This time she did vomit but she kept plunging her hands into the morass and checking every rag that she brought up out of the filth.

'M!' There was a banging on the outside of the bin and then the lid swung open.

It was Inga. 'Christ, M. Are you okay?' She put a hand over her mouth as the stench hit her.

Meredith sobbed. 'It's all I had in the world.'

'Oh M, it's only money.' Inga held out a hand. Meredith looked at it, wondering what to do – part of her just wanted to lie down and die in the filth. Inga smiled and Meredith saw the pity etched on her face. Meredith took hold of Inga's hand and let her help her up and out of the bin. A couple of passing tourists paused and without asking took pictures of her as she climbed out. Meredith couldn't help but think that they would make good posts.

She followed Inga back into the flat and took a shower. Then Inga lent her some of her purloined clothes to wear. Meredith's own were fouled and stained beyond saving.

Meredith thanked her and then left. She had found a card in her bedroom. It was the card given to her by the landlord, Carlos Llul.

The address was in the Gothic Quarter and only fifteen minutes' walk from her place in the Raval.

Meredith spent the time trying to calm herself down and rationalise. It wasn't easy. The towel, Fernández had admitted, was the only piece of forensic evidence that could tie her to Ferran's flat on the day of the murder. Without that, they had nothing. The sighting of a young woman entering the building by some geriatric pensioner amounted to nothing. With the towel, she was home free. Without it, there was the chance of a knock on the door. But if the towel was in the city dump then what were the chances that it would ever be found? Slim, but what if it was found? What if Carlos still had the bag, wondered why there was a towel in there and linked her to the murder of Amy? If he watched the TV news or read the papers, he would know about it.

She couldn't bear not knowing and not being in control of the situation. Just waiting for the knock on the door was not a course of action. Whilst there was a chance she could find it and dispose of it properly she had to act on it.

The address on the card led her to one of the dark, twisted alleys of the Gothic Quarter but one that was off the main tourist routes. It was a narrow passageway with room for maybe four people standing abreast. It screamed muggings and violence and this explained why, even on a hot Barcelona summer's afternoon, it was deserted. The narrowness did afford it protection from the sun and she welcomed the coolness of the air. Even after showering for twenty minutes she still felt soiled, and sweating on the way over here hadn't improved her sense that she was covered in a filth that she could never wash from her body.

She came to a door that had two small brass nameplates on the wall next to it. The one at eye-level was shiny and new and bore the name of Frank's Video Services. Below this was a dirty green copper plaque that stated 'Carlos Llul Abogado'. He was a lawyer as well as a landlord.

Meredith cursed. She had never had a good experience with a lawyer and now she thought back to their first meeting he bore all the usual signs: shrewdness and an eye for easy cruelty to achieve his ends.

She rang the bell for his office and from deep within the building she heard an ancient buzzer sound.

'Who is it?' asked a voice thick with tar and afternoon somnolence.

'You stole my money and I want it back.'

There was a cough or the crackle of the microphone and then the door unlocked.

Meredith pushed it open and entered the building. There was an old iron lift directly ahead but its surfaces were covered in dust. It looked as old as Methuselah and she didn't trust it. Instead, she took the stairs up two flights. She instantly regretted this as the lights weren't working and there were no windows, so no natural light other than what crept in from the yellowing skylight three floors above.

She came to the second floor and a door marked as 2-1. She rang the bell and the door was opened by Diego. He wore his hair slicked back, brilliantined and shiny and now she was close to him she saw his face was pocked with small craters. His hands were huge. *Perfect,* thought Meredith, *for crushing a carotid artery.*

He didn't say a word as he led her through an antechamber and knocked three times on a solid oak door.

'Enter!'

The man opened the door and led her into a small office. It was dark inside. The window shutters were closed to keep out any sun that made it down between the tall walls of the alley. Behind a desk full of yellow papers and a smouldering ashtray, sat Carlos Llul.

'What a pleasant surprise. Diego, please let us have some privacy.'

Diego grunted something that Meredith didn't catch and left the room, closing the door behind him.

The room was even darker with the door closed. Llul beckoned for Meredith to sit down in the chair opposite him across the desk, but she remained standing. 'I've come for my money. I know you were owed rent and they should have paid you but you stole way more than was owed. There was €5,000 in that bag and the rent owed by Spider for the whole apartment was what... €800.'

Carlos brought the tips of his fingers together and studied her for a moment. 'What bag?'

She opened her mouth but he held up a hand, stopping her. 'Relax, you mean that bag,' and he pointed to her bag, which she could now see was in the corner of the room behind him next to a filing cabinet.

Was the towel still in there? She couldn't ask. She knew that a man as shrewd as Carlos would instantly realise there was value in it if she showed any interest at all. 'You took all my money.'

He waved towards the chair. 'Please, we are not animals, take a seat.'

Reluctantly, Meredith sat down and faced him across the table. It was the first real chance she had had to look at him close up and she realised he was older than she had first thought. He was sun-baked but the troughs and folds of his dark skin ran deep and the brilliantined hair was thin and scraped back across a scalp covered in liver spots. He could easily be in his late seventies.

'You want your money. I understand this totally, but why should I give it to you?'

'I will go to the police if you don't give me that bag back.'

This caused him to laugh, a deep, lung-racking laugh, that she thought may kill him so violently did he shake as he struggled to contain his mirth. 'The police!' He held his wrists together as though waiting to be cuffed.

She looked at the bag.

He followed her gaze. 'I don't mean to mock you, but your cash, which you kept under the floorboards of a house with these types of people, this money is not from any legitimate source, come now, is it? This is money for the strongest to take and to keep. You have wasted your trip, I'm afraid. I will keep the bag of money. I thought you had a better offer to make.'

She looked around the room in desperation but there was nothing that presented itself as a useful weapon: only the usual office implements – a hole punch and a stapler on the desk. She should have stopped at Ganiveteria Roca and bought the biggest knife they would sell her.

Meredith raised her right hand to her forehead and let out a small sob. Her left hand fell upon the stapler, almost without her realising. 'It's all I have in the world,' she said in a quiet voice.

Carlos stood up and shuffled round the table. He placed an avuncular arm on her shoulder and leaned in close. 'Darling, darling, that's not true at all. You have a lot more to give.'

Slowly, he let his hand fall and a bony finger brushed her breast. She looked up at him. He was leering at her and his other hand was at his crotch.

'Can I have the bag back?'

He made a low noise in the back of his throat as he spoke. 'Less my rent and some interest, we can come to an arrangement.'

He unzipped the fly of his pants and pulled out his penis. His genitals reminded her of the rovellón mushrooms she often saw in the market during winter, lined with fine wrinkles, a dark orange colour with a central nub accompanied by a repellent odour.

Meredith smiled her sweetest smile, pressed down hard and stapled his dick to his balls.

Carlos didn't scream but made a noise like a balloon slowly deflating and dropped to his knees. She ran round the desk and grabbed hold of the bag.

She looked down at Carlos. His hands were on the stapler but she could see that the stapler was pressed down, the saggy skin crushed in its maw, making it impossible to open. He pawed at it and he was trying to say something, his voice raspy and full of pain.

Meredith picked up the hole punch.

'Diego!' Carlos wheezed out.

Meredith stood at the side of the door. The door swung open and Diego stepped through and came to Llul's side. The lawyer raised a finger to point at Meredith, who was now behind Diego, but it was too late for him to avoid the hole punch slamming into the back of his head. He fell on top of his boss.

Meredith ran out of the room, slamming the door behind her, and didn't look back as she left the office and ran as fast as she could down the stairs, out into the alley and away into the labyrinth of the old town.

23

Meredith flopped down on the crisp, Egyptian cotton bed sheets and slept. Luckily, the staff was used to sweating, red-faced guests on the verge of collapse coming into the lobby so she was sure none of them would have seen anything suspicious about her entrance.

She hadn't been sure she wouldn't collapse before she got to her room and there had been the nagging doubt that Olivia would have checked her out a day early, a situation, which if it had arisen, would have led to her complete mental and physical collapse. Luckily, that wasn't the case and she had never been so relieved as when the red light on her hotel room door clicked to green.

She had stuffed the bag in the bottom of her wardrobe whilst she considered how to dispose of its contents.

But for now, all she wanted was to sink into the bed and rest. She was tired beyond what she thought possible.

When she awoke, many hours later, it was with a raging thirst and she ran to the minibar to grab a bottle of water. As she drained the bottle in one long swig, she noticed her mobile phone was buzzing.

She checked and saw she had four missed calls. Two from Olivia, and one from a number she recognised as Inspector Fernández's, and one from Edu.

There were texts, too. Edu looking to hook up later that evening and four from Olivia asking her to call, each with more urgency, the last a simple "CALL ME!!!".

Meredith jumped in the shower and soaked off the dirt and sweat from the day. Even after fifteen minutes of blasting herself with hot water and then covering herself with the Soho House oils and lotions she still felt a molecular layer of filth was covering her skin. As she massaged her aching limbs, she had flashbacks of the bin and then the dark, hell-like office and Carlos's gap-toothed grin as he approached her.

It's all fine now, she told herself. *You've got this, Meredith. The towel is the weak link, and without that Fernández has nothing. You can concentrate on moving forward, becoming a better version of yourself.* That was all she could hope to do. Every day in every way, she would be better.

Amy's death and the events of the last week, and the last day in particular, were both setbacks along the way to becoming who she wanted to be. She told herself this and felt a little bit happier. It's all about self-visualisation and not being trapped by the past, or negative thoughts about who she was destined to be because of her genes and her socioeconomic background. She could transcend all of that.

She ignored Edu for now. She would call him later, but first, she needed to speak to Olivia. If there was a chance she could win her round, then she needed to go for it. She had a plan if she couldn't but ideally, she could work with The Squad.

Meredith put on some fresh clothes and then checked on the bag. She put the euros, towel and her sports clothes in the safe and locked it shut. Tomorrow, she would take the train far out from the city, to Montseny Natural Park, and burn the damned thing.

She called Olivia's room and she answered immediately. 'Where have you been? I need to speak to you urgently!'

Meredith arranged to meet her in reception in five minutes. When she got there Olivia was already waiting. She looked flustered and there were specks of blood on her thumbs where she had been picking at the skin.

She grabbed Meredith by the arm and led her out into the street. Even though it was 10pm the air was still loaded with heat and almost immediately Meredith began to sweat, filthy city-flecked perspiration running down her newly-oiled arms as Olivia veritably pulled her along.

'What's up?' Meredith asked.

Olivia kept walking fast through the crowds of tourists engorging the narrow streets.

'Her, that's what's up.'

'Who?'

Olivia barged into a couple of fat German girls and in response to their look of surprise gave them the finger. 'That Spanish cop, Fernández. She came to see me again today. Did she speak to you again?'

Meredith didn't mention the missed call from Fernández. 'No, I spent the day with some friends and then had a sleep.'

'Come on, we need to find a quiet bar, if that's fucking possible in this city.'

They moved down Carrer de l'Argenteria with the flow and ebb of the thousands of tourists. It took ten minutes to walk the 500 yards to the Plaça de Sant Jaume and by the time they reached there both of them were slick with sweat.

When they reached the Gothic cathedral, Meredith took control and led them to La Alcoba Azul. They entered and Jordi nodded discreetly, and she raised her eyebrows slightly in response, indicating to him that she didn't want to exchange anything more by way of greeting. They found a dark, quiet corner at the very back of the bar where there were no other patrons and sat down.

Olivia's face was flushed and red and there were dark circles under her eyes.

'Is everything okay, Olivia?'

Olivia looked around the bar and took a deep breath. 'No, everything is not fucking all right. Fernández thinks I killed Amy, I'm sure of it.'

Meredith felt a release of tension and almost smiled. She had been suspecting much worse than this. She thought that maybe she would be told to leave right away. But if they were now focussing on Olivia, didn't that make Olivia's previous comments about Meredith leaving The Squad redundant? This was in fact, great news. 'That's ridiculous, why would she think that?'

'Because I was the last person scheduled to meet her. I turned up at Amy's place at 2pm but no one answered so I thought she was out. I didn't know' – her voice cracked a little – 'that she was lying in pieces around the back of the building. But I've got no one who can verify my alibi and with the description given by this fucking old woman matching me, they are gunning for me, I can tell. Fernández came to see me today and that nice bumbling old woman act? All that was gone. She asked me directly, did I kill Amy?' Olivia slumped back in her chair. She looked exhausted and on the verge of tears.

'Jesus, she came out and asked you? That is so ridiculous. It's out of order. What did you say to her?'

Olivia's eyes flashed angrily. 'What did I say? I told her *no,* of course. That's the truth. But it's the way she looked at me when I said that. I could tell she didn't believe me. Did you find that when you talked to her?' Olivia looked at Meredith imploringly.

It was the first time Olivia had ever asked Meredith for something and she desperately wanted an answer that would help her. It was true Fernández did have a way of making you feel like you had done something although in Meredith's case of course, she had. Meredith almost sniggered. If only Olivia knew what her day had been like, what she had been through, then it would give her some perspective on her own self-pity. 'I didn't get that with her, I must admit, but maybe it's because I speak the language... I don't know.'

'Do you think that's what it is, the language barrier? Jesus, maybe I better think about "lawyering up".'

Meredith tried to look concerned. 'I don't think you need to. You haven't been arrested and you didn't do it, so it could make you look guilty. Fernández is just trying to spook us because she doesn't really have any evidence that Amy's death was anything other than a tragic accident.'

'But she seems convinced it wasn't and thinks it's one of us. That old woman saw a young woman in a baseball cap, and unless there is some unknown killer out there, she thinks it must be someone known to her, and that in this city boils down to you and me. Listen, Meredith, I have to ask you something. Tell me it wasn't you?'

Meredith held Olivia's gaze for a couple of seconds and then began to smile, and then they were both laughing.

'I know it's so absurd me even asking that, it's so fucked up, the whole thing. All this because some old dude watering his plants thinks he saw something. That's it really. But Fernández, she won't let it go,' said Olivia.

Drinks, red wine for Meredith, and a gin and tonic for Olivia, arrived.

'It is crazy, I know, but she's just doing her job. We can't blame her for that. I'm sure it will all just fade away with time,' said Meredith.

'I hope so. Fernández seems convinced one of us was involved. And here's the thing, I won't deny I did find Amy difficult at times, Christ we nearly came to blows a few times – actually strike that – once in Istanbul I slapped her, she was being such a spoiled bitch. You must have seen that side of her when you guys were hanging out?'

'She was a little bit spoiled maybe, I agree, but we never came close to hitting each other. Christ, I don't think I've hit anyone.'

Olivia leant forward, getting closer to Meredith.

'All I'm saying,' continued Olivia, 'is that if you had fallen out with her, if you did, I don't know, have a row with her at Ferran's apartment, then I would understand. Amy was a pain in the arse.'

Meredith shook her head.

'No, that never happened. I really miss her even if she was a pain in the arse. Come on, let's toast her.'

Olivia leaned back in her chair. She looked disappointed for a brief moment but quickly replaced it with a wry smile.

They raised their glasses. 'To Amy, still a pain in the arse even in death,' said Olivia. After the first drink, they ordered more and then after a couple more they found themselves laughing and joking. After the fourth drink, Meredith didn't shiver anymore at the thought of the bin and Carlos.

On the fifth drink, Meredith took hold of Olivia's hand. 'Look, this may not be the time but on the beach the other day, you said that I needed to move out of the hotel and I totally get that you need to protect the brand, but you know once this is all over, is there any chance I can become part of The Squad again? I don't know, but, even though this terrible thing has happened, I have enjoyed working with you guys so much and if there was any way I could continue that would be amazing.' She risked a smile.

Olivia sighed and then half-smiled back. 'Look, Adam is on board. It was me who was concerned about the brand and I dunno, maybe we haven't got along because I am naturally suspicious. You won't believe the number of freeloaders and scam artists there are out there. But listen, why don't you stay a few more days in the room. It's paid up anyway. Let's see how things pan out. You know we've had lots of messages asking where you are over the last couple of days on the 'Gram, so maybe we do need you.'

'That would be great, if you think it would work.'

'I was thinking of getting in some poor kid, hopefully, someone from a BAME background, you know – black, Asian minority, ethnic? You've seen all the cool brands are just pure BAME these days. But a new kid might disrupt our balance, not get us, and that's one thing I think you do have: you get us.' Olivia raised her glass. 'To you, Meredith!'

Meredith raised her glass. 'To us!'

She went to the bathroom, a tight little space at the back of the bar. Maybe, things were coming right. Olivia could see that she was Amy's natural replacement. The booze made her sway as she sat down. It had been a hard road, and it was a pity about Amy, although if only she had seen how much sense it made to have her on board then that unpleasantness could have been avoided, actually should have been avoided She should be mad at Amy but she decided to forgive her. The life she wanted was at hand and there was grace in forgiveness, she had seen that on a T-shirt somewhere, and things were going to be different from now on – grace, forgiveness and the life she deserved. She finished and dreamily walked back towards the table.

As she passed the bar, Jordi, who was polishing a glass with a rag, leaned forward and said in Catalan, 'Your friend.'

Meredith smiled, 'Yeah, I think she could be.'

He frowned. 'Do friends record each other? In her bag by her feet, it's open, she checked it when you went to the toilet, I got a glimpse, she's recording you on her phone.' He shrugged. 'Strange kind of friends you have.'

Meredith felt numb, but nodded at him and then walked back to the table. Olivia noticed her and smiled broadly. She glanced down at Olivia's feet and saw her bag was wide open – a dangerous thing to do in this city – and there was the unmistakable blue glow of a phone screen sat at the top of the bag. Olivia's eyes flickered down towards the floor. Had Fernández put her up to this or was it a frolic of her own? wondered Meredith. It didn't matter, of course, all that mattered was that Olivia wasn't her friend, never would be and she would have to think of an answer to the problem of Olivia.

For a second Meredith didn't react but then she too smiled, and it was her biggest, brightest, most perfect smile.

'Is everything okay?' asked Olivia.

'Everything is perfect, we just need to find an answer.'

'An answer to what?'

'How we are going to deal with the Amy situation and Fernández.'

'What do you suggest?'

Meredith laughed.

'Another drink?'

Olivia clapped her hands. 'That's a great idea!'

They left La Alcoba Azul at some time after midnight and stumbled out into the stone alleyways that twisted away and around from the tiny bar. Arm in arm, they walked towards the cathedral, down empty passageways walled with ancient tenements. Meredith pulled Olivia down another side passage that led them into the small square of Plaça de Sant Felip Neri.

The square was dark and lit only by two dim bulbs from ancient lamps that cast a pale light on the cold stone walls. In the centre of the square there was a small stone fountain. There

were a few people scattered around the square, sitting silently by
the fountain or looking at the grotesque pitting in the walls of
the church and school. Even though it was warm, Meredith shivered involuntarily. The atmosphere in this square had always
had this effect on her.

It seemed to affect Olivia, too. She was staring at the pock-
marked walls, at the grey and white stone which was violently
marked with the sign of war and death. 'What happened here?'
she asked Meredith.

Meredith put her hand up against the cold stone. When she
was here sometimes, she felt she could hear the past screaming.
'During the Spanish Civil War, the fascists dropped a bomb on
this square. It killed forty-two people, mostly children from this
school.'

Olivia shook her head slowly. 'That's horrific.'

Meredith leaned closer to the stone. She wanted to put her
cheek on it, as though there was relief from the incessant heat
there, but she stopped herself, conscious of how it would look to
Olivia.

'It is. What makes it worse is what happened afterwards. You
see the fascists won, as you know, and they spread a rumour that
became accepted truth: that damage you can see to the walls
here' –she caressed a blast mark – 'was caused by rifle bullets
from anarchists executing the priests of this church. They even
concreted over one of the walls so it wasn't obvious that this was
blast damage, but looked like the wall the priests were lined up
against before their execution.'

'Fake news, but at least the truth came out eventually,' said
Olivia.

'But it was believed for decades, long after the perpetrators
were dead, so it worked for them. It worked perfectly.'

'Well, I think that's a bit of an odd way of seeing it, but I suppose so. Can we go? This place gives me the creeps, if I'm honest.'

'Of course, let's go' But she didn't want to leave. She smiled, although she hid it from Olivia. She wanted to stay because this place, with its secrets, was the answer.

24

'I like the colour.'

Edu ran his hand through her hair and stroked it gently. She hadn't been expecting him this morning. She had planned to sleep off her hangover and then spend the day in her room as she was concerned that an angry Carlos and his goons would be out looking for a girl with blue hair.

So, the first order of business had been to run out to the *farmàcia* across the street and pick a new hair colour. It was time to become a blonde.

Edu had arrived shortly after she had applied the dye and had been a welcome distraction from thoughts of Fernández and Carlos.

'It was time for a change.' She rested her right hand on his naked hip and idly wondered what The Squad was doing today and whether Olivia, post-drink, would continue to be as supportive as she seemed to suggest last night.

'I need the bathroom.' He kissed her and then got up.

She heard him run the taps and then he shouted, 'There's a towel in the bath, you know this, no?'

'Yeah, I spilt some wine last night and used it to mop it up. There are fresh ones under the sink.'

'Got them!'

When he returned to the room he was grinning.

'I can't believe you get to live here.' He stretched his arms wider. 'It's fabulous. You want to see where I am living now. It's like a *favela*.'

'How come? Why aren't you in your flat?'

'Fucking police. The National Guard raided my flat and the bar last week. They are trying to disrupt our preparations for *Diada*. This year is worse than many before because they fear the return of the Terra Lliure, *cabróns*. I think they want them to return, as it would give them an excuse to crack down on us.'

'You know why, don't you? The world needs bigger villains than the real ones. Real ones are too banal, too nuanced and difficult to deal with. Why do you think serial killers are the biggest draws on Netflix and in crime fiction? So, what do you guys have planned for *Diada*?'

He laughed and jumped on the bed, grabbing hold of her. 'You'd have to torture me to get that information out of me.'

She pulled him close and kissed him deeply. She was becoming used to him being there and even his sunglasses habit was becoming bearable as she was getting to know him and understand what he meant without having to study his expression when he spoke. She had rarely given anyone this time before and she had surprised herself how he easily he seemed to fit with her. 'I prefer to use the carrot rather the stick.'

He kissed her back and then she pushed him away slightly. 'So, go on, tell me, I'm keen to hear what you have planned.'

He looked at her curiously for a moment and then propped himself up on one elbow. 'It's going to be our biggest acts of civil disobedience yet. We are blocking the autopistas in and out of the city, the train lines will be shut and we have got some big surprises planned for an art attack on city hall.'

She jokingly punched his shoulder. 'An art attack?'

He chuckled. 'Yeah, you know, paintball guns – we are going to cover it in yellow and red paint. It's going to be huge. The press will go crazy for it!'

'That's a brilliant idea. I'd love to get involved.'

He looked at her askance. 'You! You are already too much in the news. And the National Police are after us and I would have thought you have enough already with the local police here. Has there been any news on that? Ferran is still very shaken about it. He won't sleep at the apartment, you know. He says he hears screams from the terrace at night.'

Meredith looked back towards the bathroom where the towel was soaking in detergent in the bath. 'No news. I think the *Mossos* will have to just accept that poor Amy killed herself because of undiagnosed depression. It's not as sexy as murder but this Inspector Fernández doesn't have any evidence other than some old man who thinks he saw something, but this isn't *Rear Window,* you know?'

'*Rear Window*?'

'You are a barbarian. It's an old movie. A man in a wheel-chair thinks he sees a murder in another apartment whilst spending a hot summer looking out of his rear window.'

'And has he?'

Meredith stretched out and yawned. 'In the movie, yeah, but this isn't a movie. It's just the prosaic turning of life's grim wheel and Amy couldn't handle it anymore.' She suddenly felt the need for him and pulled him close.

After, she asked if he would show her where he was staying now and where they were preparing the art attack.

He agreed eagerly. It was the first time that Meredith had

shown an interest in spending time with him after they had had sex.

They got dressed, and whilst he was putting his clothes on, Meredith took the towel out of the bath and hung it over the shower screen. They left the room. Meredith put a Do Not Disturb sign on the door and then headed out to where Edu had parked his ancient Vespa.

They took off and headed north up Via Laietana. It was dusk, and the blue-red sky, the headlights of the traffic as it raced through the city, and the agile darting of the little moto as they filtered through the other cars, made Meredith feel briefly romantic. But then she thought back to Fernández and more than that, to her father, and she just clung on, wanting as always just to survive.

The place he brought her to was a small two-storey building on the corner of a block of residential apartments in Gràcia. It was covered in stylish graffiti and an old man was sitting on a stool outside smoking a cigar and reading a newspaper.

He greeted Edu and then knocked on the roller door behind him three times, and a few seconds later it was rolled up and a young woman with a straight fringe and wearing the usual accoutrements of a Gràcia bohemian – army fatigue shirt and tight black jeans and boots – threw her arms around Edu.

Meredith stood there, feeling slightly self-conscious for a few seconds, and then Edu introduced her as one of his oldest friends, Claudia.

'And this is the girl who has captured our Edu's heart! *Eres muy guapa.* I can see why he has fallen so hard.'

Meredith could see that Edu was blushing slightly and she enjoyed his discomfort, and at the same time was slightly concerned by Claudia's comments as she hadn't thought Edu saw their relationship as anything other than a summer fling. She glanced at him and winked.

'Well, he is pretty gorgeous himself but don't tell him I told you that,' she pretended to whisper to Claudia.

'He has stolen many hearts, so you' – she linked arms with Meredith – 'be careful with your own.'

'I think I'll be okay, but thanks for the warning.'

She let Claudia show her round the small warehouse. Claudia explained that it was usually used for manufacturing and storing the papier-mâché giants that were a feature of so many Catalan fiestas and also for the annual Gràcia festival which had taken place a month before and so was the perfect place for them to bring in their own 'art' supplies.

Edu walked just behind them and seemed to be enjoying the fact that Claudia and Meredith were getting along like old friends. No doubt this was some form of relationship test, thought Meredith, and she played the part to perfection, laughing at Claudia's affectionate digs at Edu and making all the right comments in praise of what they had done and their plans for *Diada*.

Claudia showed her boxes of red and yellow paint that would be used to splash the Catalan colours onto every surface not already covered with the same paint or cleaned by the city on national government orders, and boxes of firecrackers that would be used in the parade on the day itself. But the *pièce de résistance* was a pile of wooden crates covered in a green tarpaulin.

'I will let Edu show you this, as it was his grand idea and you know boys and their toys!'

Meredith and Claudia clinked together bottles of Estrella.

'Well, I told you about this, but I am quite proud of it.'

With a flourish, he pulled off the tarpaulin. Underneath were three large wooden packing cases. Edu slid the top off one of the cases and beckoned Meredith to come and look inside.

It was machine guns. Meredith stepped back. 'Jesus, you said you were going to paintball the town hall, not start a war.'

Edu laughed and pulled out one of the guns. When it was out of its box Meredith could now see that in the space behind the magazine there was a small black container where the paintballs must go, but aside from that it looked like a standard AR-15 assault rifle.

'They are good, no? We are the art terrorists!' He brandished the gun and pulled a mock aggressive expression.

Claudia laughed and picked up a gun as well. 'We are going to make the town hall red and yellow and the media are going to have to give us wall-to-wall coverage. All the effect of a terrorist attack without the violence! Good, no?'

Meredith raised her beer bottle. 'I gotta hand it to you guys it's a pretty sick stunt. When are you going to do it?'

Claudia and Edu exchanged a mischievous look.

'Early in the morning of *Diada*. Our crack team' – they both laughed – 'of insurgents will hit the town hall and other government buildings before dawn. It's going to be cool. Want to join us?' said Edu.

Meredith thought of the Instagram possibilities. It would be something Amy would have liked doing: harmless paint-balling of a building – and the photographic possibilities were amazing – with the right filters the art attack and the ensuing red and yellow splatter pattern could be quite Pollackesque. 'I think I'm going to have to pass. As you said, my profile is a bit high at the moment and it's a bit early in the morning for me.'

Claudia looked down at the floor as though embarrassed. 'We understand. I know Ferran isn't joining us because of the same reasons. It's so totally tragic what happened to your friend.'

Meredith looked away for a moment as though she were dealing with some deep and upsetting thoughts. 'It's okay, Claudia, but thank you. She would have really loved this.'

Claudia raised her beer bottle in the air. 'To Amy!'

Meredith and Edu raised their bottles. 'To Amy!'

EDU DROPPED her off near the Estació de França. She walked along the street towards Soho House, enjoying the last of the early evening sunshine. Tonight, she would speak to Olivia again and perhaps see if she wanted to go out dancing.

Suddenly, a car screamed to a halt right next to her and sounded its horn. It was a battered old Peugeot and at the wheel was Inspector Fernández with a cigarette at her lips. She hit the horn again and waved at Meredith to get in the passenger seat.

Fuck, thought Meredith, and with a sigh, she opened the passenger door and got in.

Fernández smiled at her, exhibiting her yellow tombstone teeth. 'Are you in?'

Before Meredith could answer Fernández hit the gas and the car screeched off at a speed that made Meredith's head whip back.

They swept by a traffic cop standing by his car at the intersection that led to Barceloneta but he did nothing but wave.

Fernández cackled. 'It is... what's the English word? Ah yes, it's a perk, no! They recognise my plates. Everyone knows me here!'

Meredith had no idea what to say so she just nodded.

Fernández steered the car along the Passeig de Colom at high speed, swerving in and out of traffic. 'You haven't been returning my calls, Señorita Weaver. I totally understand of course, it's like filling in a tax return, dealing with the police, no? So many boring details, back and forth. Tell me again, where's this receipt? And on and on. I hate the tax people, hate them. I really don't blame you but' – she lifted both hands from the steering wheel and Meredith found herself gripping the edges of her seat – 'we have to do these things. Life, jobs, pah, bureaucracy, I can't stand it for the truth.'

Meredith sucked in her breath as they approached the rear of a truck without braking and then at the last moment swerved to the left. For a second they were in the path of oncoming traffic before pulling back into their lane.

'I'm sorry, I've been really busy and it's all so upsetting. I suppose I thought you didn't really need me as there's nothing much I can tell you that I already haven't told you.'

The car slowed a little as they got caught in traffic near the Colom and then they stopped to let the hordes of tourists cross the road towards the Maremagnum.

Fernández turned and looked at Meredith. 'Oh no, don't think that at all. We only achieve our job with the help of people like you. Without you, we are nothing but notetakers after the event, mere observers of the passing of a person. With you, people like you, we can become part of the deceased person's story, hopefully' – she hit the accelerator pedal hard as the lights changed, sending a couple of Chinese tourists scrambling for the pavement – 'bringing it to a resolution. So I need to ask you some more questions.'

Meredith looked straight ahead as they approached the roundabout at a seemingly impossible speed. She wasn't sure whether Fernández was driving this way to intimidate her or whether this was just part of the woman's eccentric behaviour. She had been schooled in fear and intimidation by her father, with beatings, burns, verbal abuse and constant terror. She had learned to bury any feelings of fear, to mimic emotions that she did not feel, and she did so now. Meredith let her hands relax and stopped gripping the seat. 'Sure, whatever I can do to help.'

Fernández gunned the engine and then swung the car into a sharp right-hand turn into the Gates Diagonal Hotel.

'Cell phones...' Fernández took her right hand from the wheel and held up her phone. 'They are amazing. DNA and phones. They have made my life so much easier. *Hijo de puta!*'

A motor scooter had slowed to let another car into their lane.

Fernández threw her phone back into the central storage well. 'But we end up relying on them way too much and that's where I am with the phones. Listen, I will speak frankly now, maybe too frankly.' She snorted. 'Your friend, Olivia Lowe, her phone backs up her story. The signal is on her room until 12pm and then we can trace it to Ferran's apartment at 2pm and then it stays there for fifteen minutes and then it tracks back to your hotel.'

'Yes, Olivia told you this.'

'Exactly, it all fits. Unless she got someone to take her phone to the apartment after she went there at an earlier time, then she couldn't possibly be at the apartment at 12pm to kill Amy.'

Meredith looked out the passenger window at all the people going about their business, shopping, meeting friends for lunch, and she wondered if any of this would ever be possible for her. Not she wanted any of that: she needed much more. But maybe it would be nice to be satisfied with just that. 'Which is what we've told you all along. As painful as it is, Amy probably killed herself and I'm not sure what this is achieving, dragging it all out, making people think she was murdered.'

The car began to speed up again. 'You're so right, dragging this out makes it so much worse, but indulge me so I can cross my boxes and tick all my ticks, yes? Your phone also backs up your story. The signal stays in your room all day even when you said you went out to the stores in El Born and bought that... let me remember... that bracelet.'

'I just forgot to take it out.'

'Of course, of course, I would forget my ovaries if they weren't with me.' She crossed herself. 'But you see the bureaucrat's dilemma. You could have, let us say for devil's advocate purposes, have left your phone in the hotel, gone to Ferran's apartment, thrown Amy off the balcony and your phone would say you hadn't moved from the hotel all day. But of course you did move – you said at 1pm – but the store assistant said an hour later, to buy the bracelet. So we know one thing from all of this: your phone, unlike Olivia's, cannot identify your location at the relevant time.'

She said this in the same manner as she might give a child a present, as though Meredith would greet the revelation with gratitude.

'Olivia could have left her phone in her room, gone to the apartment, returned to the hotel, picked up the phone and then gone back to Amy's apartment. I'm just saying as a devil's advocate,' replied Meredith.

'No, we thought of that. The hotel system records when a hotel door is opened with the key card, not when someone leaves, and there was no record of hers being opened until her return at 3.15pm. So, unless she had an accomplice or left her phone somewhere outside her room, then this is' – she waved her hand airily – '*sin valor.*'

Meredith sat quietly for a second. 'But all this is based on an assumption that Amy was murdered.'

Fernández pressed hard on the accelerator again and received the finger from a moto driver who she cut up. 'We have a witness who will testify she was pushed from the balcony.'

'An old man.'

'Who served in the army for twenty-five years and who has excellent vision. We tested it, of course, as we know how those lawyers like to play things. I don't think he is mistaken. And nor do I think is the resident who saw a young woman, late twenties, take the lift at the relevant time. Tell me again, what was your connection with this "Squad".'

'I told you everything, I knew them briefly in Thailand many years ago and randomly connected with them again a few weeks ago.'

'Because they are working in Barcelona and now they are very successful and wealthy and you, not so much. That's right isn't it?'

Meredith shrugged. 'They've done well. I've spent my time exploring and travelling the world. Life is about choices, I guess, and I don't regret mine.'

Fernández slapped the wheel in agreement. 'That is so true unless you believe in a deterministic universe in which case we are just doomed by cause and effect to do what we do. But I don't so I believe in choices, like you, otherwise what is the point of it all, eh! So, did you choose to sell poisoned wine to tourists?'

Meredith didn't answer straight away. She was thinking and praying that the American tourists were not dead and wondering how did the police officer know about this? 'I have done many jobs whilst travelling and it usually involves sales of some sort. I work giving out flyers or getting tourists to try a restaurant or bar. And, yeah, I've worked for people selling wine. But I really wouldn't know anything about the quality of the wine so if someone has got food poisoning then I suggest you take it up with the manufacturer.'

Fernández smiled and then hit the horn at some minor traffic transgression by the car in front. 'We have a man in custody already. I think you know him, Alfonso Rivera. But I know how tough it can be making a living in this city. Rents are high and good jobs difficult to come by so I don't blame you for taking what you can get, even if some *guiris* ended up in hospital. They are fine now, by the way, if you care to know.'

'I never knew anything about any bad wine.'

'But you knew about being poor and that must have been difficult, no, when you saw your friends' lifestyles, the hotels, the money, the ease in which they live their life compared to your struggles. It was some good fortune finding them again and becoming part of their group even for such a little time. It will be difficult to go back to your life. You are going back, no?'

'The details haven't been worked out yet.'

Fernández slowed the car down. 'Because if Amy had come back, I understand you definitely would not have been staying with them. *Gracias and adios,* no? So, even though it is terrible, you now may stay and have this life. As a box ticker, you know what box that ticks? Motive.'

Meredith carried on looking straight ahead. 'I didn't kill Amy.'

'No one is saying you did! Box ticking, that is all. Don't worry, I'm not going to arrest you.' She turned to look at Meredith. 'I only do that when I have everything I need, all the boxes ticked and that is not so, yet.'

'Look out!' A young woman holding a selfie stick had stepped out into the road, seemingly oblivious to the oncoming traffic.

Fernández slammed on the brakes and the car shuddered to a stop inches away from the nonplussed tourist, who seemed unconcerned about how close she had come to dying. She leaned in and took a picture with the car as the background.

Meredith unclipped her seatbelt. 'I'm getting out. This is dangerous and unless you are going to arrest me, I'm not spending another moment in this car.'

Fernández grinned. 'I don't blame you. All my colleagues say I am the worst driver on the force. But I think I am pretty good. I always end up where I am going, no? I will be in touch and this time, please do answer my calls.'

Meredith grunted a reply and stepped out of the car. It was a good twenty-minute walk from here and it was still unbearably hot. She began to walk.

25

Meredith sat in the shade of the Bahia café terrace and sipped at her cortado.

She had been waiting here for just over fifteen minutes now. Next to her feet was a bag packed with all the essentials for a beach trip; swimming costume, book, small packed dinner and, of course, towels.

It was another sun-saturated day, although there was the first sign of a cooling in the air as September dragged the heat away and Meredith stretched her legs under the table. She liked having the day ahead of her, especially a Monday, when she could sit here and watch other, more responsible citizens, returning from a day's work whilst she enjoyed the sun and her coffee.

She had been hot, sweaty, tired and anxious after her car trip with Fernández. Two things were clear to her: the first was that Fernández thought she had killed Amy but didn't have enough evidence to arrest her yet and the second was that Fernández would not stop until she had Amy's killer in custody.

Meredith couldn't let that happen and had spent a restless night worrying about what to do. In the early hours of the morning, a thought that had first occurred to her in Plaça de Sant Felip Neri became clearer and after that, she had slept peacefully and woken rested and refreshed. She had spent the day making preparations, and, once completed, relaxing by the pool

You have to keep on moving forward, she told herself, *you move forward or you die.* She had decided to move forward once again. She had spent too long drifting, waiting for things to happen. That's the difference, the only difference that mattered, between her and Amy and Olivia. They had managed to focus earlier. They had accepted an identity and then in the spirit of the times packaged that identity up and sold it online. Amy's downfall was because she had become complacent and wanted to experiment with new identities. *She should have accepted herself,* thought Meredith. *If she had, she would still be alive.*

Meredith checked her watch again. Then she saw her.

Olivia waved and then took a seat next to her. 'Sorry I'm late. I'm keen to hear what we've got planned.'

'Like I told you, it's a surprise, but like that plaça I showed you the other night, it's worth it. Did you manage to get away without telling the others?'

Meredith had spoken to Olivia earlier that day as they swam in the pool, Meredith carving easy laps whilst Olivia performed her awkward stroke that reminded Meredith of a puppy thrown in a canal. She had asked her whether she wanted to see another secret place like Plaça de Sant Felip Neri and Olivia had told her she would love to see such a place. They had arranged to meet in the café but Meredith had suggested that Olivia didn't tell Adam or the others in case they wanted to tag along.

Olivia waved over the waiter. 'Oh yeah, I told them that I was on my period and wanted to spend the night in the room with a good book and a bottle of red. They didn't ask anything after that. Talking of wine, I'm having a glass now: can I get you anything?'

'No, I'm good,' said Meredith, pointing to her coffee, 'I had a little too much to drink last night.'

Olivia laughed. 'I go the other way, actually. Hair of the dog for me.'

The wine came and Meredith astounded herself by making small talk for thirty or so minutes whilst Olivia finished it. If you had asked afterwards what they had talked about she wouldn't have been able to tell you at all – but what was new was that she didn't find it so painful. Perhaps it was because she was getting to know Olivia a little more, and even starting to like her, or maybe it was because it wasn't small talk but rather small talk dedicated to a higher purpose.

When it came time to leave, Meredith paid, putting some cash in the tin and uncharacteristically leaving a larger tip than was customary in Spain. As they stood up to leave, she announced that she needed something from the hotel and handed her beach bag to Olivia. 'Will you take this while I run back. I'll meet you at Estació de França.'

'I can just come with you,' Olivia said.

'No, you can browse in the shops along the way.'

Olivia hesitated for a second and then picked up the bag. 'Oh well, I can do that but for God's sake don't be too long.'

Meredith called over the waiter she had just tipped. In Spanish, she asked him if he could direct her friend to Estació de França as they were parting ways now and she didn't want her to get lost in the streets.

The waiter nodded in agreement and then in fluent English began to tell Olivia how to get to the station.

She held up her hand. 'I know the bloody way. I've been here three weeks already. But thanks for your help anyway.'

The waiter shrugged and muttered something under his breath.

Meredith reached in and hugged Olivia as though they were saying goodbye forever.

Olivia hugged her back but looked slightly perplexed.

They agreed to meet at the station in fifteen minutes. As they left the café Meredith made sure to shout '*Adios*' to the waiter who looked up as she turned right and Olivia went left.

Meredith walked around the block for ten or so minutes and then made her way to the station. When she arrived, Olivia was waiting at the entrance.

'What did you need that was so urgent?'

Meredith opened her bag and showed Olivia the two bottles of cava that she had packed much earlier.

'Now you are talking! So where are we going?'

'A beach. Playa del Muerto. It's outside of Barcelona, I think we need a break from this city heat.'

'Okay, but what's so special about a beach?'

'You'll see. Come on, our train is leaving in two minutes!'

MEREDITH OPENED the second bottle of cava and filled Olivia's plastic flute to the top.

'Jesus, I'm going to be wasted soon enough,' said Olivia.

Meredith handed her the flute.

'Summer will be over soon and it will be time to step off the merry-go-round then. But for now' – she filled her glass and drank deeply – 'we drink!'

'To summer!' Olivia gave the toast and Meredith drank.

The beach was now deserted. A week earlier and they could have decamped to the *chiringuito* and had a sundowner there but now it was boarded up, awaiting the arrival of next summer.

'I almost forgot, hang on.' Meredith busied herself in the bag and then pulled out Tupperware boxes containing jamon de bellota, Manchego cheese, chorizo, a chilled ration of *pulpo*, a large *barra de pan* and a bottle of Rioja.

'Fantastic,' said Olivia.

They laid the picnic out in front of them and whether it was the sea air, the lateness of the hour or the drink, they devoured the meal quickly, accompanying it with glasses of the red wine.

Afterwards, they lay down on their towels, satiated and more than a little drunk. Meredith skinned up a joint. She hated weed but tonight was a special occasion and she knew that Olivia liked to smoke.

She lit the end and took a small toke which caused her to cough dramatically and she immediately passed the joint to Olivia who expertly sucked in a few enormous drags and then handed it back to Meredith.

This time Meredith just kept the smoke in her mouth. She already felt a little nauseous following the first drag and she knew she didn't have a head for it at all. If Olivia noticed that Meredith wasn't smoking it correctly, she didn't say anything but when Meredith handed it back to her she kept it for longer, almost smoking it down to the roach.

When they finished the joint both of them lay down next to each other, their hips and arms touching.

'You know what, Meredith?'

'What?'

'I'm sorry I misjudged you. I'm sorry for being a bitch.'

Meredith noticed that the first stars were starting to appear. 'That's okay, I can come off a bit forward sometimes and I know you were just protecting The Squad. Friends?'

Olivia's pinkie finger intertwined with Meredith's. 'Friends.'

Meredith propped herself up on her elbow and scanned the beach. There was still no one around. She wondered, should she lean forward and kiss Olivia.

Olivia must have seen something in her eyes. 'So, what was this special thing you were going to show me?'

Meredith jumped to her feet and immediately half regretted it as the booze and dope had made her a little woozy. 'Yes, we need to go now, before it gets too dark and cold.'

'What is it?'

'Come on, follow me, I'll show you.'

Meredith offered her hand to Olivia who took it. Meredith pulled her up and then led her by the hand to the water's edge. There wasn't much of a swell and the waves were lapping rather than crashing on the shore. The sea was the colour of denim and the sky bruised blues and deep oranges. It was a beautiful sunset.

'Very pretty.'

Meredith shook her head. 'No, it's not that. We have to go out there' – she pointed towards the horizon – 'so I can show you.'

'What, we have to swim all the way to the fucking sun?' Olivia laughed a little manically.

'No, just a little way out until we get to the headland there.' She pointed towards the rocky side of the bay nearest to Barcelona. The sea is still warm and it will be worth it, I promise.'

Olivia put her foot in the water. 'It's freezing!'

'Not when we get in there. Come on, I thought you wanted adventure?' Meredith took off her T-shirt and ran into the water. It was cold but she dived into the first wave and although it took her breath away at first, as always, it felt immediately better. She put her head down and struck out with a few kicks until she was twenty yards from shore.

Olivia was still standing on the beach.

'Come on in!'

Olivia looked hesitant for a second and then stepped into the waves and gingerly made her way forward until she was chest-deep in the water.

Meredith swam back until she was next to her. 'You need to put your head under and then it's not so cold.'

'Fuck you,' said Olivia, but then she ducked her head under and re-emerged a second later with a rictus grin on her face. 'Jesus it's cold!'

'But that's better now, yeah?'

'Yeah, but where are we going? Fuck, I think I just sobered up.'

Meredith didn't think Olivia looked sober: her eyes were red and she was slurring her words.

'Just a little swim, maybe five minutes.'

'I can only do the breaststroke.'

'Don't worry, I'm a good swimmer so I'll stay with you at your pace.' Meredith slowed her stroke so she matched Olivia's awkward doggy paddle.

'I always hated swimming: no books, cigarettes, booze or boys so I didn't see the point.'

Meredith laughed. Olivia could be funny. This wasn't something she particularly enjoyed, but kudos to her, she was brave and adventurous and doing it to please Meredith.

'You're doing really well.'

'Maybe you can give me some lessons when we get back.'

'I'd like that.'

As they got further out, they had to raise their voices a little and Meredith also noticed that the temperature was dropping.

The headland was a little further away than Meredith first thought but they kicked on and the waves were still slight and the sea calm.

Meredith swam easily and enjoyed the sensation of the water on her limbs as she cut through the sea. Beside her, Olivia kept spitting out water and breathing heavily.

In five minutes, they reached a point opposite the rocky headland.

'Are we there yet?' Olivia spluttered.

'Just a little further,' said Meredith.

'Okay.' Olivia's voice sounded a little weaker now.

They pushed beyond the headland and were rewarded with a view all along the coast towards Sitges and Barcelona. All the lights were coming on as dusk settled and the yellows, ambers and greens made the coastline look like a spectacular necklace strung out for miles.

Olivia caught up with Meredith and grabbed hold of her arm. She spat out some more water and Meredith noticed her legs were kicking furiously in contrast to Meredith's easy movements.

'Look,' said Meredith.

Olivia's head dipped under the water but then bobbed back up. 'Yeah, it's beautiful.'

They trod water for a minute or so longer and then Meredith noticed that Olivia's teeth were chattering. 'Are you okay?' she asked.

'Yeah, I'm good but I need to get in now. I think I'm getting a cramp... all that booze and food.' She made a valiant attempt to laugh.

Meredith kicked away from her so she was treading water a metre away from Olivia. 'Come on then, let's go.'

Olivia nodded and then began her awkward stroke heading towards Meredith and the shore. Meredith remained treading water and then when Olivia was within an arm's length Meredith put out her right hand and gently pushed Olivia's forehead.

Olivia was surprised and her head went under. She kicked her legs, sending up lots of white water and then re-emerged. 'What the fuck, Meredith! Stop fucking around. It's dangerous.'

She kicked forward again and once again Meredith raised her hand and gently pushed her back.

Down she went again.

This time it took slightly longer for her to re-emerge and there was real panic on her face. Meredith noted with curiosity how that panic contorted her pretty features into something much more grotesque. *Fear is definitely not good for the skin and would not photograph well at all,* thought Meredith.

'You?'

She tried to swim at an angle to Meredith but Meredith gave a kick of her legs so she stayed just ahead of her and again pressed gently on her forehead so she once again sank.

Olivia bobbed up again and this time she vomited water. Her eyes were wild and rolling. She tried to scream but only a squeaking sound emerged from her flapping mouth.

Meredith gave a gentle, almost loving, press to her head and Olivia sank once more.

She swam in a small circle and looked back towards the beach. It was still empty save for the two towels and the beach bag. She waited but Olivia didn't reappear and after two more minutes Meredith struck out for the shore, which took her very little time at all.

Once back on land she bundled up Olivia's clothes in her arms and then threw them in the sea together with Olivia's iPhone. She put Olivia's hotel key card in her pocket.

She then picked up her towel and put it in the beach bag. She put on a pair of plastic gloves that she had brought with her and placed Olivia's towel, the same towel she had taken from Ferran's apartment and which was now, she hoped, covered in Olivia's DNA, in a clear plastic bag and put it into the beach bag.

Meredith began the long climb back up the cliffs towards Sitges and home.

26

Meredith could tell that Adam was drunk by the way he walked, and to make it even clearer he brought his large gin and tonic from the bar into the restaurant as though he couldn't be without a drink even on such a short journey. It had been a rush, but she had caught the train just in time, stopping only briefly to stuff her sports gear into a city rubbish bin behind the station, and returned to Barcelona in time to get back to her room at Soho House, hide the towel in Olivia's room, change and then meet the others for dinner at 10pm.

Richard sat down next to her and raised his eyebrows as Adam shouted for the waiter to come over and take his order. 'Watch out for him tonight, he's pissed as a fart. We lost two sponsors today.'

Dylan grabbed the breadbasket and began chewing his way through the rolls without stopping to butter them. He caught Meredith's eye. 'High fibre, low fat. I'm moving to a keto diet next week so I need to bulk up my carbs.'

She pretended to care and smiled sweetly at him.

'Dylan seems to be taking Amy's death in his stride,' she muttered to Richard.

'I'm not entirely sure he has actually noticed. He's basically like a small child: as long as we keep him fed and watered and give him toys to play with, he will be fine.'

The waiter arrived and without asking them Adam ordered two bottles of red and two bottles of white. He rubbed his hands together. 'I know the ladies like white and this is probably going to be one of our last nights together before we return to Blighty next week.'

'Told you he was pissed,' said Richard in a low voice.

'What was that mate?' said Adam, leering at Richard over the bread basket.

'Oh, nothing, I was just wondering if Olivia is joining us?'

Adam looked at his Rolex Submariner. 'Yeah, she said she was coming to dinner. I'll ping her.' Adam sent her a text and then relaxed into his seat and into his wine glass which needed refilling almost immediately.

'Where have you been hiding all day, Meredith. I knocked for you about 4pm. Me and the boys hit some bars. It was a cracking laugh, eh Dicky?'

'It was okay, yeah,' replied Richard.

'I went for a jog, hit the beach for a bit and then came back for a sleep. Sorry, I missed you guys: it sounded like fun.'

'It was hell,' whispered Richard.

'What was that, Dicky? I thought it was good given what I've been dealing with on your fucking behalf. I thought you would have been grateful. You enjoyed it, eh Dylan? Here, let me fill up your glass.' Adam picked up one of the bottles of red.

'No thanks, mate, I'm on the protein shakes tonight. Gotta look after these guns.' He flexed his biceps and then put his palm out above the wine glass, but Adam poured the wine onto Dylan's hand anyway.

He moved his hand back and Adam filled his glass.

'Here we go. He's a mean drunk,' said Richard.

Adam leered at them and held up his glass. 'I am not a mean drunk. I am a very, very generous drunk. Here, Dicky, let me fill up your glass.'

'If you must,' said Richard.

Adam filled it up and then checked his phone. 'No reply.' He held the phone up so they could see his screen. 'Maybe Miss high-and-mighty can smell the coffee.'

'And what does that mean?' said Richard.

Adam downed his glass of red wine. 'That means we are truly fucked if sponsors keep leaving. You two just don't get the likes. We can't use Meredith because, and begging your pardon here, Meredith, Olivia doesn't fucking like you. The money well is as dry as my granny's fanny.'

'I think Olivia is coming round, actually,' said Meredith.

'Yeah, well we need to do something if we are to save this rapidly sinking ship.'

Meredith noticed other guests looking over and commenting disapprovingly at Adam's volume. She wondered whether Olivia's body had floated out to sea. Or was it even now being photographed and pored over by scenes-of-crime officers in white suits. She sipped her wine, letting it top up the faded buzz from the wine and weed she had consumed on the beach.

It didn't matter what happened to the body: things were in motion now and there was nothing else she could do. She had gift-wrapped Amy's murderer for Fernández. The towel would show Olivia's DNA, placing her at Ferran's apartment, an apartment she had told the police she had never entered, and she had obviously been so remorseful and racked with guilt and fear of being caught, that she had just got drunk and stoned and walked into the sea.

All Meredith needed now was for The Squad to keep their

shit together and she could step into the Amy-Olivia void and things could get back on track. 'Well,' she said kindly, and she smiled with her eyes at Adam, 'I spoke to Olivia last night and we kinda bonded and she totally came round to me joining you guys again. So if you want, I can start helping you take some pictures and we can see if we can get the likes back up. I speak Spanish, so we can maybe use that as well: you know how Spanish is going be the number one language in the States soon.'

'Olivia thinks we need an ethnic. She says white is pale and stale, and – don't take this the wrong way – she also thinks you may be too old.'

Meredith laughed and waved over the waiter who was speaking to the sommelier and looking over at their table. 'Well, you got to remember that our audience will age with us. They will grow old too.'

Adam jabbed a finger at her. 'That is a fucking good point!'

The waiter appeared at Meredith's side, looking sheepish. 'Señorita, would it be possible for you to ask your companions to be a little quieter as you are disturbing the other guests.'

'Whadda he say?' said Adam.

'He said you're being drunk and loud and should shut up,' said Richard.

Adam stuck out his bottom lip in what looked like an impression of Robert De Niro. 'I am drunk, this is true, but my colleague and friend died last week and my business is falling apart so I guess, Manuel' – he pointed at the waiter – 'that gives me an excuse, hey?'

Meredith asked for the menus and also ordered an immediate serving of extra bread and patatas bravas to help soak up the booze. 'And two jugs of water,' she added.

Adam stretched out his hands. 'We want the finest of everything tonight, yeah! Just like *Withnail and I*... I want the finest wines' – he hit the table hard with his fist – 'and I want them now!' The hum of conversation dropped to the silence of a car full of rubberneckers at the scene of an accident.

Meredith nodded at the waiter. 'The food and water,' she whispered, and he walked briskly away.

'For Christ's sake, could things get any worse?' said Richard.

Dylan hadn't appeared to notice, so engaged was he by Candy Crush on his phone.

Richard continued, 'Olivia keeps Adam in check. He is classic working-class stock. Just add drink and he becomes emotionally incontinent. Oh fuck, he's started crying.'

Tears were rolling down Adam's cheeks and then he let out a loud sob. The other diners were transfixed.

Meredith got up and went round the table and kneeled next to him. 'Are you okay, Adam?'

He let out another sob. Meredith could see the waiters hovering. No one wanted their dinner ruined by negative emotion. It was the opposite of all a brand hoped to do. She had already seen two kids, famous DJs, Richard had told her when they checked in, taking brazen pictures with their phones of the middle-aged man having a meltdown.

'Of course, I'm not fucking okay. I'm drunk. My friend is dead, we are all going to be ruined and now Olivia can't even be arsed. Everything is falling apart.'

She put her arm around his shoulder. 'Oh Adam, don't worry. Come on, I've got an idea. Let's get you back to your room and then get some room service sent up.'

She squeezed his shoulders and he looked up at her like a little boy being comforted by his mother. 'That would be nice, yeah.'

She helped him to his feet and linked arms with him. Slowly, she led him out of the dining room to the relieved expressions of the waiting staff.

Back in his room she helped him onto the bed and then took his shoes off.

'I'll just have a curry and some more wine,' he said in response to a question she hadn't asked.

'Sure,' she said, and she sat on the bed next to him.

In less than a minute he was snoring. She went to the minibar and took out a bottle of water and placed it by him on the bedside table and then carefully wrapped a cotton sheet around him as she knew how cold it could be when the air conditioning cranked up to deal with the heat.

And then she leant down and placed a gentle kiss on his forehead.

SHE SLEPT in the next morning and awoke close to midday with a fuzzy head brought on by the day and evening of drinking and smoking.

The first thing she did was turn on the television and check the local channels. There was nothing about a body being washed up. With the currents as they are in that area it was entirely possible that they would never find Olivia's body.

It doesn't matter either way, thought Meredith. But on balance, the lack of a body was probably better as it left open the possibility that Olivia had faked her own death to avoid being arrested. This was the type of confused narrative that suited Meredith.

She checked all the channels again, and nothing. It was possible, of course, that the body had been found and it hadn't been reported yet... But if that was the case and it had been identified then surely Fernández would have been in contact already?

Meredith checked her phone. There were no messages from Fernández but there was one from Adam. It just read:

Sorry for being a wanker. Shooting postponed for today. Squad time tomorrow.

There were also two messages from Edu asking her what she was up to but she ignored those for the time being. Instead, she sent a message to Olivia's phone. It helped build a story.

Hey, missed you at dinner last night. Fancy grabbing some lunch? M xx

She had a vision of Olivia's phone screen coming to life at the bottom of the ocean and startling a fish. This caused her to giggle. Adam's message was just what she had wanted, he had included her in The Squad itinerary again, even this hangover-postponed one. And without Olivia he would need her even more.

Meredith showered and then got dressed and for extra verisimilitude, she went to Olivia's room and knocked on the door. A cleaner was passing when she did this which just showed fortune favoured those who paid attention to such little details.

After that, she sent Olivia another message asking her to contact her later for drinks if she couldn't make lunch. Then she decided to go and get some brunch herself as she found she was suddenly famished.

Meredith wandered through the Gothic streets until she found a small square next to the old Roman wall. She took a seat at one of the metal tables outside and when the waiter came, she ordered scrambled eggs, with jamon, and foie gras. She washed this down with two cups of strong coffee and then a brandy which she nursed as she sat looking out across the square.

After her meal, she stretched. It was all just a matter of keeping her nerve now and she was sure that wouldn't be a problem for her at all.

A man walked slowly and deliberately across the square, with a rolling gait. She recognised the man instantly and the fear and terror rooted her to the spot even though her brain was screaming *Go, go, go!*

There was a medical dressing on the back of his head. It was Diego.

She slammed back the rest of her brandy and thought about her options – she could scream, get the owners to call the police, but what then? Fernández would be called, no doubt, and then Carlos may mention the bag and its contents, money and the towel. She remained sitting as the man walked up to her table and stopped.

'You are to come with me.'

'If I don't?'

'Your friends will pay the price and I will break one of your arms right now.'

Friends? Fuck, Inga must have talked. She had known that Meredith was staying at Soho House and Carlos Llul had obviously put the heat on her to tell him where she was.

She stood up, unsure whether her legs would support her, but the shaking had gone. At least now she didn't have to worry about what would happen if Carlos Llul found her. She was about to find out.

27

'All animals are afraid of pain, even those, who like you, are without normal feelings.'

He was right. Meredith was frightened. She was sick with anxiety and she wanted to be anywhere but here, back in Carlos's office, with its shutters keeping out all the natural light.

On the desk in front of him was the stapler and the hole punch. He hadn't mentioned them yet but there they were.

She didn't say anything but instead glanced to the corner where Spider and Inga were sitting. Both of them looked terrified. Spider had a black eye and a vicious looking cut on his lip. Diego stood behind them.

'So, tell me, are you afraid?' Carlos smiled at her, his face becoming a mass of lines like crumpled brown wrapping paper.

She looked again at Spider and Inga. Inga looked down rather than return her gaze. 'Yes, I'm afraid of what you will do to me.'

Carlos nodded serenely. 'For you, it is fortunate that I am a man with certain values that would be sneered at today by the likes of you and your friends here. I believe in honour and as you can see, I have not harmed your friend here because she is a woman and I do not hit woman.'

Inga was shaking.

'And what about him?' asked Meredith.

'He is less fortunate. You know what you did to me and Diego here and you know that you must pay for this.'

Meredith leaned forward in her chair. She tried not to look at the stapler and the hole punch. 'I can give you the money, the €5,000 that was in the bag. It's yours.'

Carlos chuckled and held up a mobile phone. 'After you attacked me, I found out who you were from your friends here and although I am old and can't pretend to understand how this' – he waved the phone – 'makes you money, I can see that you have money and the price of my leniency is set accordingly. To be clear, you will bring me €50,000 within three days or Diego will ruin your face with that.' He gestured at the stapler. 'And one thing I do recognise is that this new business on the internet is the same as the old business, and without your face, you will be nothing.'

'I don't have that kind of money. I don't have any money. I was only helping them out. The Squad are the ones with money. They don't give me anything.'

Carlos held up a finger to his lips. 'Shush, you stay in Soho House. The people you work with flaunt their wealth online. You have access to this and you will bring it to me by Friday or... well perhaps a demonstration, yes? Diego, if you would be so kind.'

Meredith watched frozen with horror as Diego swiftly pulled out a box cutter and before anyone could react, slashed it across Spider's face. Before he felt the pain a curtain of blood began to descend from the slit described across his face from above his right eye, across his nose and down to his chin.

Inga screamed and then Spider did so too. Carlos raised a hand.

'Be quiet or there will be more.'

Diego handed Spider a cloth. He held it to his face and then began to rock back and forth in his chair.

'Do you understand me and understand what will happen?'

Meredith nodded.

'You have three days. We will be watching. Diego, show them out.'

Outside, Spider sat down on the pavement and just stared into space. Inga was crying, dark smudges of mascara turning into long dirty streaks down her cheeks.

'What are we going to do?' said Inga.

Meredith looked at her curiously. 'What do you mean "we"?'

Inga seemed shocked. 'You heard him: if you don't get that money, he is going to hurt us.'

Meredith was thinking. She understood clearly, unlike Inga, that they would have to leave Barcelona and never come back. It was over for them here. But, unlike Inga and Spider, she couldn't leave, not with Fernández on her tail. She was stuck.

She started to walk out of the alleyway.

Inga called after her, 'What should we do?'

Meredith looked back briefly. 'Run,' she said, and then turned away.

Inga began to sob but this time Meredith didn't look back. They were all on their own now.

28

Meredith didn't feel better after her second martini but the third brought a dulling of the fear and she knew that a fourth would put real distance between her and anxiety.

She played with the stick, twirling the olive around in the glass and enjoying the oily slick it left on the surface of the drink. It made her feel in charge of this moment. The warmth of the alcohol in her veins contrasted with the cool of the hotel's air conditioning, making her the master of this environment for this precise time. *Maybe this is what mindfulness is all about,* she thought. *Martinis are a quicker way of arriving at peace than meditation.*

'That looks like a fine drink. I'm on duty, but why not!' Fernández slipped onto the barstool next to her and beckoned the barman over.

'Inspector, how are you? You should have one, it makes things a lot warmer in this goddamned icy air conditioning.'

'Another two of those,' said Fernández to the barman, pointing at Meredith's martini, and she twisted the stool so she was facing her.

Meredith kept facing forwards towards the bar. Fernández could wait if she thought she would play her game and beg for a treat.

'We can't seem to contact Olivia. Have you seen her today?'

'No,' said Meredith.

'Where have you been today?'

Meredith snorted with laughter as an uninvited image of Spider's flesh opening entered her mind. 'Just hanging with some friends.'

'And they will confirm this?'

'Yeah, why? What is it you think has happened now?'

'Señorita Lowe hasn't been seen since yesterday. Your friends are worried.'

'She's a big girl, I'm sure she's fine,' said Meredith, and she took a sip of the fresh martini. 'Are you not going to taste your drink?'

Fernández didn't look away. 'I'm here to conduct a search of her room. My officers are doing that right now.'

'And yet here you are with me.'

Fernández smiled. 'And yet here I am with you. Why do you think that is?'

'You like martinis?' Meredith laughed at her own joke and then shivered involuntarily. It was way too cold in here. She raised a finger and pointed at the air conditioning unit. 'Too cold,' she shouted at the barman. He nodded but didn't do anything about it.

'I think the temperature is fine in here. Are you feeling okay, Meredith?'

Meredith looked down at her glass. What would happen if she just smashed it into Fernández's face? 'I'm just fine and dandy, yeah. So, why are you sitting here with me then, if it's not for the martinis? Do you need a friend?'

At that moment Fernández's police radio crackled and a

voice that Meredith assumed to be Miguel's said they'd found something and she was to come up right away.

'I'll be back,' said Fernández.

'I'm sure,' said Meredith and then finished her drink in one long hit.

IT TOOK two days for the lab tests to come back and prove that it was Olivia's DNA on the towel from Ferran's apartment. Miguel and his team had discovered the towel stashed at the bottom of the wardrobe and Fernández hadn't returned to finish her drink.

The search for Olivia had begun immediately and had made the national news with regular bulletins speculating on her whereabouts and linking her disappearance to Amy's death, which had been given renewed vigour as a formal murder inquiry was announced with plenty of salacious photographs, new and old, culled from Instagram and splashed all over the media.

Fernández told the remaining Squad members to stay in the hotel if at all possible, to avoid the scrum of photographers and press that besieged the entrance. Policemen were guarding the entrances, too. Fernández said that they were to keep the press away but Meredith couldn't help but worry that she had posted them there for other reasons.

Another consequence was that their numbers had gone through the roof. The likes for all their old posts were astronomical and Adam was being bombarded with offers from new, more edgy brands who wanted to be associated with what the press was calling the 'Instagram Murder'.

There was an international manhunt for Olivia as her passport was missing. The prevalent theory – once the information about her phone records was leaked, which showed that her phone had a non-standard termination of its connection to the Sitges mast, indicating that it had not been turned off as usual by the user – was that Olivia had killed herself because of her guilt at murdering or accidentally killing her best friend.

The night that the tests confirmed that it was Olivia's DNA on the towel they had all got together for a drink in the rooftop bar. It was a sombre occasion and Adam had been drunk again. He was determined that Olivia couldn't have been involved in Amy's death but when Richard had mentioned that sometimes she had been jealous of Amy's success as the face of The Squad, he had put his drink down and retired to his room from whence he had not emerged since.

Being trapped in the hotel did have one unexpected advantage. It meant that when the deadline came and went for Meredith to deliver the €50,000 to Carlos, she could feel relatively secure in her gilded prison. Inga and Spider's fates were unknown to her but she hoped Inga had heeded her advice and left the city.

Meredith passed the time updating The Squad's Instagram feed with photos they hadn't used from previous shoots. Adam wouldn't leave his room to take any more shots.

She had approached Dylan to sit for some more photographs. He was doing his usual lap after lap of the rooftop pool and she had knelt by the edge to try and speak to him but he had ignored her, instead grinding out seemingly endless laps with his metronomic front crawl, even though she was sure he had seen her. She had asked Richard if everything was okay with Dylan.

He replied, 'Dylan's not in a good place, darling.'

'Why?' she asked as just the two of them shared cocktails one evening.

'Because he blames you for everything that's happened. He says that everything turned to shit once you turned up.'

'Amy had contacted Ferran before I even knew you guys were in the city.'

Behind Richard, a group of teenagers settled around the daybed next to them. They were giggling and taking pictures of each other.

'Yeah, I know, but like I explained, he is Australian so it's less about what's up here' – he pointed to his head – 'than how he feels in his gut.'

A series of pops from Champagne bottles being opened came from the group next to them and Richard cast them a dirty glance. 'YouTubers.' He almost spat out the words. 'No doubt they'll be up to some horrendous prank involving torturing a homeless person. I can't stand them.' He raised his voice and shouted at them, 'Film us and I'll get you turfed out, all right?'

This was greeted by a forest of raised middle fingers and one of the younger black girls shouted, 'Fuck off, grandad!'

'Kids today,' muttered Richard.

'You're twenty-eight,' said Meredith.

'I know, it's fucking ancient. Come on, let's get pissed whilst we wait for our freedom.'

THE NEXT MORNING Meredith awoke with a horrifying lassitude. At first, she thought it was simply her hangover biting and causing her to feel as if it would be impossible for her to ever leave her bed. She wondered whether this was guilt. She knew what guilt was, of course, and intellectually had observed it in others, but she had never felt it in ways that she had read about or observed.

She wanted Inga to be okay more than she wanted Inga to suffer at the hands of Carlos. But if the Swedish girl was harmed then Meredith wouldn't feel as though this was her fault, and some sort of burden, like hunger or pain, that she should inflict on herself. It would simply be cause and effect, avoidable if people had made different choices.

Like Amy. She easily could have worked with Meredith and Meredith would have been happy to accept any type of role, but she didn't and, well, things happened.

Life was about evolving and Meredith had tried to work with The Squad and become part of a group. Amy should have tried making a similar evolution.

Meredith would have stayed in bed all morning but the damned air conditioning rendered her environment unbearable. It was so icy it made her blood chill. She had set it on twenty-two degrees but still it pumped out frozen tendrils that felt like they were clawing at her skin.

Eventually, she could stand it no more and jumped out of bed and turned the unit off. Within minutes the hotel room began to heat up, making her brain swell.

She considered having a drink. There was a chilled Penedès in the minibar, but it was too early and although she didn't usually mind drinking alone, today, she felt the need for company. She called Edu who answered eagerly on the second ring.

'Meredith, how are you? I see your Squad on the news already twice today. There was a picture of you on the beach and you looked so beautiful.'

'I'm well, thanks. I was wondering if you fancied coming over to the hotel? I'm a total prisoner here at the moment and I could use the company. We could have lunch on the terrace.'

In the background, she could hear the sound of power tools and laughter.

'I'm so sorry but it is impossible today. We are preparing for the *Diada Nacional de Catalunya* and I'm needed here.'

Meredith had known he would say this, but still, she was

disappointed. She was getting used to him being around and maybe this was what it meant to have a relationship that wasn't just about sex. He irritated her to hell but yet she still wanted him to just be here with her.

'You guys must have been super-bummed when Al-Qaeda took out the world trade towers and ruined September 11th for you.'

He chuckled. 'It's good to celebrate something positive and our brand of art terrorism is better than theirs, no? You are funny Meredith. It's one of the reasons I love you.' He didn't seem embarrassed by his dropping of the L-bomb but maybe it was just a translation issue. She ignored it.

'Okay, well enjoy your fun and I'll catch you on the flip side.'

'We will, and if you can slip away from the hotel you know where we will be at 4am tomorrow morning.'

'Yeah, yeah, have a great time without me.' She put the phone down and rolled back onto the bed.

Even wearing nothing it was too hot without the air conditioning but she wouldn't put it back on again: it made her anxious. So instead she lay there wondering what to do. She had no more cards to play. Olivia's body hadn't been found. And if it was found, the story told itself. Jealous Olivia got into a fight with her friend, killed her on purpose or by accident and then killed herself because of the guilt. That's what people did, it was almost classical Greek tragedy and it spoke to the ages and to all common sense. But Fernández was the problem. She knew, somehow, she knew and she wouldn't rest until Meredith was in jail.

But what could she do? She could only lie here in this room and broil in the heat. If she left the hotel the press would follow her and worse may be waiting. It was six days since she had been due to pay Carlos the money. Wouldn't it just be her luck to avoid the police but to be killed by some two-bit South American gangster due to the many fuck-ups of Spider and Inga. She almost hoped that they had been caught by Carlos.

There had been one call from Inga the day after the money was due, but she hadn't taken it and no message had been left. After that, she had blocked her number.

She lay on the bed for hours, not sleeping, but just breathing and looking up at the ceiling. Meredith realised that she needed someone to be here with her and that she was not enough on her own. Belonging to The Squad had given her purpose but perhaps if this slipped away it didn't matter. Edu had said he loved her and she had heard this from others over the years, said in passion, said in seriousness but never before had it made her not want to laugh at the person saying it. He had said it without expectation or hope, but rather matter-of-factly as though it were just acknowledging the way things were for him. Meredith wasn't sure she was capable of love. It seemed as alien as guilt to her but she was missing something, of that she was sure, and perhaps this absence once filled, perhaps that was love or as close as she could get to love.

At some point in the afternoon, she drifted off.

She woke, covered in sweat and breathless due to the oven-like heat of the room, to the sound of the hotel phone ringing loudly.

She answered it. It was Adam. His speech was slurred. 'Listen M, you gotta come to my room now. That Inspector Fernández is here and she has got some guy with a briefcase here, yeah. Chop chop, she says.'

'I'll be there right away,' replied Meredith. She quickly jumped in the shower and blasted herself with icy water and then slung on some denim shorts and a crisp white T-shirt. She hadn't eaten anything all day but the shower had made her sharp again and she was pleased that Fernández had arrived. It meant things were coming to a head.

FERNÁNDEZ GREETED her with a big grin and an effusive hand-shake. 'Thank you so much for your time again Senorita Weaver! We have all of you here now, and the others have already helped us, so it is just you left now.'

Adam was slouched in an armchair. He looked and smelt drunk. Richard was sitting on the bed and his expression gave nothing away whilst Dylan was standing and she could see he was full of nervous energy.

'Hey M,' said Adam, and he gave her a pathetic little wave of his hand and she nodded her head by way of reply.

Richard nodded and Dylan just stared at her with hostility.

There were two other people in the room: Miguel, Fernández's assistant and a younger woman in a sharp black suit that looked too much for this weather. There was a large black leather suitcase by this woman's feet.

'Is there any news? Have you found Olivia yet?' Meredith said.

Fernández's eyes sparkled in amusement but her expression remained calm and professional. 'Alas, no, but we have some very interesting developments. I wasn't happy with the testing on the towel. We outsource the testing and you know how things can be sometimes. You want a second opinion if your car is broken and for me, the same was true of the towel. I sent it to another lab and there were some very interesting results, oh yes. You see, they found another set of DNA on the towel which is interesting, no?'

Meredith used every muscle in her face to keep her expression calm. 'Interesting, of course, but it could be Ferran's, I guess?'

Fernández pointed at Meredith. 'You are like me so much! I thought that and we have his DNA on file, but unfortunately not. We checked and it is not his so I need your DNA, Meredith. To rule you out, of course, as it would be impossible for your DNA to be on the towel taken from the apartment by the killer.'

Meredith felt her legs wobble but she focussed on her core muscles and told herself to stand up straight like her father used to tell her. Her legs had wobbled back then. She had even wet herself but she had learned to keep her back stiff and her head held high.

'Are you arresting me?'

Fernández burst into laughter and turned to Miguel. 'Arresting her! What for? No, no this is entirely voluntarily, in order for us to carry out our work and focus our resources appropriately. The checking of boxes, it continues! All your friends have given a swab. It's a simple swipe of some cells from your cheek, and we were hoping that you will help as well.'

Was it possible she had touched the towel on the beach? She had been so careful not to and yet the only DNA that should be on there was Olivia's. She had washed the towel before taking it to the beach so no one else's DNA should be on there. If there was other DNA it must be hers. She had slipped up and how could she explain that away?

Meredith thought about launching into a spiel about privacy and human rights but she looked around the room at everyone's eyes on her and instead she gave Fernández her biggest grin possible. 'Abso-fucking-lutely! Anything, anything at all I can do help, I want to do it. We need to catch this fucker and get Olivia back.'

'This is Señora Cortez and she will take the sample.'

The smartly dressed young woman opened the leather case and took out a small plastic bag. From the bag, she produced a swab. 'Can you open your mouth, please.'

Meredith opened her mouth wide as instructed and the swab was inserted. She felt it scrape alongside the inside of her mouth, taking her guilty cells, and then it was gone and in a new bag.

Fernández looked at her. All the usual merriment in her eyes had disappeared and Meredith realised for the first time that this was her real face, hidden behind the eccentricities in the same way that Meredith hid behind her smile. Meredith knew then that Fernández saw her just as clearly and she shivered because this woman was the first person, perhaps since her father, to see her this way.

'Thank you all for your help. We will have the results within twenty-four hours so you can sleep well knowing that we will rule you out of our investigation.' She never took her eyes from Meredith as she spoke.

29

The others had retired to the terrace bar after the swabs were taken but Meredith just couldn't bear the thought of the conversation that would ensue. Adam's drunken, self-pitying rants, Richard being wry and ingratiating and Dylan saying nothing and sending her hostile vibes.

Instead, Meredith made her way downstairs to the Square Bar and ordered a martini. It duly arrived and she sat on one of the stools looking at it. The bar was full of a couple of parties, including the Youtubers who Richard had told off the night before. They were talking and having fun, clearly enjoying each other's company. Meredith was only a few feet away and could hear the warmth – sometimes there was gentle mocking, but overall the affection they held for each other was clear.

She was a few feet away but it may as well have been a thousand miles. She was alone and in less than twenty-four hours she would be arrested and who would vouch for her and her life? Her family had disowned her after her father died. They blamed her for his death and it was true she was responsible although the son-of-a-bitch had truly deserved it. Friends? She had none. Inga, if she was sensible – and Meredith did think she had the necessary smarts to focus on survival – was one of just a succession of flatmates, none of whom she kept in contact with, and Olivia and Amy were both dead. It had been possible that they could have been friends: she had liked them both and wanted to impress them but they had made that impossible.

The only person who might come to see her in her cell would be Edu. He wouldn't forsake her, not right away, although time would tell how he felt as the evidence mounted against her as she knew it would. But at first, he would help her and be her friend.

She took a sip of her drink. There was nothing else for her to do but wait.

AFTER THE ONE DRINK, Meredith had come back up to the room. She had a feeling it would be the last time for a while that she would be staying in such luxurious accommodation. The air conditioning remained off and she stripped down and lay back on the bed, enjoying the sensation of the Egyptian cotton on her bare flesh. At some point, she fell asleep.

She woke at around 2am, the sheets congealed around her in a sweat-infused heap. She padded to the minibar and took out a bottle of water and then came back to bed. She noticed that her phone had a new message. She picked it up and checked it. It was from Edu and the message simply said:

join us xx

It had been sent fifteen minutes ago. She knew where they were, they were in Plaça de Sant Jaume, ready to carry out their red and yellow paintball attack on the town hall, their art terrorism. She could join them, maybe it would be one last piece of fun before the cuffs were slapped on her tomorrow. What did she have to lose? But she knew she would never see him again. She had only one choice left and that was to run.

Meredith got dressed quickly and then she packed a small bag, making sure she put her passport in there and also Olivia's. She had taken it when she placed the towel in Olivia's room. It had been beside the television and she wanted the police to think that Olivia had fled town. It had seemed like a good idea but now it was one more thing she needed to dispose of. She added a change of clothes and then her envelope stuffed with the €5,000. She took a last look around and then she left the room.

It was just before 3.30am but the hotel was still busy, the bars full, the sounds of parties and fun. It was a Friday but every night in this city was the same. Meredith would miss it, would miss what she now realised was important, the sense of being part of a greater thing than herself. But she would find another city.

She walked briskly past the guests, almost all worse for wear from drink or drugs, or both, who staggered uneasily past her, to their rooms or to other rooms, to drink, make love, be alive. She tried not to be envious. She needed to focus on reliance, on herself, on escaping and not looking back. It's what Inga should have done and what she had to do.

She noticed one of the receptionists look up as she headed for the doors and she wondered whether the receptionists had been tipped off to alert Fernández when she left the building – but this was beyond her control and therefore beyond her worry. Confidently, she pushed open the doors and stepped out into the night.

No journalists were waiting for her outside. This had been her fear, that they would be waiting with cameras, and that they would follow her, making her escape impossible, but the story seemingly didn't justify twenty-four-hour coverage. She was sure they would be there in force tomorrow, no doubt acting on a tip-off from the *Mossos*, that arrests were going to be made in the Instagram Murder case.

Meredith smiled to herself. Maybe this could work.

She plunged into the heart of El Born, taking the narrow, tight alleys, the ones avoided by the tourists because of their fear of what may wait for them in the shadows. There was always the chance of a mugger waiting for a lost, drunken *guiri* but Meredith fancied her chances against the usual stoned Moroccan teenagers who hunted in these streets.

Her plan was straightforward. Walk to Estació Sants and catch the 5.15am train to Tarifa in the south of Spain. From there she could catch a ferry to Tangiers hopefully before the DNA results came in and before there was a block on her passport.

Instead of crossing Plaça de Santa Maria which would still be bustling at this time of the morning, Meredith cut through the narrowest, darkest alleyway, one she would normally avoid. No moonlight penetrated here and the only illumination was from the dim orange glow of the occasional lamp behind windows high above her in the walls of the Gothic stone apartments that towered overhead.

The alley was quiet and afforded her passage parallel to Carrer de l'Argenteria which would bring her out onto Via Laietana and from there she could use more back alleys to get out of the Barri Gòtic and move northwest across town to get to the station. She didn't want to catch a cab and she had plenty of time to walk across town.

Meredith made her way up the alleyway, her footsteps echoing on the stone walls. Somewhere overhead a man shouted furious nonsense. A dog barked.

She realised that there was now another sound. There were other footsteps, echoing in slight syncopation with her own. There was someone else in the alleyway with her. She looked behind but after ten yards or so the alley was in darkness. She listened, there was nothing, and then she heard them – footsteps again, this time quicker and coming towards her.

For a second, she was frozen to the spot waiting for whoever was coming – but then her legs responded and she spun round and began to run as fast as she could down the alley away from her pursuers.

Meredith ran hard and fast but she could hear the sounds of pursuit and they were getting closer. As long as she could get out of the alleyway, she stood a chance, and if she could get to Plaça de Sant Jaume then it was possible Edu and his gang would be there by now.

She risked a look round and was horrified to see, only twenty or so paces behind her, the huge bulk of Diego and another scrawnier, rat-faced man, bearing down on her. The press had vacated their watch on the hotel but Carlos had not and now she would be punished for not paying over the money.

At the end of the alley, there was a brighter patch of light where the alley opened out onto a wider street. She was nearly there when her heel slipped out of her shoe and she stumbled. If she had fallen to the ground, she would have been done for, but she managed to regain her balance, kick off her shoe and burst from the alleyway into a crowd of young men just ahead of Diego and his colleague.

The bunch of lads were drunk and the sudden appearance of a beautiful young woman in their midst led to a barrage of catcalls and whoops.

Diego and Ratface came barrelling out of the alley and halted in front of the boys. Meredith stood behind the stag party who, seeing a frightened young woman being pursued by two intimidating-looking men, closed ranks in front of her.

'Give her to us,' said Diego. Behind him, Ratface produced a flick-knife and clicked it open, revealing a nasty-looking blade.

One of the young boys, maybe nineteen years old, and quite drunk, squared up to Diego. 'We don't like men who chase woman so why don't you fuck off!'

Diego's head caught him square in the nose and the young man was unconscious before he hit the floor. The other four men charged into Diego and Ratface and Meredith saw the blade flashing back and forth and the boys began to fall.

She ran, leaving behind her the sound of screams and cries for help.

Meredith didn't look as she crossed the wide Via Laietana but she heard a car, presumably a taxi, blaring its horn at her. She was breathing heavily now as she ran up the slight hill and suddenly, she was at Plaça Jaume. Frantically, she looked around but there was no sign of Edu. The square was quiet and empty save for a small group of homeless people or junkies away in one corner.

'Holá, Meredith,' said a voice from behind her. She turned around and there was Diego. There was blood on his face and he was panting.

Behind him, Ratface was walking up the street. He was still holding the knife.

Diego took out a handkerchief and wiped the blood from his face.

'I can get the money tomorrow. I'm just on my way to meet someone who can help me, actually.'

Diego laughed. 'Oh, it's too late for that. I can see you are running. Give me the bag.'

Meredith clutched the bag tightly to her chest. It contained her every worldly possessions, the passports, and her money. If she lost it, she would be doomed.

Diego shook his head and turned to Ratface. 'Raoul, if you please, the face.'

Ratface stepped forward and raised the knife. Meredith braced herself for the pain of flesh opening up.

And then he squealed as a projectile hit him hard in the face and exploded in a garish yellow flash. He staggered backwards clutching at his eyes.

Diego began to speak, but as he opened his mouth it was hit hard by another missile which burst, covering his teeth and gums with red paint. Meredith saw one of his teeth fall to the ground.

And then came a fusillade of more paintballs splattering over Diego and Raoul, who backed away covering their faces with their hands. The attackers were remorseless and switched their fire to concentrate on the undefended bodies of Diego and Raoul.

They screamed in pain as the paintballs smashed into their faces and then their bodies. At such short range each hard plastic ball must have felt like a rubber bullet.

Meredith watched the attackers – Edu, Claudia, and two others – who were at her side now, firing, and she realised that they must have been what she thought were the junkies hanging around in the corner of the square. They had been getting ready to start their art attack on the town hall just as she came running.

Diego and Raoul ran off down the street towards Jaume metro.

Meredith flung herself at Edu and put her arms around him. 'Thank Christ. You saved me.'

He grinned. She could see that he had enjoyed every moment. 'Who were those guys?'

'It's a long story.'

Claudia spat on the ground. 'Fucking men!'

Edu held up his hands.

'Okay, not all men,' said Claudia.

'You're missing a shoe,' said Edu.

Meredith smiled. 'I'm a regular Cinderella.'

'Shit,' said one of the other members of Edu's gang.

A police car had entered the square and its blue lights were flashing.

Edu grabbed hold of Meredith's hand. 'Split up, meet back in Gràcia.'

He led her down past the Gothic cathedral and into the labyrinth of streets of the old Jewish quarter surrounding Plaça de Sant Felip Neri. The others dispersed down alleyways as they ran until Edu and Meredith were suddenly alone. As they jinked down another impossibly narrow alley Edu suddenly pulled Meredith close and kissed her hard.

She kissed him back, and for a second she forgot about everything, but then they stopped at the sound of a distant police siren.

'Do you have a car?' Meredith asked him.

'Yeah, it's a shitheap but I have a car.'

'Will you drive me to Tarifa?'

'What, now?'

She grabbed hold of his hips and pulled him close again. 'Yeah, right now. Will you take me?' And she kissed him again.

30

E du hadn't lied. The car was a piece of shit.

It was a faded blue Citroën Xsara that was old in the early 2000s and it had no air conditioning. They left Barcelona at 4.30am and by 10.30am the heat inside the car made it feel like a blast furnace. They drove with the windows down and the crappy fan blowing warm air in their faces in an attempt, with copious espressos, to keep them awake as they made the ten-hour journey from Barcelona to Tarifa.

The car stank with their sweat and also the smell of a thousand other summer days' sweat and dirt, which was triggered by the blazing sun and the heat from the engine. But it was a car and it was moving away from Barcelona.

Meredith had told Edu all about Carlos and the money, leaving out, of course, anything about the real reason why she had needed to get the bag back. He had become very angry when she told him about Carlos trying to sexually assault her and for one moment she had thought he was going to turn the car back and get his friends together to deliver street justice, but she had explained to him she just wanted to get away for a while, that Barcelona had become too much, too hot, too dangerous.

He had eventually calmed down and the monotony of the drive and the heat had proven to be a calming as well as a stultifying influence.

'I'm sorry you didn't get to plaster the town hall with your paintballs,' she said to him once they had cleared the city limits.

He had winked at her. 'Social justice was delivered, no? It means so much more when it is personal. And as for *Diada*, there will be another one next year and another the year after that. I would much prefer to spend the time with you, like this.' And he reached out and placed his left hand over her right hand.

And when the sun came up and he put on his Ray-Bans she didn't mind so much.

She had slept and when she woke, they were high in the Serranía de Ronda mountain range. Meredith had left the route in Edu's hands, and the romantic that he was, he had avoided the autoroutes and driven a more scenic route, taking them up past Benehavís. He said it wouldn't add much time on at all and they would still be able to make the ferry to Tangiers. The country up here was sublime. They passed through cork forests and stopped for coffee at a small *pueblo blanco* which hung high and parched on the side of one of the mountains.

While they sat watching the vultures climb on warm updraughts of air he leaned across the table and put both of his hands on hers. 'Listen, why don't I come with you to Morocco? We can take the car across and drive it down south. I have friends who have done this before. We can drive to Marrakech and then just keep going until we hit Dakar. I've always wanted to go to Dakar, though I never knew it until now.' And he grinned and then looked at her hopefully.

Meredith didn't know how to respond. Her plan had been to land in Morocco and then fall into the backpacking scene where she could be anybody, just another privileged lost girl travelling the world and picking up trinkets. Nobody gave them a second glance. But without him, she would have been maimed or worse by now, and she realised that what she wanted from The Squad wasn't money and fame, but a sense of belonging, a place, and somewhere to call home.

She squeezed his hand back and smiled without thinking. 'I think that would be awesome. I'm ready for a new adventure.'

She meant it but didn't know what would happen when they reached the port. If the DNA tests had come back then it was possible that Fernández would have gone to the hotel to arrest her and when she found out she wasn't there she would surely put an immediate call to flag her passport at ports and airports and that would be the end of things. She had considered using Olivia's passport but that was also bound to be flagged already so she would dispose of that on the ferry, if they got on, by throwing it overboard.

And when they landed in Morocco, should Edu find out about the DNA results, she could explain to him that there was a mistake and if he didn't believe her it would be easy to get away from him there. Yes, it could all work. There was a way it could work.

He kissed her across the table and she felt, for a moment, happy.

Back in the car, Meredith kept the radio tuned to a music channel which had a continuous diet of classic rock tunes, which she enjoyed. However, the real reason she wanted to listen to the news bulletins was to hear if there were any developments on her case. But there was nothing. As they began to descend, via a series of switchbacks, to the plain and Tarifa, she began to feel more confident that they would make the ferry and get on it before the DNA results were back. She also kept an eye on her mobile phone as she was sure that Fernández, upon discovering that Meredith was no longer in the hotel, would call her immediately.

About halfway down the mountain, there was a loud bang and the car lost traction and slid across the road before coming to a stuttering halt on the verge with Edu barely in control.

'Shit,' he said.

They both got out and Meredith could see straight away that the rear passenger side tyre was flat.

Edu said, 'Won't take me a minute to fix it. *No hay un problema.*' And then he went to the boot of the car and opened it. He took out a black cloth bag and then set about jacking up the car. 'Can you pass me that tyre iron,' he said, after the car was jacked up.

Meredith, who had been admiring the sublime view out to the Mediterranean, wandered back over to the car and picked up the tyre iron from the ground behind him and passed him it. He was sweating heavily and his check shirt and jeans were stained with the red dust that covered everything on the mountain. Since they had stopped there had been no passing traffic and the only sound was that of a million cicadas, the ubiquitous soundtrack to this intense Spanish heat. He loosened the wheel nuts and then handed her back the tyre iron before removing the wheel. Meredith wandered back over to the edge of the road and looked out across the slope that tumbled down to Tarifa and the sea. They had plenty of time to catch the ferry.

'Meredith, what's this?'

She turned round and saw that Edu was standing at the rear of the car looking into the trunk. Meredith sauntered over to join him and slipped her arm around his waist. He moved away brusquely and then she looked in the trunk and saw why.

Her bag was open, the stack of banknotes visible and there on the top, where he must have put it after looking at it, was Olivia's passport.

'How can you have Olivia's passport?' He began to back away from her, a look of confusion on his face as he came to terms with what this must mean.

She raised her left arm and outstretched her palm in a 'keep calm' gesture, but he knocked her hand away.

'It's nothing Edu, I can explain it all,' she said, and slowly stepped towards him.

'Nothing? You can only have that, if...' He paused. 'The police think she is on the run or has killed herself. But if you have her passport that must mean... fuck...' He looked at her with wide, confused eyes.

She swung the tyre iron and it connected, with a dull thud, to Edu's left temple. He sank, almost in slow motion, to his knees, and then he tried to say something to her. It may have been, 'I love you,' but she wasn't sure that she hadn't just imagined this. She swung the iron once more and hit him again. He slumped, with a ghastly thud, to one side.

Meredith felt sick in a way that she hadn't before but she had to act quickly. She grabbed him by his heels and dragged him to the side of the road where a minute before she had been admiring the view. The edge dropped away here into a dense scrubland with thick bushes and she rolled him over. His body fell a few feet and then stopped.

She considered climbing down and covering him up but he wasn't visible from the road and it would take someone standing on the side of the road in this exact spot to find his body so she left it as it was. It was the right thing to do, she was sure.

She needed to tighten the nuts on the rear wheel and then lower the jack and once she had done that, she checked the area. Apart from the wheel marks, you would never know anyone was here and they would be gone after one quick rainfall.

Meredith jumped in the driver's seat and began the drive down to Tarifa.

31

M eredith had no choice but to present her own passport to the border guard. Olivia's would have undoubtedly triggered a warning.

He grunted and looked at it, his eyes hidden behind mirrored sunglasses, and then he looked at the computer screen in front of him. *This is it,* thought Meredith. There would be another look and then he would make a call and ask her to step out of her car. From there it would be windowless offices, vans and then a courtroom and finally a small cell to hold her until she was in her fifties, if she was lucky.

She smiled at the guard but he was too busy checking the screen to notice. If he asked her to get out of the car, she could just gun the engine and swing the car around, make a break for it and go out in a hail of gunfire or worse, be wounded and then arrested. But she knew this wouldn't happen, she would just wait here for her fate.

He turned his head away from the screen. A middle-aged, paunchy man, probably bored with his job, his family, his life choices and heading for a cardiac event. This was the man who would deliver her to justice.

She saw herself in the mirrored shades, two images of her face reflected back at her. She tried the smile again and even in the lenses it looked the most real, beautiful thing she had ever managed. The guard made a deep noise from his throat and then handed back her passport.

'Have a pleasant trip,' he said, and then he tried a flirty smile of his own that revealed nothing but nicotine-stained teeth.

Meredith slowly drove the car forward, joining the rear of the queue of vehicles waiting to board the ferry to Tangiers. There were many old cars, filled with families, eating, arguing, laughing, and camper vans with friends and lovers, and hers seemed to be the only vehicle with a sole occupant. She sighed and to kill time whilst she waited for the ferry to start boarding, she tuned the radio into a news channel and checked her mobile phone. She had considered turning it off, but what was the point? Her passport use identified her location and she would throw her mobile phone from the ferry, together with Olivia's passport, so she could not be tracked in Morocco.

She managed to catch a news bulletin but there was still nothing about the case so she assumed the DNA result had not been released yet.

She opened Instagram and The Squad's profile. The last picture was of her, Olivia, Dylan and Richard sitting by the pool at Soho House. They were all grinning and Dylan was holding up two fingers behind her head. She scrolled down, revealing more of The Squad's history, the early images of just Amy, Olivia and Richard. They grew younger and happier as she scrolled. Eventually, the earliest images were just of Amy alone at the start of her online journey. Meredith came to an image, it must have been four years old, of Amy, sitting outside a coffee shop in London, sipping a soy latte and she had foam on her lips. She was smiling with her eyes and it was the type of innocence that sold well and would eventually lead to Adam's attention and many followers.

But here she was not alone of course: there was someone behind the camera. Olivia in all probability.

And that was the trick, Meredith had come to realise, as she sat in the car, in the heat, waiting to board a ferry that would take her away from Spain and away from people. She had had nobody and never would. She had come close with The Squad and then Edu but now she was alone.

But maybe that wasn't the case.

Annik, the painter she had met at the MACBA outside of Tangiers, and in the bottom of Meredith's bag was the drinks mat with her address on it.

The car in front of her suddenly started and its rear red brake lights came on, as did all the others ahead of her. Meredith turned the key and Edu's Xsara juddered back to life.

Slowly, the cars began to move forward. And then Meredith noticed that stationed just before the ramp were two armed police officers. These were of a very different type to the border guard. These men looked alert, toned and professional. One of them looked at the occupants of the cars and the other was scrutinising the drivers. Each of them held automatic weapons and they looked poised and ready. Was this it then?

Meredith let the clutch go and inched the car forward.

At that moment a message notification flashed up on her phone. It was from Fernández. She reached down for the phone which was on the passenger seat and put it into her lap.

She was the next car in line and her stomach felt like it was cramping with anxiety. Carefully, and trying not to stall the car, she drove forward.

One of the policemen was young and had a square chin and dark, pitiless eyes that betrayed no emotion.

It was hot and her window was already rolled down. The

policeman looked in and then winked at her. 'Just checking for terrorists. You go right on, Señora.'

She smiled at him and he blushed. 'Thank you,' she said, and as the car moved forward, she let out a breath of pure released tension. The car bumped as it hit the steel ramp that led to the bowels of the ferry and then she was inside and it was dark and cool in here. She brought the car to a stop and switched off the engine.

Meredith picked up the phone in her lap. She knew that she could still be stopped at the Moroccan border or the police could just board the ferry and pull her off. She hesitated for a second and then opened the message.

DNA on the towel was a false positive. Nothing further needed from you at this time. Fernández.

She leaned back in the seat and was rewarded with a scent from the headrest that was the ingrained smell of Edu's cologne and sweat. She wondered how long it would take for his smell to disappear from the car, from the world. Only a matter of weeks, she thought. It was a shame about Edu. She could maybe have loved him or pretended for a while, but he was gone now and until she met Annik, she was alone. It was the way it had to be.

Meredith watched as the passengers in front of her left their car. There were two small children; a boy and a girl, a wife wearing a hijab, who looked harassed as she tried to marshal the children who had immediately started to fight. And then the father stepped out of the driver's side and he smiled, a smile so genuine, so full of love and pride. It was a smile that no one else saw, including his wife and children, apart from Meredith, and she began to cry.

THE END

Printed by Amazon Italia Logistica S.r.l.
Torrazza Piemonte (TO), Italy